THE NEW YEAR'S EVE MURDERS

THE NEW YEAR'S EVE MURDERS

THE THIRD KIT & MARY ASTON MYSTERY

JACK MURRAY

Books by Jack Murray

Kit Aston Series
Mysteries
The Affair of the Christmas Card Killer
Taken
The Chess Board Murders
Tin Pan Alley
The Phantom
The Frisco Falcon
The Medium Murders
The Bluebeard Club
The Tangier Tajine
The Empire Theatre Murders
The Newmarket Murders
The New Year's Eve Murders
The French Diplomat Affair (novella)
Haymaker's Last Fight (novelette)

Bobbie Flynn
A Little Miss
Murder on

DI Jellicoe Series
A Time to Kill
The Bus Stop
Trio
Dolce Vita Murders

Agatha Aston Series
Black-Eyed Nick
The Witchfinder General Murders
The Christmas Murder Mystery
The Siegfried Slayer (Oct 2023)

Danny Shaw / Manfred Brehme WWII Series
The Shadow of War
Crusader

El Alamein

Jackmurray99@hotmail.com

Cover by Jack Murray after J.C. Leyendecker

ISBN: 9798867939366
Imprint: Independently published

For Monica, Lavinia, Anne, and Baby Edward

The Party Poopers

Kit Aston........................*Dashing, highly intuitive, amateur detective and former spy*

Mary Aston....................*Beautiful, brave and brilliantly smart*

Agatha Frost..................*Kit's aunt*

Alastair Aston...............*Kit's uncle*

Inspector Flynn.............*A detective*

Bobbie Flynn.................*Journalist daughter of Inspector Flynn*

Amory Beaufort...........*Party host*

Dick West.....................*Former friend of Amory*

Chester Lydgate............*Former friend of Amory*

Ethel Barnes.................*Chester's date for the evening*

Freddy..........................*Amory's butler*

The Troopers..............*Four-man band playing at the party.*

Detective Nolan............*Young detective at Midtown precinct*

Captain O'Riordan........*Senior detective at Midtown precinct*

Laura Lyons...................*Dick West's date and former girlfriend of Amory*

Colette Andrews...............*Beautiful young woman, former girlfriend of Amory*

Two of these people will die.

1

RMS Aquitania: 30th December 1921

It takes a brave man to admit when he's wrong; it takes an even braver one to tell his wife when she is. Kit Aston was in just such an unenviable position with Mary. Kit was a man that had faced the worst that the German army could throw at him, in Flanders. He had helped Alexander Kerensky escape from the Bolsheviks during the Russian Revolution. He had faced peril on many an occasion since the War. In short, it is safe to say that Kit Aston was a man who had looked death in the eye and, while not exactly laughing, had proved equal to the task of surviving. Fashions may change, so too scientific laws, even genders, but the one thing that remains constant is a husband's desire to have an easy life.

There was only one road a man such as this would take when confronted with the ultimate test of his mettle.

'I'm sorry, Mary,' said Kit dejectedly. 'I wasn't much help to you there.'

Even men of unquestionable valour know when a white flag must be hoisted. The shortest route between two points is a straight line, as the saying goes. It was simply easier for Kit to apologise, for Mary's over-optimistic assessment of her bridge hand, than point out where she may have reined in her ambition.

Mary was magnanimous in accepting Kit's *mea culpa*. A good wife always forgives her husband when she's wrong. Perhaps there was just a hint of a hidden smile in her eyes when she said, 'You did your best, darling. The cards weren't with us.'

Which was probably the point that Kit would like to have made to Mary when he asked her to explain why she bid as if she was holding the poker equivalent of a Royal Flush.

The other two players, participating in the post-mortem, were Colonel and Mrs Sedgwick-Harris. They had brutally routed the Astons, in a manner that would have had Attila the Hun covering his eyes in horror.

Mary politely declined the offer of a return match, deciding that her wounded soldier's confidence would need a little nursing. The treatment Mary had in mind was somewhat different from the ministrations she had practised on the front in 1918, when she had first met Kit, but she had every conviction that they would result in a complete recovery for the patient.

A few minutes later, Kit and Mary stood on the deck and gazed out into the ink-black night. The chill burned their skin causing them both to cling to one another for warmth, as much as for the sheer pleasure of holding one another.

'It was good of you to take the blame in there. I suppose I was a bit of a clot,' said Mary, grinning ruefully. When it comes to apologies, women will rarely take a direct route. Instead, circumnavigation is usually the preferred road; an approach that is wholly reliant on the short attention span of men. This rarely fails. Heart melting in the heat of the love he felt for Mary, Kit kissed her, thereby ending any further post-mortem on their woeful showing at the bridge table.

'What shall we do now?' asked Mary.

Kit had some ideas on this subject, but decided against suggesting them, lest it be seen as an attempt to extract further concessions from her. Perhaps later.

'Let's go for a walk. It might warm us up a bit,' he suggested.

'Good idea.'

They walked along the deck occasionally nodding to other passengers they'd met on the way over, on a journey that had begun five days ago on Boxing Day.

'When do we arrive in New York?' asked Mary.

'I imagine in less than eight hours,' said Kit.

It was around ten at night as they promenaded. They would arrive in New York on New Year's Eve. A long day and night lay ahead for them.

'I'm looking forward to the party,' said Mary, 'but I am worried we'll both be horribly tired.'

'We can rest in the afternoon,' said Kit. 'We're away for a month. There'll be plenty of time to see the city. No need to rush and see everything on the first day.'

Mary grinned like a child on Christmas Eve. This was exactly what she wanted to do. See everything immediately. Yet it made sense to be sensible. This was a trip she had been looking forward to for weeks, ever since Kit had suggested it. She had visited New York once before, almost two years previously, but that was en route to San Francisco. There hadn't been the time to see the sights. This time they would be able to enjoy the city fully. Although it had been a wrench to leave her family behind at Cavendish Hall, her family home, she was going to see her other family. And she couldn't wait.

'I hope they've organised an itinerary for us, social, cultural and otherwise.'

'Knowing them, it will all be in hand,' said Kit.

2 7am

New York: 31st December 1921

The last time Mary had arrived in New York, she caused something of a commotion, as a combination of her looks and proximity to nobility had the waiting pressmen in a lather. The arrival of the Aquitania on New Year's Eve was a little more understated. A combination of foul weather and the prospect of a long evening ahead had dissuaded many pressmen or photographers from waiting to record the arrival of notables on the liner.

This suited the Astons down to the ground. Kit glanced up at the leaden sky, noted the fact that his eyeballs were frosting over and immediately scanned the quayside for a friendly face. He spotted a man dressed in a costume that Americans thought English chauffeurs wore. He was holding a handwritten sign which read:

CHRISTOPHER & MARY ASTON.

This made Mary smile affectionately. Kit waved over to the man and then pointed to a customs hut that he and Mary had to visit before they could join him in the car. The man offered a salute.

Fifteen minutes later, the American customs official deemed Kit and Mary trustworthy enough to be allowed into the country. They headed out into the open air which appeared to have grown colder in the few minutes they had been inside.

The chauffeur came over and introduced himself as Lester. Kit shook his hand, which required little effort as most of his body was already shivering in the cold.

'I hope we didn't keep you waiting too long. It's a bit on the chilly side.'

'You can say that again, bud,' grinned Lester before realising he was speaking to English nobility. 'Hey, sorry, I forgot myself there.'

'Don't worry,' said Kit. 'I've heard worse, trust me.'

'And that's just from me,' chipped in Mary.

Lester took one look at Mary, and it took a great effort on his part to stop himself wolf whistling. Kit could see the reaction on the chauffeur's face and smiled. If Mary's sister, Esther, had come, as originally intended, then he'd probably have fainted. As it was, she and her husband, Richard Bright, had other reasons for not coming. Sometime in early summer that reason would hopefully be delivered safely to an ecstatic mother and father.

'I spoke to the people at the boat. Your luggage will be sent on, but I am to take you directly to the Hotel des Artistes.'

'Hotel des Artistes, sounds interesting,' said Mary. 'Is it really full of artists?'

Lester nodded, 'It is. Writers too. One of the most famous artists in the country lives there, Charles Dana Gibson.

You're staying in his apartment, I understand. Anyway, let's get to the car before we all freeze.'

'Good idea,' said Kit, following the American towards the large black car waiting on the quayside.

'There's someone waiting for you in the car.'

Kit and Mary looked at each other in surprise. It was barely seven in the morning. It struck them as a little early for anyone to have come to greet them.

They reached the car to find, to their surprise, sheltering from the sleet, an old friend.

'Ella-Mae,' exclaimed Kit. Mary brushed past Kit and climbed into the car. She gave Ella-Mae a hug.

'Oh Miss Mary, it's so good to see you,' said Ella-Mae.

Kit, still standing outside the car and somewhat blocked-off in terms of climbing in, glanced at Lester, who was observing the greeting. Kit rolled his eyes. The chauffeur grinned in sympathy. Kit murmured to himself, 'Good to see you too, Kit. I've missed you.'

'Oh shush, you, sir,' said Ella-Mae. 'Don't think these old ears can't hear everything you're saying and everything you're thinking.'

'I never doubted it,' responded Kit, climbing into the automobile at long last. He kissed the old housekeeper on the cheek. 'So how are my dear aunt and uncle?'

'Bickering as usual,' came the reply.

This was not quite true. Both Agatha and Alastair, Kit's aunt and uncle, were fast asleep in the warmth of the apartment they'd rented for the month. It had been left to Alastair's housekeeper to do the honours of greeting the couple. This had been done at her insistence, not Alastair's who'd dismissed the idea as "soft". However, after several decades as master and housekeeper such distinctions had become blurred. Now, they resembled nothing less than a put upon husband and a dominating wife.

The arrival of Kit was deemed by Alastair as something akin to the US Cavalry arriving. He was besieged by his sister and housekeeper and needed the odds to be evened up. As much as he adored his sister, Agatha had rather a singular view of how things should be done. She and Alastair would discuss any given issue, then they agreed that Agatha was right. As a decision-making process, what it lacked in democratic construction was more than compensated for by its efficiency. To be fair to Agatha, Alastair rarely gave much consideration to anything and usually just argued with her for the fun of it.

Lester was under instruction not to arrive at the building before eight. The drive from the harbour was probably going to be close to an hour anyway. This would give him a chance to show Mary a bit of Manhattan and also allow both Agatha and Alastair a chance to get more sleep.

Fifteen minutes before Kit and Mary's car pulled up outside the Upper West Side seventeen storey building, Agatha was out of bed. She immediately sent word down to the kitchen, on the second floor, that they should send up some coffees and brioche. An unusual feature of the building they were in was the lack of kitchen facilities in the rooms. Instead, residents could either eat in the restaurant or order food, which was sent up via dumb waiter.

Order made, Agatha washed and dressed, in readiness to receive Kit and Mary. The last time she had seen them was a rather more exciting trip to Morocco than she had intended. A week or two spent on the run from the police was not an ideal way to holiday. Thankfully, she had managed to avoid arrest and stop a potential revolution.* She hoped, for once, that she could see the young couple and avoid some of the usual trouble that seemed to come their way.

Agatha had had her fair share of adventure over the years. Now in her seventh decade, she was more aware of her age. She had moved to the south of France to live out her remaining years, she hoped, in peace with her two great friends, Betty Simpson and Jocelyn, "Sausage" Gossage.

Since returning from Morocco, she and her friends had managed to avoid trouble before she had come over to the United States, just before Christmas, to spend time with her brother in San Francisco. The plan was to meet with Kit and Mary, in New York and then depart with them on the Mauritania, towards the end of January.

Agatha wandered over to the window and risked a glance down. Almost immediately she stepped back. They were at least eight floors up. The automobiles, far down below, seemed like nothing less than insects crawling around the street. This was a little bit much, especially so early in the morning. She would never understand the American penchant for building so high. She much preferred the European style of low-rise buildings, which rarely exceed five storeys. This was, to her mind, a much more sensible, more human and considerate way of living.

From one of the three bedrooms, she heard the noise of the male of the species slowly awaking from its slumber.

'Hurry up, they'll be here for eight.'

'Yes, yes, all right, I'm coming,' came the reply of a sixty-year-old teenager from the bedroom.

Mary was delighted by the trip through Manhattan. Lester had clearly done this many times before and was an assured guide and added even to Kit's knowledge of the island. On top of this, Lester was an avid boxing fan and provided Kit with an eyewitness view of the current world heavyweight champion, Jack Dempsey.

'I saw him against Carpentier,' explained Lester. 'The man is a killer. I've never seen anything like him in the ring. The French guy showed pluck…'

'He fought against the Germans,' pointed out Kit.

'I know,' nodded Lester. 'I think I'd rather have taken my chances against them than Dempsey though. You know, they booed Dempsey on the ring walk. The crowd were on Carpentier's side.'

'Were you?' asked Kit, genuinely surprised by this.

Lester used his hand to indicate that he could have gone either way. Then he pointed up, to a tall grey building which came into view as they passed away from Central Park and pulled onto west 67th Street, a narrow tree-lined road. Mary looked out of the window at the building. It was very much in the New York style with just a hint of Gothic design, around the large window of the second floor.

Soon they were out of the car and braving the icy rain, falling in sheets. A doorman tipped his hat to them as they rushed up the steps.

'Sorry about the weather,' commented the doorman, as he held the door open for them.

'We're British,' replied Kit. 'This is what summer looks like.'

The comment drew laughter from the doorman, 'Then you'll feel right at home here, sir.'

Lester took them up to the twelfth floor. The lift doors opened, and they walked along a marble corridor to a dark mahogany door. Kit rang the buzzer. Moments later the door opened to reveal Alastair.

'Kit, my boy,' grinned Alastair, shaking Kit's hand firmly. Kit's uncle was in his early sixties, bald with tufts of silver hair either side of his ears. His face was permanently set in a relaxed smile and a look that seemed to have a beatific enjoyment of the nonsense he was hearing around him. Following the handshake with Kit, he gave Mary a hug and a kiss while Ella-Mae earned a scowl. The ageing housekeeper returned the compliment.

Agatha came over and went to Mary first. There was no English reserve in the greeting. They hugged and perhaps a discreet tear was shed. Agatha would want nothing less, than to hug the young woman that she had come to view as a daughter. Certainly, any tears were discreet enough to be hidden from male view.

'Christopher,' said Agatha, giving her favourite nephew a look of studied disdain. 'Still as skinny as ever.' This was hardly fair, but Agatha never liked to hand out compliments to men when an insult could suffice instead. Kit laughed and hugged her anyway. This secretly delighted Agatha and she showed it by saying, 'Unhand me you lout.'

Kit and Mary stood back to look at the apartment.

'You're not staying with us,' said Agatha. 'We've organised for you to take the room of an artist, who lives on the floor above.'

'Oh yes, Lester mentioned someone called Charles Dana Gibson,' said Mary.

'Yes, that's him. Charming fellow. Rather good artist too,' said Agatha. 'I told him all about you, Mary. I think he'd like you to pose when he comes back at the end of the month. He's famous for his pictures of girls. The Gibson Girls I believe they're called.'

'Really?' exclaimed Mary, with a little more enthusiasm than Kit would have liked.

'I'm not sure I like the idea of some artist wanting to paint Mary,' said Kit.

'I don't know what you have in mind, Christopher, but she'll have her clothes on,' said Agatha rolling her eyes.

Mary grinned primly up at Kit, which was a lot less reassuring than it should have been. So much so, in fact, that Kit burst out laughing and murmured, 'Minx.'

'That's one of his over there,' said Agatha, ignoring her nephew and pointing to the wall.

All eyes turned to a small, black-framed picture of no more than twelve inches square. It showed a young woman's face and was drawn with pen and ink. Mary, joined by Kit, moved closer to view it better.

'It's lovely,' said Mary.

'Yes. Well, in that case, I hereby give you my permission to pose,' announced Kit. He was laughing as he said this.

Mary curtsied in response, before saying, 'I'll see if he does nudes, all the same.'

'Witch,' grinned Kit. Then he turned his attention to Agatha and asked, 'So, what have you organised for us tonight?'

'A murder mystery,' said Agatha.

**The Tangier Tajine (Kit Aston Mysteries Book 7)*

3

Kit was the first to speak, after the shocked silence that followed Agatha's announcement. He glanced from Agatha and then to Alastair, to assure himself that they were serious and then he said, 'There hasn't been a murder?'

'Correct, dear boy,' said Alastair. 'There hasn't been a murder. Your aunt's penchant for the dramatic knows no bounds.'

'So, there hasn't been a murder,' confirmed Mary.

'Not yet anyway,' said Agatha, her eyes on Alastair. 'Nothing so drastic. There is a young man on the floor above us who is a writer. He is throwing a murder mystery party. We all have to read a short story that he has written and then, at the dinner party, we will offer our solutions to the case. Sounds rather intriguing, don't you think?'

Mary's face erupted into a smile. This met with Agatha's approval. Kit was little more unsure.

'It doesn't sound in very good taste, Aunt Agatha,' pointed out Kit.

This was met with a pout from Mary and a 'pah' from Agatha. Clearly the ladies were all for it. Alastair lit his first cheroot of the day. He merely shrugged. By any stretch, Kit was outvoted. Even so, the idea sounded like it would be fun. He wasn't particularly keen on dancing in some club that evening. Having a prosthetic limb did limit his mobility around the dance floor somewhat. With each passing year the popularity of more energetic dances than the foxtrot appeared to be growing. Perhaps, an innocent murder mystery evening might be preferable.

'Very well,' said Kit breaking into a smile. 'When do we see this literary tome?'

'Oh, we have it here already. Amory sent us down a copy yesterday.'

'Amory?' asked Mary.

'Amory Beaufort, the young writer I was telling you about,' replied Agatha, turning to seek out the manuscript. 'He brought an extra copy for you and Kit.'

'How on earth did you get to meet this young man and end up talking murder?'

'Oh, Charles introduced us before he left for New Rochelle. He has another place up there.'

'Charles? You mean the artist chap?' asked Kit.

'Yes,' said Alastair. 'When Amory heard that your aunt was a 'lady', so to speak, he was positively insistent that we join him and his friends for the party. Of course, when he heard you were coming that set the seal on it. A famous lord and amateur detective.'

'Hardly famous,' said Kit.

'You'd be surprised, my boy. He'd certainly heard of you. Yes, poor boy was almost pawing the ground in anticipation. I wouldn't be surprised if he pops down to say hello to run his eyes over the runners and riders.'

'How do you mean?' asked Mary.

'Oh, Americans can be quite competitive,' pointed out Alastair. 'I imagine that the first to come up with a winning solution will have bragging rights. It would be good to have a British winner.'

'Of course,' agreed Agatha. 'Can't have the Americans winning.'

'Revenge for 1783?' suggested Kit. 'That'll teach them.'

'Don't be facetious, Christopher,' scolded Agatha. She pretended not to notice that Alastair and Mary were smiling.

Alastair blew a smoke ring and then said, 'I wouldn't be surprised if Amory has a little wager on the outcome with his friends. Who knows? If he likes the cut of the English representative's gib, he might put a few dollars on the unknown outsider.'

'I thought you said I was famous,' said Kit.

'I was talking about Mary,' laughed Alastair. He grinned triumphantly at his nephew.

'It sounds intriguing,' said Mary. 'What is the story like?'

'Well, I doubt he'll win many awards. It's a little in the manner of Scott Fitzgerald, I don't know if you read his last novel.'

'I did,' said Kit and Mary in unison.

'I gave it to Kit,' said Mary. 'You know what he can be like. He seems to regard his presence in the twentieth century as a mistake and don't start him on modern literature.'

Kit gazed affectionately at Mary and replied, 'There are some compensations to growing up in this century.'

'I shall feel ill soon,' said Agatha. Then a thought struck her. 'By the way, I meant to ask. Did you not bring Sammy?' Kit and Mary glanced at one another. There was a moment's silence. Then Agatha took Kit's hand, 'I'm so sorry.'

Kit inhaled deeply. The little Jack Russell had died a few weeks previously. He still felt the pain of losing his friend from university.

'Yes, we lost him. It was rather sudden, but I don't think he suffered,' said Kit.

Mary put head against his arm. She said, 'Simpkins misses him horribly.'

Agatha seemed emotional also. She asked, 'Did you bury him...?'

'Yes,' nodded Kit. 'He's beside Talleyrand and Dumas.' Agatha smiled at this, and her eyes misted over as memories crowded her mind of the two Bassets she'd had as a young and, then, married woman. Her reverie was interrupted by the sound of a buzzer.

'Someone at the door?' asked Mary.

'No, coffee,' replied Agatha before going on to explain the dumb waiter system in the apartments. 'The button is on the wall here. You just turn it on and off. All powered by electricity. Marvellous really. There's a rope here too as a backup in case the power supply is interrupted.'

'How modern,' said Mary. As Ella-Mae brought a tray containing coffee and cakes down from the second, duplex, floor of the apartment.

'After we have our coffee, we'll take you up to your apartment. Charles left us the keys. It's much the same as ours which belongs to a friend of his, called Robson. You're on the same floor as Amory, you'll be glad to hear.'

'What's he like?' asked Mary.

'Well, you'll find out soon enough,' said Agatha, handing over the manuscript to Mary. 'Good-looking, smart. I think he fancies himself a little like Oscar Wilde. He's certainly not that, but likeable. Here's the short story.'

'Have you worked out the solution?' asked Kit, opening the first page.

Agatha pursed her lips and raised her eyebrows. She responded, 'It's not exactly laid out on a plate for you. I think the idea is that we all read it and then ask him some questions about what happens in it. He'll provide more meat to the bones.'

The title of the short story was *The New Year's Eve Murders.* This seemed suitably melodramatic, without ever overstepping the bounds into lurid.

'We can read it later and then, I suppose, we'll compare notes?' suggested Kit.

'Not quite,' said Agatha. 'There is a twist to this particular tale.'

Kit and Mary looked up sharply. Both noted that Alastair was grinning, like a Cheshire cat being handed his fourth gin and tonic.

'Apparently, we are going to be in teams. He asked me what I would like to do?'

'And what did you suggest?' said Kit, fixing an amused eye on Mary.

'Well, I thought that you might like to team up with Alastair…'

'While you and Mary…'

'Excellent,' said Mary. 'Boys against girls.'

Agatha clapped her hands and said, 'That's the spirit, Mary. I knew you would approve.'

'May the best man win,' replied Kit pointedly. Mary scrunched up her face at this and then shot Kit in the head with her forefingers and thumb.

As Agatha had suggested, the apartment was very like the one downstairs, except it was full of the artist owner's works. The walls were lined with pictures of the Gibson Girls. Kit had to admit he was very talented. The drawings showed, mostly young women dressed in the modern fashions of the day, starting from the turn of the century to more flapper-like creatures. The women seemed to Kit to be like Mary. Young, beautiful, assured, unselfconsciously confident, but without arrogance.

'You don't mind if I sit for him?' asked Mary, taking Kit's hand.

'No, don't be silly, of course not. He is rather good,' answered Kit. He went over to a table and picked up a photograph. It showed a tall, urbane man in his late fifties, with a handsome woman that Kit suspected was his wife. He didn't seem like a dissolute pre-Raphaelite, keen to persuade a young girl to shed her clothes, on the pretext of creating great art. Quite the opposite, in fact. He looked more like the owner of a large bank.

The bell rang, just as Kit was receiving further reassurance, as if he really needed it, of Mary's undying fidelity. Their suitcases had arrived. Much to Kit's initial surprise, Mary had not packed too many. Then he realised that this may have been an excuse to investigate the shops on Fifth Avenue, of which she had heard great things from Esther, who had been there just before summer.

The bell hop left, considerably richer than when he had arrived. As he left, Kit noticed that a few people were arriving at the apartment situated at the end of the corridor. They were carrying furniture and what looked like musical instruments. Perhaps, there would be dancing after all. Overseeing matters was a black manservant. He was around Kit's age. Their eyes met briefly. Kit smiled and the man bowed slightly, before returning his attention to directing the considerable amount of traffic entering the apartment.

Kit went back inside to carry the cases into the bedroom. The room was large, with high ceilings. The décor, like much of the apartment, was in the modern art deco style, which Kit was slowly becoming used to. While he quite liked the minimalism, which was quite male, he still had reservations about its aesthetic appeal.

'Looks like we will have music tonight. I saw a lot of activity out in the corridor,' said Kit.

'It must be quite a large apartment. Perhaps, we should say "hello" and introduce ourselves,' suggested Mary.

Kit was less keen on imposing but, before he could say anything, they heard the buzzer ring.

'I'll assume that's not the dumb waiter,' said Kit. 'I'll see who it is.'

A few moments later, Kit opened the door to find a young man standing there, holding a bunch of pansies. He was as tall as Kit, with a face almost feminine in shape. He was one of the most striking people Kit had ever met. He wore a bright red coat that would, unquestionably, have met with the approval of the young and the fashionable disapproval of the old.

'If you are not Lord Kit Aston then I'm ringing the police,' said the man with a grin, revealing very white, even teeth. Kit assumed this was Amory Beaufort. He was tall and slender with dark curly hair, symmetrical features and long eyelashes draped over bored blue eyes. He was so upper class American he almost seemed as if he was parodying English nobility.

Kit looked at the flowers and replied, 'A man bringing flowers for my wife? I shall have my seconds speak to yours. What weapon would you like to use?'

'Sarcasm,' replied the man, before adding, after a beat, 'dipped in poisonous irony.'

'To the death?'

'Always.'

'Well you better come in and give these to Mary. Are you Mr Beaufort? I'm Kit Aston.'

Mary appeared at this point, causing the man to stop quite theatrically. Mary noted the sudden stop. Her eyes narrowed and she leaned her shoulder against the wall.

'I may have made another conquest,' she said, drily.

'You have,' said Amory. 'Is it too early to ask you to run away with me?'

Mary made a show of studying him, slowly, before replying with a frown, 'Do you like German poetry?'

'*Ja fraulein.*'

All three broke out into laughter and Amory Beaufort stayed for half an hour, which was enough time for him to whet their appetite for the evening ahead. Kit walked Amory to the door as the visit drew to a close. Outside in the hallway, there was a delivery of flowers arriving to the door of Amory's flat.

'Duty calls, I shall see you later.'

Kit watched Amory approach the delivery man. The door to the apartment opened just as Amory said, 'I'll let you in.'

Kit shut the door at that point and went to join Mary. They both lay down on the bed to rest. A long night lay ahead of them.

4

Frederick Hughes had first arrived in New York when he turned eighteen. That was fifteen years previously. He'd heard there was a place in Manhattan that would accept someone like him. That place was Harlem. For a country boy from Alabama, Harlem was quite a shock.

Almost his first act upon arriving in the city was to save an old man from being beaten up by two drunken white youths, out for some fun. Freddy was not a fighter, but he was tall and well made. He knew enough to send the two kids away, with a bruise or two.

The old man was grateful. Very grateful. He sized Freddy up in an instant and offered him a sofa to sleep on. Freddy accepted this, gratefully. He didn't have money and had even less of an idea on how he would earn any.

The old man found him work in a kitchen at a swanky uptown hotel. Freddy was overcome with appreciation. The next thing that the old man did was teach Freddy how to read and write properly. Freddy's education had ended around the time he was ten. He'd been sent to work in the fields. The south may have lost the Civil War yet, somehow, the message had not been received in that part of Alabama. Things had hardly changed there in a hundred years and Freddy was not prepared to wait for the day that they would.

He did what he had to do. He stole some money from the man who was employing the black fieldworkers. Employing was perhaps putting it a bit too strongly. He gave them enough to subsist on, but no more, while he made a fortune from his cotton.

He boarded a moving train and joined half a dozen other boys like him on their way to the city. He was the only one that made it. The others were caught as they neared New York, having not taken Freddy's advice to jump from the moving train a mile outside the town.

By the time he reached New York he'd run out of money and the shoes on his feet were in tatters. Meeting the old man was probably the best thing that had happened in Freddy's young life.

He stayed with the old man for two years. The old man ran a library in Harlem, supplied with books given by rich, liberal benefactors. Every day, Freddy would devour the books in the library. Every evening he would work almost twelve hours, late into the night, in the hotel kitchen. He would fall onto the couch around four every morning and sleep for five hours, before joining the old man in the library.

Youth can do this. Often youth has to. Energy pulses through your veins when you are young, like an electrical current, until one day life and responsibility slowly weaken the body's vitality and old age brings its comfortless embrace. Freddy survived a year in the kitchen before chance offered him an escape route. Short of staff in the restaurant, the *maître d'* suggested that Freddy be given a chance front of house. His good looks and almost noble bearing had marked him out from the others in the kitchen. Freddy had a natural grace and a manner that was polite but never servile.

The additional money from the role, mostly from tips, gave Freddy his first dilemma. He had saved enough to move out of the small apartment he shared with his original benefactor. But the old man was slowly succumbing to infirmity of age.

Freddy chose to stay.

Another year went and then another. He stuck with the old man and then he no longer had to. The death of his first real friend was a release for Freddy, but a shock none the less. Freddy paid for the funeral at the Abyssinian Baptist Church, and it seemed half of Harlem turned out to see the old man off.

Freddy never went back to the apartment. Instead, he quit his job as a waiter at the hotel and became the manservant to one of the hotel's regular customers, Albert Beaufort. He moved to Long Island and stayed in the Beaufort mansion for four years until he, too, passed away. This time it was not old age, but Spanish Flu. It nearly killed Freddy, but he made it through. Just when Freddy thought that he might have to leave the life of vicarious luxury he enjoyed, Beaufort's son, Amory, asked Freddy to join him in Manhattan in 1920. Freddy went.

The two men shared Amory's apartment in Manhattan, at the Hotel des Artistes. Amory was dedicated to a life of socialising and yet more socialising; he felt as if he, personally, had invented the Jazz Age. Through Amory, Freddy met many men and women who would one day come to define the era: the Fitzgeralds, Dorothy Parker and Harry Crosby.

On the morning of 31st December 1921, as he watched men file into his master's apartment to make it ready for bringing in 1922, Freddy realised and felt grateful for how far his life had come. Even the men taking orders from him, all of them white, did not blink at hearing a black man tell them what to do. How different life was here, compared to Alabama. Prejudice existed in New York. You could never escape the colour of your skin entirely, but it was an undercurrent, rather than a threat, that carried the real risk of death.

Freddy watched as a man wheeling a trolley with pots containing Cyclamen, Snowdrops and Pansies came in. Amory loved to have flowers in the house. So too did Freddy. He loved the delicate fragrances that represented such contrast to the stale smell of sweat he'd grown up with living in the south. There, people slowly soured in the sun. In New York, he had been cultivated and had grown. With the right nurture, anyone could grow and become beautiful, just like a flower. He truly believed this.

The man delivering the pansies was new to Freddy. He was tall and rather cadaverous. Freddy stopped him and asked, 'Where's Gus?'

'Who?'

'Gus normally brings the flowers.'

'I don't know any Gus. I'm Phil,' said the man. There was just enough irritation in his voice to warn Freddy not to push the issue. Then he noticed the card sitting in one of the pots. He stooped down and picked it up. Written in a very feminine hand was the following:

Seeing as you like flowers so much...

Freddy smiled at this. Amory had so many female admirers. It was difficult to keep up sometimes. Amory knew this. He was rich, handsome and young. He could have his choice and he couldn't help himself. His apartment should have a revolving door installed; Freddy would sometimes say archly to him.

Amory would laugh. He didn't disagree. Yet behind the clear blue eyes of the satyr, there was a sadness too. Freddy had seen it appear unbidden from time to time. Of course, he would never mention it. Instead, he would stare disapprovingly at Amory and say, "you need to settle down young man".

Freddy saw Amory come into the corridor from another room he had gone to visit. He was standing in the corridor behind the new delivery man. Alongside Amory, Freddy saw another man. He was as tall as Freddy and just as noble in his bearing. Freddy's eyes met those of the new man. The man nodded to him then returned to his apartment. The door closed.

'Someone's ordered me flowers,' said Amory, brushing past the delivery man. 'Put the pansies in my room, would you?'

Phil, the delivery man, fought back his initial instinct to tell the negro to get back to his field. He wasn't prejudiced, or so he believed, but some of them seemed to be getting a bit uppity. He wheeled the flowers into the apartment and stopped to take in its opulence.

It was a beauty and no mistake. Just like the guy had said it would be. He ventured further in and saw some men setting up a drum kit. Phil could not believe that somewhere like this would be owned by a negro. The man, who had asked him to bring the flowers up, brushed past him and trotted up the stairs. From the landing, he gazed down at Phil with a superiority that was not something he'd had to learn. It was something into which he'd been born. He looked like Douglas Fairbanks' better looking kid brother.

'Can you bring the yellow ones up here? Do you know who ordered them?' asked the man.

'I was just asked to deliver them, I don't know any more than that,' replied Phil, a little cowed by the evident superiority of the man staring down at him from the second floor of the apartment.

'Hurry up and bring them up here, will you?'

To be fair, it was difficult to know where else he could put the flowers. The apartment was a like a jungle. Phil had never seen so many flowers in one apartment. If it hadn't been for the fact that he could see the man looking down from the balcony was clearly the owner, he'd have said that the apartment was owned by a female.

'Pansies,' said the man. 'My favourite. Bring them up to my bedroom. I wonder who they are from.' He shook his head, as he considered the question, then decided there were more important things to be getting on with.

Tommy 'the Trump' Jackson watched the flowers being wheeled in by Phil. He glanced towards the drummer, Arnie Nichols and made a shape with his mouth. Arnie smirked and continued fixing a high hat to the rest of his drum kit.

'You never bring me flowers, Lanky,' said Tommy, to a man propping a double bass against the wall. The "Lanky" in question was a man named John Towers. He was six feet five, yet so skinny he might conceivably have fought at bantamweight, if he had been capable of punching out of a wet paper bag. He couldn't. Pugilism's loss was music's gain. His nimble hands danced over the double bass' strings like a ballerina on a hot plate.

The final member of the "Troopers" was Albrecht 'Fritz' Keeler. Like the other members of the band, he was an outsider, but this time it was nationality, rather than skin colour, that made him so. Fritz was a German by birth and by philosophy. He managed the band's schedule and, since joining them eight months earlier, he had doubled the number of engagements and helped their reputation no end, by the simple arrangement of having them turn up on time and not high. He ignored the flowers, until he saw the owner of the apartment appear.

This was the first time he'd seen Amory Beaufort. He was like a god looking down from Mount Olympus. He was about to mention the fact to his bandmates when he decided there would be no point. They were decent players and, better still, they did as he said. But classical mythology was not their thing.

'May I?' asked Fritz, sitting down at the large, black, grand piano near the foot of the stairs that led up to the balcony.

A curt nod from the balcony was confirmation enough. Fritz lifted the lid and played a few notes. It was perfectly in tune. He began playing a tune that had been in his head for a few days now. Sometimes he and Tommy would write the odd song together. Tommy was proving to be quite an agile lyricist while Fritz provided the tunes. Between them, they had written some numbers that were being introduced into their performances, alongside the standards that they played. They were good enough not to be noticed. Far from being a bad thing, Fritz took this as a positive. If no one noticed, then it meant that they were good enough to earn their place alongside more established tunes.

He started humming a tune that came into his head and then picked it out on the piano. Lanky glanced in his direction. He said, 'What's that?'

'I don't know,' came the honest answer. Fritz's accent was heavily accented. He'd been in America just eighteen months now. His English had always been good and now it was excellent. He'd never sing like Tommy unless they did that comic song they'd always talked about. It wasn't time yet for it. Too soon after Flanders. Perhaps one day they would though. He was sure Americans would enjoy hearing a German, with a heavy, accent singing a number making fun of his new country.

Just not yet.

Arnie had nearly completed erecting the drum kit, so Fritz walked over towards the window of the apartment and stared down at the narrow street below. He never had enjoyed heights and what he saw gave him a light-headed feeling, that went all the way to his feet. He stepped back and backed into someone. He turned around and found himself staring up at Zeus.

Fritz, it must be added, was around five feet five. He stared up at most everyone wherever he went. Zeus gazed down at him with an amused expression.

'A bit high?' asked the man.

He would be when their performance was over, but that was another story. Fritz smiled and repeated something he heard Lanky say often, 'You could say.' It wasn't exactly clear to him what he had said, as idioms were something he was still getting used to, but it seemed to amuse Zeus.

'I'm looking forward to tonight. Should be interesting,' he said enigmatically. Zeus stepped away from Fritz and went over to one of the two dozen potted plants with flowers that were strewn around the apartment, making it look like the gardens of Versailles. He took the stem of the cyclamen and smelled it. 'What time will you start?'

'We were told around six, for a half hour, just for the arrival of the guests. Then around eight thirty, for another hour and then from ten, until midnight.'

'Yes,' said Zeus, looking up from the cyclamen. 'That sounds about right. There's an envelope with the money in the drawer here. You can take it whenever you want.'

Fritz smile and replied, 'It's good of you to trust us.'

Zeus left them to go back upstairs. Fritz glanced to his fellow bandmates who all nodded. He, immediately, went over to the sideboard with the flowers. He opened the drawer. Inside was an envelope. He lifted it up. Underneath was a sheaf of papers. Fritz read what the top piece of paper said:

THE NEW YEAR'S EVE MURDERS by AMORY BEAUFORT

As Zeus had disappeared, Fritz glanced up to check he was gone. Then he picked up the story and showed it to the other band members. He smiled and shrugged.

'It seems he's a writer,' said Fritz replacing the papers.

Tommy had seen the title and said, 'Throw it over here. I wouldn't mind a read of that.'

5 THE NEW YEAR'S EVE MURDERS by AMORY BEAUFORT

All the world's a stage,
And all the men and women merely players;
They have their exits and their entrances;
And one man in his time plays many parts...

William Shakespeare

I THE THREE MUSKETEERS

The first day at a new school is terrifying, by any measure. For Dexter York it was particularly so. He was going to a private school. He'd never been a boarder before. That was for rich kids. His family were certainly not that. They weren't quite the wrong side of the tracks, but it was close enough for him to be worried about how he would be received.

He was almost thirteen years old. A prodigy or so he'd been told by his headmaster. Dexter knew he was different from the other kids in the school. Always had been. Whenever older kids would come to you demanding help with homework, then you knew you were smart. Some he helped because he liked them. Some of them took the wrong tone.

He dealt with them. After this, the kids at his old school did not mess him around. Besides, they liked him. He played on the football team as a running back. The fastest kid in the school they said, but Dexter suspected Joey was faster.

His mom and dad saw him off, much to his mortification. He could see the other parents, the other boys looking at his folks and he knew that trouble lay ahead. It took until lunchtime on the first day.

It was a tall kid who came strolling over. He was slender and, by any standards, he was a good-looking boy. An angel. Yet, the smile on his face was diabolic. Dexter had been here before. It was time to ensure that people understood what the acceptable tone of conversation should be.

'Who are you?' asked the boy, in a careless enough manner to suggest that he really didn't care what the answer was. Dexter was caught between being rude there and then or, at least, trying to be polite. A few boys were with the young prince. Dexter wondered if they would lay into him too.

'Dexter,' he said. He didn't bother asking the boy's name. His eyes bored into the other boy. This seemed to amuse him, but Dexter sensed he was slightly unsure now.

'Were those your folks, or staff?' asked the boy. There was just enough innocence in the question to disguise the sneering intent. A few boys sniggered.

Dexter was getting bored with this. He stepped forward, to within a few inches of the boy. By Dexter's reckoning he was giving him three inches in height, but Dexter was more powerful and had been in a few fights. He fancied his chances.

'Why don't you get on with what you came here to do?' snarled Dexter.

The punch was telegraphed. It had started out twelve years previously from a boy born within a week of Dexter. It connected with thin air.

Dexter took a step back and clouted his rival on the chin. The boy hit the ground with a thud but was up in an instant. They normally stayed down when Dexter caught them like that. Dexter knew he was in for a fight. He quickly went into a crouch, his fists up by his face. The other boy rubbed his chin. He tuned to his friends and grinned.

'That was some punch,' he said to them. They looked a little confused.

One of his friends, a little stouter than the others said, 'Why don't you leave him alone Archie? What's he done?'

The boy Dexter had hit, Archie, glanced towards Dexter and grinned. He said, 'Dexter, you say? I'm Archie.'

Archie held out his hand. After a moment's hesitation, Dexter shook it. Dexter glanced towards the boy who had acted as peacemaker.

'Thanks,' said Dexter, holding out his hand.

The stout boy smiled back at him and rolled his eyes. He said, 'You have to ignore Archie. Likes to test the mettle of the new boys.'

'Did I pass?' asked Dexter.

'Flying colours. My name is Chad Lyons,' said Charlie. They shook hands and the friendship of the three boys was sealed.

II THE STATE PENNANT

The friendship between the three boys grew from this moment. For five years they were inseparable. Archie was the leader, no doubt about that. He was the smartest boy in the school, even Dexter had to acknowledge this, although he did have a blind spot, when it came to mathematics. Chad and numbers was a marriage made in heaven. As good as Dexter was in this subject, he had to admit, Chad was something else again.

Another area where Chad excelled was sport. He was the strongest boy in the school and dominated all the field events except the javelin. This was Archie's best event. His wiry frame seemed perfect to propel the javelin prodigious lengths. Dexter was the fastest of the three, marginally quicker than

Archie over the hundred, but no one could touch Chad over the first fifty. Then he would burn out.

This year, at Haley Academy, was a vintage year. For the first time, they had a shot at winning the pennant. Archie was natural leader and his golden arm meant he was the quarterback. Dexter's speed and power made him a natural running back and sometime wide receiver.

Chad enjoyed hitting people. Hard. He was a line-backer, who developed a fearsome reputation for turning over quarterbacks. The finals beckoned. One problem faced them though. The Academy was small and had never won before. Their opponents were the reigning champions, with a long tradition of victory in the State Pennant.

Fourth quarter, after a closely fought match, saw the two teams separated by a touchdown and two points. Haley Academy had put in a heroic performance, but it seemed likely they would fall just short. There was barely a minute left on the clock, and they were on their own twenty-yard line. Touchdown was so far away it may as well have been in a different state. With just over one minute left on the clock, the team formed a huddle around Archie.

'What's the plan,' asked Dexter.

Archie gazed around at the exhausted faces of his men. To attempt to make progress up the field would be madness. Their opponents were simply too big and too strong. They had to gamble.

'I have an idea.'

'Go long?' asked Dexter.

'No, they'll be expecting us to do that.'

'Here's what I have in mind.' He told them and the team laughed in disbelief, or perhaps it was relief.

The two teams lined up facing one another. The ball came to Archie. Without looking he immediately released the ball to his right. It landed in Chad's hands. He tore ahead into the empty space. No one would catch him, at least for the first thirty yards. This was when the second part of the plan came into force. Chad immediately released the ball, rugby-style, to his right.

Dexter caught the ball and dashed off the remaining forty yards to touch down and bring them to within two points of victory.

The match restarted. The clock ticked away inexorably. As if the referee needed any help, the Haley Academy crowd counted down the clock on his behalf.

THIRTY, TWENTY-NINE, TWENTY-EIGHT...

Their quarterback fumbled. Chad was on him. This was the first time in the match he'd got near him. The ball was in his hand, and he had fifty yards to travel.

Then it was forty yards.

TWELVE, ELEVEN, TEN...

They caught him on the ten-yard line. He collapsed to the ground in a heap.

FOUR, THREE, TWO

The Haley Academy crowd erupted into a cheer, as much of relief as joy. Haley had fought heroically but they had, unquestionably, lost.

Archie called the team into a huddle. He saw tears streaming down the eyes of his men. He put an arm around Chad who was crying uncontrollably.

'Men, I'm proud of you,' he began. 'Lament not. I've never been so proud of anyone as I am of you right now. What we have done will be spoken about for generations at Haley. No prouder words will be spoken, from any student, than to say, I was there the day they played the Pennant.'

The team cheered Archie and themselves. Dexter cheered too, stirred by Archie's words but also laughing too. He caught the eyes of Archie.

There was a ghost of a smile on his friend's lips. The first shadow fell between them in five years.

III PRINCETON

It was towards the end of their first year at Princeton, when Archie hurried towards the rooms he shared with his two friends, carrying his latest acquisition. The sunlight seared the sidewalk, making Archie wish he'd brought something to shade his eyes. But, then again, it was worth seeing the reaction of passers-by to his clear blue eyes. He dashed up the stairs to his room, hoping the boys would be there.

Bursting through the doors, he caught his two friends, neck deep in their books, preparing for the first-year exams. He'd done next to nothing, of course. English Literature was one of the easier options he could have chosen, and he'd read the books that he'd be examined on, ten years earlier.

'Look what I bought today at the auction,' announced Archie. He was brandishing a pair of pearl-handled colt revolvers.

'Good Lord,' said Chad, somewhat appalled by the two weapons. 'Do they actually work?'

'I was told they do. They used to be owned by Pat Garrett.'

Dexter, who was sitting on the bed, law book in hand, erupted into laughter. Archie began laughing too.

‘Did the auctioneer say that these are the weapons that killed Billy the Kid?’

‘He did,’ laughed Archie. ‘I couldn’t resist when I heard that.’

‘Did they really?’ asked Chad, always the most querulous of the three. A pillow hit the side of his head, thrown by Dexter. ‘That’s a “no”, then,’ laughed Chad.

Archie glanced down at the newspaper Chad had been reading. The headline was particularly large. He bent over and spun the newspaper around. A man named Princip had assassinated Archduke Franz Ferdinand.

‘Looks like war,’ said Archie. Then he rolled one of the revolvers gunslinger style around his finger. ‘I’ll be ready.’

The three boys’ chuckles turned into uproarious laughter when Francis, the houseboy, entered the room and saw the guns. His eyes widened in horror, and he ran out shouting, ‘Laud, they goin’ to kill me. They goin’ to kill me.’

A few of the other fellows entered their room, to see what the commotion was all about. The first was the Englishman they called Lord Fauntleroy. Whether he was a lord, or not, was up for debate, but he acted like he was nobility, and everyone liked him well enough for all that. His conversation had a certain verve, that went down well with Archie. The Redcoats had been defeated, said Archie, let bygones be bygones.

IV HELEN

The three years that followed at Princeton went by in a flurry of parties, broken hearts and mild intoxication. To be rich, to be American and to be young, at that time, would have made even Wordsworth reconsider his original views on time and location.

As bachelors went, the three boys were both desirable and distinguished. In Archie's case, very rich too, but that was merely the cherry on a rather attractive cake. And the girls rarely went hungry when he was around. He absorbed himself in alcohol, to an extent that would have had Dionysius shaking his head sadly.

And then everything changed.

Chad met her first.

Helen du Bois.

No one ever believed the family was really called this, but it suited them. They gave the impression that they were old money from the south. Chad didn't care. Her purpose in life was to make men miserable. In this she was strikingly successful

He wrote to his friends, over the summer, about how he had met the most beautiful girl he'd ever set eyes on. Her hair contains sunlight, he cooed in one letter.

Archie and Dexter ribbed him in their letters back to him. He told them they would meet her when they returned to Princeton, after the holidays. As it turned out, Archie was late back to the college, as he had been over recent terms. He was guaranteed to finish top of his class, no matter what. He was the outstanding student of the year. Everyone said he would be a writer.

By the time Archie met Helen, Dexter had already stolen her from Chad.

The conversation, when she'd told him, had been devastating. Chad would play it in his mind for years.

CHAD: I love you, you know, old thing.

HELEN: Oh, you are divine, Chad. I love you too. You're such a good friend.

CHAD: I could be more than a friend you know.

HELEN (*clapping her hands enthusiastically*): Yes, like a brother. My brother Chad. I spent the night with Dexter, you know. We held each other for all of the night. He's such a sweet boy. A gentleman. I like him so.

Her words stabbed away at him remorselessly, as only disinterested women can. She hardly stopped to breathe until, finally, he was able to escape, bloodied but unbowed, to fight another day. And then came the moment when his world came crashing around him.

And Dexter's too.

V THE STORM

Chad had put a brave face on things. It was true that he and Helen had dated, but things had not progressed as he thought they would, he told Archie in confidence, in their rooms, on Archie's first day back at Princeton. And he liked Dexter.

'When do I get to meet this gal?' asked Archie. Dexter was noticeably absent when he'd returned.

'This afternoon,' said Chad with a sad attempt at enthusiasm. 'We'll go for a jigger. She won't eat an ice cream, of course, but she likes to take some of mine or Dexter's.'

'Can we make it tonight? Is there a dance anywhere?'

'Yes, at the tennis club. I'll let Dexter know.'

The sky bled black, without stopping for any twilight. There was a storm brewing. Thundersnow they said. But youth cares little for such distractions. The young men wore black ties and the young women hardly anything at all, despite the snow falling.

By ten in the evening, there was no sign of Archie. Chad, as ever, made excuses for him.

'He's tired,' he said, not quite believing it himself. He was more accepting of his friend's innate selfishness than Dexter.

Helen didn't really care about Archie anyway and said so. She was already the subject of many admiring glances from the young men and envious looks of the young women. This was what she lived for.

Taking Helen on the dance floor was an exercise in patience for Dexter. Within a few moments, someone would cut in and ask to dance with her. In the end, Dexter avoided dancing. Helen didn't mind. No one could see her when she was on the middle of the floor.

Archie arrived just as the storm broke. It was almost as if he were waiting for the moment it would do so, thought Dexter afterwards. How very like Archie.

The crack of thunder brought practised screams from the ladies who were immediately comforted by men, chuckling to one another.

Archie emerged through the door as the thunder rolled. He fixed his eyes on Helen and she on him. He glided over to his friends and took Helen's hand. She gave it willingly, as Dexter looked on.

'So, you are Helen,' said Archie. She nodded, but said nothing, waiting for him to make his next move. He stared at her coolly, taking in her moonlight-infused hair, her large eyes and the lips, that had probably been kissed by a hundred men. 'Let's dance,' he said without acknowledging Dexter.

Before she could refuse him, not that she would have, he led her onto the dance floor. They walked through the throng of bodies but, instead of stopping, they kept going through to the other side and out onto the terrace.

Helen was curious now. She gazed up at him and felt a little small. Her mother had warned her against college boys. For the most part, she had followed her advice and dated young men. Rich young men. Archie was like no one she had ever seen before. The mocking smile. The clear blue eyes, that seemed to understand her, undress her and leave her feeling vulnerable and desired.

She saw the sadness in his eyes, as he stood there, and it reflected her own.

'You're beautiful, I suppose,' said Archie.

'You don't seem sure,' answered Helen.

'Beauty should not be obvious.'

'What should it be?'

'A puzzle, a mystery, a question rather than an answer, anticipation rather than consumption.'

'I never want to marry,' said Helen.

'I hate convention,' responded Archie. 'I don't want to fall in love with you. I despise predictability.'

'It's so banal. Love, that is.'

'If I were to kiss you now, it would destroy me. A part of me would die,' announced Archie.

'Would it?' she asked hopefully.

'Yes, forever.'

They walked back to the dance floor and went in different directions. Helen returned to Dexter. She ignored the question in his eyes. It was the same question. Always. From all men. All except one. For the first time she had met someone just like her. Who needed no one. And now she needed him. She looked at Dexter and said, 'I don't love you.'

She walked away from him, leaving Dexter open-mouthed. Chad looked on in astonishment.

'I say,' was all Chad could muster at that moment. They watched as Helen walked towards the French doors, that led out to a patio, where all the lovers went to gaze at the moon, search for shooting stars and make wishes.

She found him sitting on top of the balustrade, calmly smoking a cigarette. Without moving his head, his eyes flicked upward as he watched her approach. Around her the crowd whirled and shifted. Light filled her hair and made her seem like an angel.

'You came,' said Archie.

'I've kissed dozens of men,' said Helen, with her arms stiff by her sides, like an obstinate three-year-old.

'I really want to kiss you Helen,' said Archie.

'I want you to kiss me.'

VI WAR AND OTHER MATTERS

Dexter and Chad both enlisted after graduation that autumn. It seemed the thing to do and they did it, with all of the enthusiasm of lost men. Archie stayed with Helen. The same Helen he had stolen from Dexter two months earlier.

Dexter had put a brave face on it, but he was heartbroken. It was impossible to be angry with Archie for long. If Chad could forgive, well, darn it, so could he.

In the period after Archie had taken Helen from him, he concluded that he had done the right thing. He realised now that he detested Helen. He'd been blinded by her beauty. Yet now when they met; he was struck by how her voice bubbled with stupidity. She had no women friends, only male admirers.

He would have warned Archie about her, but he sensed that possessing Helen was just another way to make manifest the ultimate love of his life: himself.

Their parting of the ways came not because he had stolen his girlfriend, it came not because of his refusal to enlist. It came because, as with most things, he was probably right, but he made you feel small and insignificant when he was.

'You are both fools,' said Archie, as he watched his friends pack their trunks. In a few days they would be at the army camp. Lord Fauntleroy was with them. He was returning to England, he said. No one believed him. Chad had heard a rumour that he was going to Hollywood.

'Perhaps we'll be on the same boat home,' said Fauntleroy.

'Perhaps,' said Dexter.

Archie picked up the two pistols and pretended to shoot the houseboy, who was tidying their room. A wide smile appeared on Archie's face as he did this. Francis scuttled out of the room, leaving the job half done.

'I wish you wouldn't do that,' said Chad irritably.

'Do what?' asked Archie.

'Point those things at him, you know how nervous he is.'

Archie looked at the two handguns, allegedly owned by Pat Garrett. Unconsciously, he had been twirling them and using them to point at his friends and Francis.

'They're probably not loaded,' said Archie.

'You mean you haven't checked?' exclaimed Dexter. He remembered a night a few months previously when they had fired them for the first time. It woke half the college and resulted in the police raiding their room. They never found the weapons. Archie never said what he'd done with them.

There was a wild look in Archie's eyes as he spoke to them.

'I wish you wouldn't go.'

Dexter didn't respond. He was trained in law, but he knew better than to argue with his friend.

'It's too late,' pointed out Chad. 'If we bail out now we'll go to prison.'

'Let's go to Canada,' suggested Archie, impractical as ever. 'Imagine. We'd be on the run together.'

'We'd be on the run,' said Chad. 'You'd be on holiday.'

'Come on. Where's your sense of adventure?'

'What about Helen?' asked Dexter, at last.

The wild look reappeared in his friend's eyes. He shook his head and replied, 'No, just us.'

'What's wrong?' said Dexter. A frown appeared on his forehead.

'Helen's not well, you know. I blame her mother.'

The three boys had all met Mrs du Bois. She was someone you met once and avoided thereafter. All pitied her husband. He had married her beauty and now had a lifetime to regret his mistake. Helen was becoming the image of her mother.

'Let's go for a jigger,' suggested Chad. He knew that ice cream would be in short supply soon.

Dexter patted his friend's waist and said, 'Are you sure. I can see the sergeant major taking one look at you and making your life a misery.'

Chad laughed good-naturedly, but his suggestion carried the day. They went into town, to the ice cream parlour and ordered the biggest jiggers they could have.

'What are you going to do while we are away?' asked Dexter to Archie.

'I shall coin a few shallow epigrams, clothe them in a plot and try and sell them to a magazine or two. *Harpers* have asked me to send them something.'

'What will you write?' asked Chad.

'About the subject I know best: tragic love.'

Dexter wondered what Archie knew about love but refrained from saying.

VII NEW YEAR'S EVE

The bitter, tragic end to the last night of 1917 contrasted with the riotous, joyful party that had preceded it and made what happened all the more painful for those who were there.

'I have presents for you,' announced Archie as they dressed up for the evening. From his beaten leather saddle satchel, he extracted three, silver hip flasks. Written on the hip flasks were the names of the Earp brothers: Wyatt, Virgil and Morgan. They were the three who had faced the Clanton gang at the OK Corral. This brought a chortle from Chad, who immediately claimed the one marked 'Wyatt'. Dexter picked one up absently and nodded his thanks.

'Well, look at us,' said Archie. They were all dressed as Cowboys. Fauntleroy walked into the room, without knocking. He had this habit, which initially annoyed everyone, but now they were used to it. He was dressed as a sheriff.

'Are we off then?' he asked.

'We are,' said Dexter.

The Comanche Club was a war party without the war. A club dedicated to a sacred time before civilisation made the native people of America uncivilised. The band played ragtime music and the cowboys and the Indian girls, danced like the world was going to end the next day.

'Where's Helen?' asked Dexter when they arrived. 'No one will notice her late entrance,' he added looking around at the crowded delirium of the Princeton students.

Archie smiled enigmatically at this, which made Dexter wonder what they had planned. Something was afoot.

Half an hour later there was still no sign of Helen. Dexter and Chad were worried, but Archie just sat drinking a highball and smoking his cigarette. There was hardly a care in the world to be found in those blue eyes.

At last there was a short break in the dancing.

It was 11:30pm. The floor cleared just as Helen arrived. It was almost as if she had been waiting for her moment. She strode past the table where the boys were sitting, without even the merest hint of a glance at Archie, who smiled at her as she went by.

She was wearing Archie's raincoat which was soaked through. And she was barefoot which surprised Dexter. She had a small headdress with black-tipped white feathers. All eyes in the club were on her as she walked to the middle of the dance floor. A loud murmur greeted her arrival. She began to make strange jerky movements. Her head butted forward and back, and she hopped from one foot to another. As suddenly as she had started, she stopped. She stood tall. Everyone's eyes were upon her.

Then she threw off the coat.

Her pale white skin glowed in the dim light. A shocked silence fell over the club followed by uproar. Before anyone could react, she ran off the dance floor, through the French doors and into the night.

Dexter stared at the dance floor and then turned angrily on Archie. Their eyes met. Dexter was the first to look away.

'We must find her. She'll be arrested like that,' said Dexter, alarmed and angry.

Chad was furious, too. He turned on Archie, 'What did you say to her. Archie? Did you make her do that?'

Archie shook his head and shrugged casually.

'You wouldn't understand,' he said calmly. His blue eyes fixed, unrepentantly, on Chad, challenging him to argue the point. For once, Chad was ready for an argument.

'Try us,' yelled Chad. His eyes were bulging and a vein in his neck throbbed angrily.

'Let's go,' said Dexter. There was no time for discussion. They had to find her. 'Where will she go? Where do you usually go with her, Archie?'

'Lots of places, Dexter. She likes being in public if you take my meaning.'

Dexter and Chad's chests were heaving in hatred.

'Where?' snarled Chad, his face inches away from Archie.

'The lake sometimes. We like the old bandstand, too. We had a round of applause once, Chad; imagine that. The end zone on the football pitch, Helen liked it there. The symbolism.'

'Stop,' roared Dexter, gripping Archie by his shirt. He was about to hit him when Fauntleroy grabbed him by the arms and pulled him away.

'Dexter, enough. We have to find her,' said the Englishman. 'Did you see her eyes?'

Dexter could not tear his eyes away from Archie, but then he recovered his composure and looked at Fauntleroy.

'What do you mean?' he asked, confused and feeling a little stupid. He, like every man in the club, had not been looking at her eyes.

'I think she was on something,' said Fauntleroy. 'And that dance she started. It was strange. I saw it once before at one of those shows, you know, with people who knew Buffalo Bill.'

'We need to find her,' agreed Dexter. He turned to Archie, who was still smiling. 'What have you done to her? Where is she?'

'Come now,' said Archie. 'A beautiful girl like that, should be easy enough to find. It was the Ghost Dance, by the way, Fauntleroy. Very good. Didn't think you had it in you to spot that.'

'Why did she do that?' asked the Englishman.

'Why indeed. You need to find her, methinks, sire,' replied Archie, turning towards the clock on the wall. 'Twenty minutes from midnight. I really would be on my way, boys.'

'Why?' demanded Dexter. 'What will happen at midnight?'

They went to look for her. All of the time aware that, as the seconds counted down to midnight, something terrible would happen. A dozen of them helped in the search. The rain didn't help. They went everywhere that Archie had said and others that he hadn't.

They couldn't find her. And then it was too late.

They say she shot herself at midnight. The houseboy found her in the Archie's room. She was holding the pistol that Pat Garrett used to kill Billy 'the Kid'.

Don't believe that story either.

The End

6 2pm

It was two in the afternoon when Kit awoke to find himself alone in the bed. With a middle-aged groan despite only being thirty-two, he rose and propped himself up on one elbow. Mary was sitting by the window, wearing the blouse she had worn that morning coming from the boat. Her legs and feet were up on the table as she read the short story of their party host.

'How is it?' asked Kit.

'Interesting,' was the only answer Mary could think of at that moment. 'Do you want to read now?'

Looking at Mary's legs, which ran all the way to a blouse, that ended around her waist was a decidedly more enticing prospect to Kit than reading just at that moment. He declined politely.

They remained in exquisite silence for the next ten minutes, as Mary read the manuscript. Then Mary shuffled the papers and lobbed them onto the bed for Kit to read. He'd have liked at least another hour of staring at Mary, but it wasn't to be.

'Must I?' he complained with a grin.

'You must,' said Mary. 'We have to go down to Aunt Agatha at four and then onto the party for six. You need to read it and be ready.'

'You'll fix my tie?' asked Kit, scanning the cover. He began *The New Year's Eve Murders.* He said as he picked up the sheaf of papers, 'I don't suppose the butler did it?'

'Hard to say. I'm not sure I've ever actually read a story where the butler is the murderer. Perhaps someone should write a story like that. It might be original.'

'In an unoriginal way.'

'Exactly.'

Mary left Kit in peace to read the story, while she went to attend to her makeup. She rarely wore much makeup and abhorred the vampish styles that seemed to be becoming the rage. One Theda Bara was more than enough.

From the bathroom she was able to gaze out at the Manhattan skyline. The weather had barely improved from the morning and she was glad to be inside tonight rather than braving the crowds and the cold.

Fifteen minutes later, she returned to the bedroom to find Kit with the manuscript on his lap. It looked as if he'd finished. She stood in the doorway and leaned against the door frame. This would give Kit a perfect view of her slender figure.

'So, who did it?' she asked slowly.

Kit smiled up appreciatively at Mary for three beats longer than what protocol deemed necessary.

'I'm not sure I should say, as you are, after all, on a different team.'

Mary scrunched up her face at this unhelpful response. She undid the first button on her blouse.

'Not a word shall pass my lips,' said Kit resolutely, putting his hands behind his head.

Mary undid the second button.

'You realise that this rather incentivises me not to tell you immediately, but to resist,' pointed out Kit.

'I rather like it when you resist.'

At a certain point it became too hard to resist further.

Around three thirty, Mary made her way down to her aunt's apartment. Alastair opened the door and grinned a grin that was, even by his standards, rather effusive. In his hand may have been a contributory factor.

'Is that?' began Mary.

'Yes, it's a gin,' answered Alastair. 'Let me get you one. Where's Kit?'

This was interesting as, only a year previously, the United States, for reasons surpassing common sense, had collectively decided on an act of unparalleled self-harm. They had prohibited the sale of alcohol, thereby contributing to the growth of an illicit trade on drink, the rise of organised crime and, in the process, turned millions of Americans into *de facto* criminals.

Agatha appeared at that point also clutching some liquid sustenance. She saw Mary's eyes drawn towards the glass and then shrugged.

'I gather there's a policeman attending this evening so we may as well have a few snifters now.' Mary grinned conspiratorially at this. Then Agatha added, 'Come into my room for a moment, I want to show you something.'

Mary followed Agatha into her bedroom. It was a good-sized room with wooden panelling. It provided a wonderful view of Central Park. In the drizzle.

'Now, have you had a chance to view the manuscript?'

'And Christopher?'

'Yes, he read it after me.'

'What were his thoughts?' asked Agatha.

Mary coloured a little and turned her attention to the view.

'He wasn't very forthcoming initially,' began Mary.

Agatha snorted at this and gave Mary a deliberately long look, 'Well, if you weren't able to ease a confession out of him using what you were born with, then you're not half the woman I thought you were.'

In fact, Kit had wilted, more than once, under the intense interrogation from Mary and happily revealed what he was thinking.

'Well, the first comment he made was on the title.'

Agatha made a noise, that was perilously close to dismissal, before saying, 'I think we all noticed that only one death had occurred in the story, nor was there any suggestion of another. So far, so obvious'

'True, but it was the way he said it.'

'You think he's worried this is only a prelude to a murder yet to occur.'

'Yes.'

'I've been wondering about that, too.'

'What about Uncle Alastair?'

'Alastair fully intends letting Kit do all the work. He won't admit it, but he has yet to guess the killer in any book we've jointly read,' said Agatha.

'And you?'

'Need you ask?' said Agatha draining the rest of her gin. The bell went as she did this. Then she added drily, 'Our conscience has arrived. You should have had a snifter when it was offered.'

The two ladies returned to the living room where they found an uneasy silence between uncle and nephew.

'I fear I owe you five dollars,' said Alastair glumly.

'I told you,' said Agatha triumphantly.

Kit immediately guessed that he had been the source of the bet.

'I fear I've let you down Uncle Alastair,' grinned Kit unrepentantly. 'Did you really think I would drink alcohol made by some gangster?'

'Never dear boy, but just once, I wish you would show a chink of imperfection to make us mere mortals feel less like...'

'Heels?' suggested Mary.

'Precisely,' agreed the Alastair. 'Anyway. I would like to plead some mitigation before I receive sentence from my all-too-good nephew.'

'Go on,' said Kit, genuinely curious.

'Follow me,' said Alastair, ignoring the murmured "are you sure?" from Agatha. This was greeted by an amused frown from Kit.

Alastair led them towards a cupboard. They opened the door. What they saw made Kit and Mary both gasp. The space was piled high with bottles of wine, of gin, of vodka. There must have been a couple of dozen bottles, stacked on shelves around the room.

'The owner is an old friend of mine. We saw the direction that the country was taking, years before they decided to impose Prohibition. I advised him to stock up. He never regretted it.'

Alastair, like many wealthy Americans fond of retaining a legal link to the convivial past, had simply stocked up their reserves, perfectly legally, in the hope that they would outlast the Draconian law.

'He's always been rather grateful for the idea and said I could avail myself any time I was in New York. I might add that this is all perfectly legal Kit.'

Kit remembered his uncle's well-stocked cellar. What his uncle said was correct and Kit decided not to argue the point. His life was privileged, and this was just a further example of it. He let his uncle pour him some gin.

'So, we will be dry tonight, you think?' said Kit, trying the gin. He nodded appreciatively to his uncle.

'Well Amory, rather like myself and my friend, has his own stash. I'm not sure he'll feel able to share it if this police detective is in attendance. I rather think he'll need to test the water, so to speak.'

This was certainly an area where they would have to tread carefully. Kit had no doubt that many policemen in the country continued to enjoy alcohol. He had no doubt that a small group were profiting from Prohibition. There was probably a smaller group, who stood resolutely in favour of the law and would not allow liquor to pass their lips. Kit and the others could not risk that the policeman in attendance this evening was one of those "hold outs". 'Have you met any of the guests coming tonight?'

'No,' confirmed Alastair. 'We are going into the unknown. I don't know anything about them, except our police party pooper. I think I rather dislike him already. Now tell me, before your aunt tries to wheedle it out of you, who did it and why?"

'Mary's already taken a run at that.'

‘I don’t doubt she succeeded too. The spirit was willing I’m sure,’ said Alastair, eyeing his nephew wryly.

Kit thought about the pleasant afternoon he’d enjoyed and laughed. He said, ‘The truth is I’m not sure, but I am a little worried by what lies ahead. The story was a little opaque and if it weren’t for the title one would say – what murder? But then the title is plural not singular, yet only one person died in the story.’

‘Yes, your aunt was concerned about the title and what it meant. Did nothing else occur to you?’

Kit nodded and replied, ‘Let’s just say, I’m curious about the people we are meeting later.’

‘I am too, but I know you. You have a reason for saying this,’ said Alastair.

Kit glanced sideways at Alastair and replied, ‘I have a feeling, despite what you just said, we’ve already met one of them.’

7 5:30pm

Inspector Flynn was one of the youngest men to have made this rank in the history of the New York Police Department. He'd made it just a month shy of his thirty-fourth birthday. That was twenty-five years ago. He was a big man, but not physically. He had charisma and an air of authority that was recognised, and acted upon, by all who knew him.

There were two exceptions to this: his late beloved wife Nancy and his daughter, Roberta.

His daughter was only called Roberta when he was exasperated with her, which was often, and Bobbie the rest of the time. Bobbie, meanwhile, was called 'Red' by almost everyone else who knew her, except a couple of old aunts. Even her uncles called her Red and she had a lot of adopted uncles in the New York Police Department.

'Are you ready yet?'

This is a cry that occurs the world over as the exasperated male waits, once more, for his partner in life to do whatever it is 'they' do. In fact, the speaker was Bobbie Flynn, and she was calling from the living room of their Brownstone house in Greenwich Village.

Flynn admitted defeat, once more and walked into a large rambling living room that was bestrewn with books, which seemed to cover every inch of table, sideboard, and floor.

'Can you do this tie? I've never liked it.'

'So you keep telling me. Why don't you buy a new one?'

'Your mother liked it.'

'I can't think why.'

Bobbie quickly fixed the tie and then stood back to admire her father. He suited the tuxedo. His silver hair and twinkling blue eyes invested him with a certain craggy nobility. Yes, she was proud of her father. More than this, she adored him.

Flynn, he preferred being called Flynn, even by Nancy, due to an intense dislike of his Christian name, studied his daughter. As ever, he felt enormously conflicted by the sight that greeted him. By any measure, she was striking. Red hair erupted from her head like molten lava. Unlike many of the girls who had taken to wearing bobs, she kept her hair unfashionably long.

Thankfully, her temperament did not match her colouring. She was nobody's fool, but nor was she a storm about to be unleashed. This was one blessing. Otherwise, he suffered like most fathers must do, when they see their daughters date men who are palpably unsuitable. This probably encompassed the whole of mankind.

She was twenty-two now. At some point, he knew he would have to shift his current position and begin to do what his wife would almost certainly have done: matchmaking. Had he not married Nancy when he was twenty-three and she, twenty-one? So long ago and yet nowhere near long enough.

He'd lost her two years earlier. Without Bobbie, who knows what he would have done? Yet, he heard Nancy's voice every day when he listened to Bobbie. He saw her smile when Bobbie smiled. The hair was different. Bobbie had the Flynn colouring, but everything else was Nancy.

Perhaps, who knows, there would be someone of interest at this party.

Dick West was wondering what sort of women would be at the party. He wasn't going to take any chances. His date for the evening was an old flame at a loose end like himself. They came together every so often when romance had failed them, or they had failed it. One last look in the mirror before he left his apartment, on East 59th Street and then he was off.

He was twenty-five now. There were just some hints of age on his fine features. He retained the good looks he'd always had, but they were slowly being blunted by an overindulgence in alcohol. He had barely drunk before going to the War in nineteen eighteen. He'd barely stopped since returning. Some weekends, he did little else.

Monday to Friday he tempered his drinking. He had a living to earn. He'd trained as a lawyer at Princeton and passed top of his class. He enlisted soon after the Lusitania sank.

The drinking and the War were intertwined, but not for the reasons that most people, who knew of his problem, suspected. The real reason he would never reveal.

He nodded to the doorman at his apartments and hailed a taxi. He would travel uptown a few blocks to his old school friend Chester Lydgate. They had been at school together and then college. They had so much in common. Life had not been handed to them on a plate like Amory. Of course, they had never resented Amory's wealth. They had enjoyed being in the glow of that particular sun. Princeton had been one long party that had cost them relatively little. At least, until the end when it cost everything.

They only had a few blocks to travel, but the cab took an age.

'You'd have been quicker walking,' said the cabbie, while chewing a cigar.

'Don't I know it,' replied Dick. 'We need you after.'

'Your money,' said the cabbie, still chewing on a cigar.

Chester Lydgate turned to his date for the evening, Ethel Barnes. He pulled his chest in, no mean feat these days and said, 'How do I look?' He spoke rather jerkily as if he were worried that the person would lose interest by the time he'd finished.

Ethel was a friendly-looking young woman with fashionably short hair and small, rather kissable lips and long legs. These were her best features along with her long slender dancer's legs, a fact often remarked upon by the many men she had dated, but who, thus far, had not committed further.

'Swell,' said Ethel, blissfully unaware that this could refer as much to a waistline that had expanded considerably since he'd left the army, as his manly appeal. Chester, however, did pick up on the double meaning but smiled gamely. He always did. He rarely seemed to take offence at any jibe, especially about his weight. He wasn't a hypocrite in this regard. This was the result of a generous, convivial nature and a complete inability to resist temptation. If alcohol was Dick's Achilles heel, then food was Chester's.

He regarded Ethel in her new green dress. She was standing in the middle of his large apartment on West 54th Street. Someone like Ethel fitted in well here. Smart, funny and immensely likeable. Not a classic beauty, of course. But then again, nor was he.

'You don't look half bad,' he said admiringly. He meant it. Her lips were, unquestionably, kissable and, who knows, maybe he would find that out tonight.

'Do I look half good?' asked Ethel wryly.

'Yes, you do, Eth,' said another voice. A second young woman appeared. Like Ethel, she was in her mid-twenties, slender with cool blue eyes, that had seen a lot more of life than she would ever admit to. This was Laura Lyons.

'Laura, I was just telling Chester how swell he looked.'

Chester and Laura's eyes met. Both recognised, immediately, that the description was as unfortunate as it was apt. Chester had the good grace to chuckle which allowed Laura permission to grin also.

'When is Prince Charming coming?' asked Ethel.

The ringing buzzer provided its own answer. A servant came into the living room of the apartment, to announce who the caller was.

'Mr West, sir. He's on his way up.'

'Good, we can have a stiffener now. I'm not sure if Amory is dry or not these days. Anyway,' added Chester conspiratorially, 'I'm bringing some insurance.'

He extracted a small silver flask from his breast pocket and grinned.

'Don't worry,' said Chester. 'I wouldn't dream of excluding you.' Then he handed both Ethel and Laura small copper-coloured hip flasks. 'I imagine Dick will have his own.'

Ethel threw her arms around his neck and kissed him on the cheek. She said, 'You really are the berries, big boy.'

This drew a laugh from Laura and an embarrassed smile from Chester, who never quite knew how to handle it when women praised him or made fun of him. It usually amounted to the same thing. Amory's face flashed before him. He *always* had something to say. Invariably, it would sweep women off their feet. It could be banal, outrageous, anything really. Amory would make it sound like the smartest thing in the world, or the most lurid.

He always felt so leaden by comparison to his friend. A lead weight. Heavy. Awkward. He made Amory shine all the brighter.

Just then, Dick came into the living room. Dick saw the silver hip flask in Chester's hand. He extracted a similar one from his pocket and said, 'Snap.' The two hip flasks glinted in the light, before the two men put them away into their breast pockets. 'So, have I missed anything?' said Dick, smiling to the ladies.

Suddenly, one of them gasped, Dick saw her eyes looking towards Chester. Laura had her hand to her mouth. Dick turned to Chester and saw what had upset the two ladies. The stem of Chester's glass had snapped in his hand.

Blood was on his hand, running through his fingers and dripping onto the floor.

'So you've read the story then,' said Dick drily.

8 6pm

Kit and Alastair went to the apartment, at six o'clock exactly. This was at Alastair's insistence. He took a peculiar joy in surprising people this way, as hosts invariably assumed everyone would be fashionably late. He was wrong. When Freddy opened the door and invited Kit and Alastair in, there was a band already playing music and Amory was standing by some flowers, that Alastair probably should have recognised but didn't. He was holding what looked like a High Ball.

'Care to join me?' were his first words as he gestured with his eyes towards the drink.

'I'd love to,' said Alastair. 'I'm not sure about my nephew. Kit?'

'A conscientious objector?' smiled Amory. Then he added, 'I do keep a wine cellar at my Long Island home, and I brought a few bottles over for this evening. It's perfectly legal to drink alcohol that was purchased previously, if that would make you feel better.'

Kit laughed at this and said, 'It would, rather.' Amory nodded to Freddy who immediately disappeared into a small room before returning moments later with a glass of red wine.

'This prohibition is getting out of hand,' said Amory. 'Getting so people can't enjoy themselves. Now what did you make of the story?'

Alastair turned to Kit with raised eyebrows and said, 'I'll let my staff deal with this query.'

Kit smiled towards his uncle, before sampling the wine. It was excellent.

'It's French. We have a cellar full of it at my family home on Long Island, as I say. When I'm running low, I pootle along and pick up a few cases.'

'Thank you,' said Kit. 'To answer your question, I was intrigued by the addition of the character, Lord Fauntleroy. He seemed an afterthought.'

'Why?'

'For a number of reasons. The tone of that section strikes me as at odds with the rest of the story. He doesn't appear to have any role in the proceedings, beyond providing you with an opportunity to make some jests, at the expense of the English and our class system.'

'I hope you didn't mind?' asked Amory, genuinely concerned.

'Far from it. I imagine you understand class very well in the classless society that you profess to have here.'

Amory laughed at this before asking, 'Have you discounted him as a suspect?'

Kit nodded at this. Then he added another thought, 'It is an intriguing piece.'

'I suspect when you say "intriguing" you mean that it raises more questions than it answers.'

'Correct, but I'm sure the guests will help fill some of the gaps, when they arrive.'

'I have a feeling you've done this before,' smiled Amory, unperturbed by Kit's assessment of the piece.

He was looking at Kit and smiling, but there was something in his eyes. Had Kit been asked to pin down what he thought it was he would have said intense sadness.

'By the way, Aston, there was an Englishman who claimed to be titled. I'm not sure anyone believed him, but he made a decent fist of it. Kept it up for three years. Can you guess what we nicknamed him?'

Kit laughed at this, but assumed the question to be rhetorical and did not answer.

Amory chuckled also before adding, 'Was it that obvious that many of the characters in the story might be guests this evening?'

Behind Kit the sound of the door opening distracted everyone for a minute. Aunt Agatha and Mary walked into the apartment. Agatha scanned the room and noted they, Kit and Alastair, were the only guests to arrive so far.

'So, the people in the story haven't arrived yet?' asked Agatha, looking around the empty apartment.

'Ahh, said Amory. 'Apparently it was.'

Mary stepped forward. She was wearing a long, silver dress that was cut rather lower than Kit might have liked, outside the privacy of their apartment.

Amory took both her hands and greeted her with a kiss on each cheek. 'Mrs Aston, if there is a more beautiful lady in New York at this moment, then I will eat my hat. Your dress is divine, but I was hoping you would be more immodest.'

Mary laughed at this. Any more immodest, thought Kit and the police inspector would have arrested her for indecency.

'No offence,' added Amory, looking at Kit.

'None taken,' said Mary as her eyes narrowed, in a manner that suggested Amory was already on borrowed time.

Amory turned to her and grinned and then looked at Kit. Once more, Kit saw the sadness, lurking deep within those astonishing blue eyes. 'I wish I'd met you both years ago. Now, I'm glad the British contingent is here. As you know, I've invited a police inspector along. I've not met him before, but his daughter and I are good pals. If I could ask you to finish your drinks. We'll have to see which way the wind blows before we have some more. If you are desperate and, looking at Alastair, I think I can see someone who is fond of a snifter, then I'm sure Freddy can help you, when matters come to a head.'

Everyone laughed at this, none more so than Alastair.

Kit noticed an interesting print on the wall, near the dining room table. A small plaque underneath gave its title as *The Ghost Dance by the Ogallala Sioux* – Frederic Remington. Kit heard Amory address him.

'I'd love to have the original,' said Amory. 'I do have a Remington nocturne in the bedroom. I'll show it to you later if you like.'

'I would like that very much,' replied Kit. 'I must say, I'd love to acquire a Remington myself. I've always been fascinated by the Old West. This is a rather sad picture though when you think of what happened.'

Amory's face grew serious. He replied, 'I agree. Shameful in fact. The Cavalry murdered hundreds of these poor people just because they performed this dance. I wrote an article about it recently and how Indians think of death. It's rather fascinating. I'll show you sometime.'

'Yes, I would love to read it. I'm afraid I can't say, with regard to this incident, that we've been any better in Britain. In fact, we've some episodes in our history that beggar belief.'

'Amritsar?' suggested Amory. Just at that moment, Kit could see the sadness return to his eyes, and he seemed all the more human for it.

'Amritsar,' nodded Kit. There was a typewriter underneath the Remington print. Kit pointed to it and asked, 'Do you type?'

Amory laughed, 'Lord no. I dictate to a secretary, who comes in every couple of days.'

They both moved away from the area by the picture and went to the centre of the room. As they did so, there was a knock at the door. Freddy went hurrying to the door to greet the next guests. The first through the door was an attractive young woman with auburn hair. Her eyes fixed almost immediately on Mary. She was followed by an older man. Freddy made the announcement.

'Miss Roberta Flynn and Inspector Flynn.'

Flynn glanced at Freddy and nodded gratefully at him, for not mentioning his first name. Amory went over to them immediately and kissed Bobbie on both cheeks before shaking the hand of Flynn. Then the introductions were made.

'Red, why don't you and Mary get acquainted. I was just telling Mary that I doubted there was a more beautiful girl at any party in New York right now,' said Amory mischievously.

'And I doubt there's a bigger fraud in New York right now than you,' said Bobbie drily.

Mary erupted into a peal of laughter and decided that she and Bobbie would get along just fine. She took the young woman's arm and led her away from the group.

'I can see I have a comrade in arms, against your friend's nonsense,' said Mary.

'He means well,' said Bobbie. 'He's been waxing lyrical about having real-life lords and ladies attend his party. I love Amory, but he's an inveterate snob.'

Mary gave Bobbie a sideways glance when she said 'love'. Bobbie picked up on this and grinned.

'Let me be more specific. I love him as a friend, but I would never date him. To know him is to know him if you take my meaning,' she explained.

'How do you know him?' asked Mary, now very curious.

'I work on a newspaper. He contributes short stories to the paper and, shall we say, more philosophical pieces. The short stories are fun, but the other articles show how clever he is.'

'How exciting to work on a newspaper, though. I love to hear of women doing these jobs. Not before time,' said Mary excitedly. Bobbie's face fell a little at hearing this. Mary frowned when she saw this. The tone of her voice changed as she asked, 'What do they have you doing?'

'Obituaries. I want to do crime, but they won't let me near that.'

'Red has an unhealthy fascination with death. I blame her father,' said Amory approaching them. Bobbie looked at Amory strangely.

'I would have said it was you, Amory, who had the fascination with death,' said Bobbie.

'You have me there, Red,' replied Amory cheerfully.

Agatha and Alastair noted the look of distaste on Flynn's face, when Amory offered him a lemonade. This brought a wry smile from Alastair. Flynn accepted the lemonade and glanced towards Kit, Agatha, and Alastair. It looked as if he was regretting every second of coming to the party.

'I think you and I are in a race Inspector Flynn, to see who can rid themselves of their tie first,' said Kit, with a grin.

Flynn smiled back and rolled his eyes.

'Is it that obvious?'

'How is the lemonade, Inspector?' asked Alastair, a malicious grin on his face.

This brought a scowl from Flynn, and he set the glass down a soon as Amory left them to join the young ladies. Agatha spoke for the first time at this point.

'I notice that Amory didn't mention your Christian name, Inspector.'

Flynn rolled his eyes again at this.

'I'm happy with Flynn,' he said curtly. Then, with a rueful grin he said, 'I never liked my name. Flynn works just fine.'

'Or Inspector?' probed Kit.

It struck Flynn that he had never thought of this before. He turned to Kit and said, 'I don't want to make people feel uneasy.'

'We'll call you Inspector Flynn then. You'll have your name, but we'll keep you off balance at the same time,' said Agatha mischievously. Flynn had the feeling that this lady tended to get her own way, and, on this occasion, he was rather glad of it. He grinned at her in a submission. He looked around at the apartment. It seemed to Kit that he had never been before.

'A lot of flowers,' said Flynn in a manner that a man might adopt if asked to give an opinion on make-up. 'There's probably a nice apartment underneath this vegetation.'

'Oh there is,' said Alastair. 'Why don't you come with us? Agatha and I will show you the one directly below. It's identical in every way except for the forest. Leave these young ones to chat amongst themselves.'

Flynn glanced towards Alastair and Agatha. They were closer to his generation, older even, and this had the benefit of not making him feel like a fish out of water.

'OK.'

They made their way out of the apartment, with Freddy opening the door for them. The lift opened immediately, and they descended one floor. A few moments later Flynn was looking at Ella-Mae who opened the door and then frowned at Alastair. Alastair did what he always did when confronted by his housekeeper. He scowled back at her. This amused Flynn and he nodded to the housekeeper, who looked at him suspiciously.

The apartment was similar in design to the one above, but devoid of flowers. It was very male, and he liked it all the more. Then he spotted the reason why he had been brought downstairs.

Sitting on a table, in the middle of the room, was a bottle of red wine, gleaming invitingly in the low-level lamp light. Alastair grinned at him and shrugged his shoulders.

'It's Californian. I've been living there for around thirty odd years. I have quite a collection.'

'Californian?' asked Flynn stepping forward and lifting the bottle up.

'Try some?' asked Agatha. It sounded more like an instruction than a question.

Moments later, without a sound, Ella-Mae appeared. She had three wine glasses in her hand. Her eyes shifted towards

Alastair and narrowed. She regarded him in a manner that someone might when encountering Satan in the desert, holding a glass of water when your tongue is a little dry.

'Well, if you insist,' replied Flynn.

'That's the spirit,' said Alastair delightedly.

Kit joined Mary and the two ladies by the window of the apartment. Rain was lashing the apartment window, like it had a blood feud with its owner. It was almost biblical, and the group paid silent homage to Mother Nature in a foul mood.

Bobbie Flynn broke the silence, when she fixed her eyes on Amory and said, 'Now this short story of yours; what's that diabolical mind of yours cooking up?'

Amory held his hands up as if someone had a gun on him. He was the picture of mock innocence which only confirmed that he did, have mischief in mind. Kit noted that he seemed more relaxed with Bobbie and wondered if there was something between them. Oddly, she seemed, even on short acquaintance, a girl who could handle herself against attractive cads. If Kit didn't miss his guess, and he rarely did, Amory was just such a man.

Amory intrigued him though. Like Wilde, he tossed off epigrams he'd prepared earlier, with wilful abandon.

'I love the flowers,' said Mary looking around the apartment. It's so rare to meet a man who appreciates such things. She looked pointedly at Kit and smiled. Kit shrugged at this. He wasn't about to make a hypocrite of himself and deny it.

'I'm a sensualist. I love beauty,' replied Amory.

'You are beauty,' retorted Bobbie, drily.

'I won't deny it,' laughed Amory, yet one suspected he believed it. The lack of false modesty actually made him more appealing. He'd realised this from a young age. He knew he was good-looking. He knew he was smart. Pretending to be anything other than this would have been untrue to himself, so he'd decided to be everything he was and more.

'I am like a beautiful flower,' continued Amory, adopting a balletic pose. 'Colourful, fragrant and an adornment to any room that I enter.'

Mary chucked at this while Kit had to wonder if he meant anything else by this. Yes, flowers were beautiful, but all too soon they wilted and died.

The buzzer rang at this point. Freddy was by the door in an instant, opening it to a group of well-dressed young men and women. One of the men marched ahead of the others. He was handsome, well-made and had clearly submerged himself beneath half a dozen drinks. He scanned the apartment and smiled drily in approval. Then he fixed his eyes on Amory.

'Hello Amory,' he said. 'Your suspects have arrived.'

9 6:45pm

Soon after the arrival of the last four guests, The Troopers stopped playing, and took their first break. Amory had organised for them to have meals in the second-floor restaurant. With a nod towards their host, they exited the apartment, to take the elevator down to the second floor.

When most people enter an elevator, they immediately lose their voice. Not so the Troopers. To a man they were laughing at their good fortune, all except Tommy 'The Trump' who seemed a bit more philosophical.

'That English dame is something else,' said Arnie Nicholls, the drummer.

John 'Lanky' Towers agreed but thought the cop's daughter edged her in the beauty stakes.

'That's 'cause you married a redhead,' pointed out Arnie, nobly defending his choice.

'My wife's no more a natural redhead than I am, believe me,' laughed Lanky.

'I like the other two girls,' said Fritz.

'You would,' said Lanky, laughing. 'They could be German Fraus.'

'You mean Frauleins,' said Fritz, and explained the difference to the others. They reached the large restaurant and were led by a waiter to their table.

'Everything OK Tommy?' asked Arnie, noticing their trumpet player seemed unusually quiet.

Tommy smiled and shrugged, 'Oh you know. Families. Can't live with them. Can't live without them.'

'Say that again,' agreed Arnie. 'How's that song coming along, the one you were humming earlier?'

Fritz extracted some paper from his pocket and held it up and said, 'Tommy has given me some lyrics.'

'Already?' laughed Lanky. 'What's it called?'

'*Blue Nights*,' said Tommy, smiling a little embarrassedly.

Back in the apartment, Agatha, Alastair, and Flynn made their reappearance and further introductions were made. Agatha glanced over, meaningfully, towards Kit after she had met the four new arrivals. Kit responded with a half-smile and a raised eyebrow. Agatha did not look happy at all.

If Agatha was not happy, Bobbie Flynn wore an ever-bigger frown. Her eyes narrowed when she saw her father, who had been away for around twenty minutes. She took his arm and led him away from the crowd.

'Have you been drinking?'

'Whatever gives you that idea,' said Flynn with the wide smile of man who is at peace with the world.

Bobbie frowned at him and then said, 'I can see that those two old people are a bad influence. You of all people.'

'Don't be such a prude. Anyway, it was fine bottle of Prescott Ash 1915. Very nice indeed.'

'You drank a whole bottle with them? In twenty minutes?' exclaimed Bobbie, angrily amused.

'It's been a while,' pointed out Flynn gleefully. 'Anyway, it's a stupid law. Causing more problems than it's worth.'

'I know,' agreed Bobbie. 'Look, that's not why I brought you over here. Take a look around you.'

Flynn scanned the apartment before declaring, 'Too many flowers. You have strange friends.'

Bobbie shook her head in frustration. She said, 'How did you ever make Inspector?'

'Your mother was of a similar view, anyway, is there a point that might be reached soon?' retorted Flynn. Like any father, he enjoyed arguing with his daughter, when the subject wasn't important.

'The people. Can't you see? You are a bit of a goofer, aren't you? Look around you at the people.'

'They're your friends.'

'They're certainly not. Only, Amory,' said Bobbie, a little more defensively than she'd intended.

'So? They look like the usual Broadway crowd.'

'Look again,' instructed Bobbie.

So Flynn looked at Kit who was chatting with Amory and the burlier of the two new arrivals, Chester. The other man, Dick, was sitting with the young woman he had come with. He looked like he was already tight. He was also holding a glass of gin. Flynn wasn't in the mood to be a hypocrite, so he let that one pass. They would all probably be drinking sooner or later.

Then it hit him.

'Oh,' he said, looking at his daughter.

'Oh, indeed,' said Bobbie. 'I don't like this. Not one bit. I'm going to speak to Amory. If this is his idea of a joke, then it's in very poor taste. Excuse me Flynn.'

Flynn smiled at his daughter. She had taken to calling him Flynn also, just like her mother. They were alike in so many ways, except one. That one thing is the one you least want your child to have. Like him, she was curious to the point of obsession. She'd have made a great detective. He hoped she never would. The things he'd seen still gave him nightmares.

Amory laughed at Dick West's comment of "suspects". It sounded a little forced. He shook hands with Dick. With Chester he seemed a little bit more warmly. Chester grinned at Amory.

'You're looking well, Amory old boy. Can I introduce you to Ethel Barnes.'

Ethel stepped forward and held out her hand. Then she frowned slightly.

'Haven't I seen you before?' said Ethel. Her eyes narrowed as she studied his face closely.

Amory kissed her hand and said gallantly, 'If you had I might have bagged you before Chester.'

Chester smiled nervously at this. He'd had enough of that to last one lifetime. He said, 'Well, Amory is partly responsible for us meeting, Eth. I went out with him to see *Ziegfeld* and afterwards Amory and I ended up in a bar. He pointed you out and said to me, "Ches, if you don't talk to that girl and ask her for a date then I will", so I marched right over and did just that. I suppose I have Amory to thank.'

Ethel was delighted by the story. She stood on tiptoe and pecked Amory on the cheek. She said, 'Don't take this the wrong way Amory, but I'm glad you didn't come over. I like Ches just fine.'

'We all do,' agreed Amory, before his eyes shifted over to the other new arrivals. A hint of frost seemed to descend over his exquisite features. He took Laura Lyons hand and kissed it very carefully.

Laura smiled slowly and said, 'Long time no see Amory.'

Dick looked rather taken aback too, that his date for the evening knew the host. In fact, he did not look pleased by this. While women tend to be interested in a man's future, a man is more interested in a woman's past. That Amory knew Laura was plain for all to see. Now one question burned in Dick's mind, as he looked sullenly at Laura.

It was clear to Kit and Mary that there was an "atmosphere" between the men. This was hardly surprising, given what Amory had written. For all that, after some initial hesitation, Chester and his girlfriend, Ethel, seemed to settle down while some frostiness still remained from Dick.

Amory's initial response to Dick's line, about being suspects, had been to laugh it off and say that it had been too long. Kit wondered how long that meant. Given the rather icy air between Dick and Amory, it was clear they may not have spoken in quite some while.

Had they fallen out over the girl who had died? Kit was in no doubt that Helen du Bois had a real-life counterpart. He pondered if she had died in mysterious circumstances. It made him wonder if the purpose of the dinner party was, in some way, to understand better what had happened and, perhaps, to bring to a close a tragic event.

He awoke from this reverie when he became aware that Chester was speaking to him.

'Have you met the King?' asked Chester. He seemed a friendly sort, probably smarter than he looked.

'I've been in his company and been introduced, but I haven't had any conversations with him.'

'I thought all you chaps were hand in glove together.'

Kit laughed at this before replying, 'Not since the Knights of the Round Table.'

Amory had not spoken in at least two minutes and, like the addict that he was, he needed a fix. Hearing his own voice was his poison of choice. He had spotted Bobbie glaring at him. The light of love was certainly not in her eye. Moments later, having gained his attention, he saw her march over to him.

He said to the others, 'You'll have to excuse me, Nemesis approaches.'

Kit glanced and saw the policeman's daughter coming towards him. It wasn't just outside that a storm was brewing, if the look on Bobbie Flynn's face was any guide. His eyes flicked away from Bobbie towards her father. He was with his aunt and uncle. There was a glass of wine in his hand. Kit smiled and imagined how that might have happened. Either his aunt had verbally bludgeoned him into drinking, or his uncle had followed the maxim of catching more flies with honey. His money was on the latter. The police inspector did not strike him as a man who was easily cowed, even by English aunts of a decidedly decided nature.

'I want a word with you Buster,' snarled Bobbie at Amory. 'I'm taking my dad out of here. We've got better things to do than be part of some sick game of yours.'

'I could almost fall in love with you for saying this,' said Amory. 'My marriage offer still stands; you know.'

'What marriage offer? I think it was something else you were proposing, and the answer would always be "no", Amory.'

Amory grew more serious, which made Bobbie pause for a moment. Had she been too hard on him? It was Amory after all. He normally seemed so harmless. He was like a child who had been gifted the face of an angel and the brain of a mad scientist or German philosopher. From what she had seen, he seemed to treat women well and they never spoke ill of him, even when he remained tantalizingly out of reach. She knew his type and yet, at the same time, she knew he was unique.

'Was there a real murder, Amory?' asked Bobbie.

'That's what we're here to establish, darling.'

'What else are we here to establish?' asked Bobbie.

Amory's lips curled into a smile, but his eyes seemed curiously devoid of any light. He was like an actor trying to remember his lines.

'You'd make a great reporter, Red. I hope those fools at the paper realise that. I've tried telling them,' his voice drifted away a little at the end. It sounded almost wistful.

Bobbie felt her anger with Amory subside a little. He had that ability, sometimes, to let his guard down and become more human. He'd always supported her at the newspaper, where he was treated as some kind of minor deity. Although he was not a salaried employee, he contributed regularly and his arrival at the offices hastened half the female secretarial staff over to the floor where he met with Thornton Kent, the newspaper editor.

'I know you do,' said Bobbie trying to regain some of her initial fire but, as ever, she realised that Amory had, somehow, snuffed it out.

'You'll thank me for this one day, Red,' he added, enigmatically.

Something in the way he said this made Bobbie stop and she felt a chill descend on her. She was about to ask him what he meant by this when Freddy spoke to the assembled group.

'Ladies and gentlemen, dinner is served.

10 7:30pm

A small apartment, New York: 31st December 1921

She was angry with herself. News Year's Eve and she was on her own indoors doing what? She should be out with her friends or with her family. Yet a part of her had known all along he was a louse. He was good-looking and he had a way with words, but a louse is a louse is a louse. She knew this but had still not acted on her instincts. Why do we do this, she wondered? Women could be such fools. It's not as if we could not see what men were like. We knew. Yet still we believed we would be the one to change them. How naïve. No, she thought, let's call it what it is.

Stupid.

She was beginning to hate the small apartment. It's just a short-term thing, honey. Trust me. I've got something big coming, then it's uptown for us, kid. Wasn't that what he'd said? Of course he did. They all do that. First it's the flattery. Then it's the promises. By then you're beginning to give away what's important. You're committed, but the voices inside you are whispering. Now they're shouting.

You fool.

The room was dark but illuminated by a long line of gaily lit buildings outside. She switched on the light and took it all in. The place she was living in was a small apartment with furniture borrowed from dumps, bought from junk shops or simply found on the street. It seemed as if she was seeing the place for the first time, and it appalled her.

Outside a police siren screamed at the moon. She felt like doing the same. Paint was peeling off the walls and she was convinced she'd heard suspicious rustling the previous night. The rustling of rats under the floorboards. She looked out the window and watched as cars slashed through the rainwater on the road.

She felt like an exile from her own life and family and friends. How had she let this happen? Passion was what reckless people called love. She had felt passion, a sense of freedom when she met him. Now the passion was spent and, what was left was an empty void, where tenderness should have existed.

What should she do? That was the key question now. At the very least she would wait until he came back. Then she'd decide. Decide? No, tell him. tell him straight.

Then go.

A new year was coming, and she was going to start it in the right way. Stop making mistakes. She was getting good at that. No more wasting her time on men who were not worth it.

Well, this would be her last mistake.

11 7:30pm

After Amory had left the group, Kit suggested that they join Agatha, Alastair and the police inspector. He quite liked the look of the old detective and wanted to get to know him better. Chester and Ethel agreed immediately.

'This is my aunt and uncle, by the way,' said Kit as they approached the group. With the introductions made, Kit pointed to the wine glass in Flynn's hand and said, 'I see you have found out what a bad influence my uncle is.'

Flynn frowned and nodded, but there was a glint of humour in his eyes.

'I'll send him downtown when I finish this,' said Flynn.

'I wish you would,' said Agatha.

Alastair was unapologetic, 'I shall speak for the poor huddled masses, whose only vice has been cruelly ripped away from them by men who will, no doubt, continue to enjoy said vice while the working man must make himself a criminal to do so too.'

'Hear, hear,' said Flynn and clinked glasses with Alastair before adding, a little wistfully, 'I must be heading off soon. I said I'd pop in to see some of the boys working tonight. Maybe we can pop Alastair into one of the cells.'

'It wouldn't be the first time,' replied Agatha. Alastair grinned proudly at his 'record'.

Chester chuckled at this and said, 'I hope next time I'm busted in some low speakeasy that you're the arresting officer, Inspector Flynn.'

The group chatted about the ridiculousness of the law. While Flynn did not say anything, directly, to oppose the law he had sworn to uphold, nothing in his manner suggested he in any way supported it.'

After a few minutes Agatha, with all of the patience that had marked her life thus far, said, 'So, what on earth are we to make of this story?' She spoke in hushed tones so that Amory, who was nearby with Bobbie, would not hear them.

Any answer was interrupted by Freddy's announcement. So they adjourned to the long dining table near the window. Amory came over and began to direct people to where they should sit.

'We'll take the first course, which I gather is going to be an old American delicacy, which I hope appals our European guests: devilled eggs and stuffed mushrooms. I can see Freddy is ready to serve it.'

Amory sat at the head of the table near Kit who found himself beside Bobbie Flynn. Mary was on the other side of the table but further down. She was beside Dick West who had, thus far, said little to anyone. Alastair was on the other side of Mary, which was a relief in case Dick continued to be uncommunicative. Agatha was beside Chester, who sat between her and Bobbie Flynn. To Agatha's right was Flynn.

The dinner table was laid out with beautiful silver cutlery and the three plates on each place. There were three glasses per person, two for wine and one for water. Freddy had already served the starter wine, a Fumé Blanc.

Kit watched as Freddy expertly served the eggs from a silver platter. His fingers adroitly manipulated the spoon and fork in a manner that Harry Miller, Kit's former manservant-turned-policeman, had never quite managed to do. Kit often joked about Miller's failure in this, given his ability to crack a safe. Miller pointed out that safe cracking was not only about manual dexterity, and it was rarely done in front of a dinner party. Kit realised he missed his old friend and comrade. The man who had saved his life one night in France.

'I hope you don't mind if I don't say grace,' announced Amory. '*Bon Appetit.*'

'*Bon Appetit,*' chorused the dinner party. All except Dick, who held up the wine glass.

'Your good health,' said Dick, and proceeded to drink all of the wine in one gulp.

As they ate the first course, conversation at the table was confined to small groups, formed of the people sitting near them.

'Mary tells me you are a journalist,' said Kit to Bobbie.

'Obits,' said Bobbie glumly. 'I want crime, but, I suspect, my dad might move heaven and earth to stop me covering that beat.'

Kit laughed at this before replying, 'I suppose men can be over-protective of family.'

'Daughters, you mean.'

'And wives,' added Kit. 'Mary and I have been involved with the police a few times in England. Mary's put herself in a few dangerous situations, which had me pretty worried.' Bobbie regarded Kit strangely. It was as if she didn't believe him. 'You seem sceptical,'

'I didn't have you down as a crime-fighter, never mind a husband who would allow his wife to do anything more dangerous than choose her next dress.' When she'd finished saying this, she put her hand to her mouth, eyes wide with shock. 'Oh my goodness, that must sound horrible. I'm so sorry.'

Kit waved his hand and grinned back at the young woman, 'Don't worry. I think, when you get to know Mary better, things will become clearer. You know that we met in France. She ran away from her home to nurse near the front.'

The young American was stunned by this. She turned to Mary who was trying and failing, to engage Dick West in conversation, at the end of the table.

'Looks like she had better luck with you than she's having now,' said Bobbie, grinning. Kit chuckled at this. Then Bobbie asked, 'I'd love to hear more about how you met.'

Mary, as Bobbie had noticed, was getting little from the man she was sitting beside. He clearly resented being at the party and there was a sense of desolation in his eyes. If this man was Dexter from the story, and Mary strongly suspected he was, it was clear that he had never forgiven Amory. Yet, at the same time, he could not resist his former friend's gravitational pull. Rather than attempt small talk, she decided to go on the attack. She was not, to all intents and purposes, the adopted daughter of Agatha, without taking on some of her characteristics.

'So, how do you feel about your role in the short story? You were Dexter, weren't you?'

Dick glanced sideways at her with a half-smile. He attempted to point a finger at Mary and said, 'Very good. I like your style. Your husband is a very lucky man.'

'Did you love her?' asked Mary, unwilling to let go of his attention.

'Who?'

'The woman who was Helen du Bois?'

The smile left Dick's face. Mary sensed a coldness descend over him and she immediately regretted being so direct.

'Forgive me. That was uncalled for. I'm sorry.'

'He killed her. Whatever he says. He killed her,' snarled Dick and then he turned away and filled his glass with more wine before Freddy could do this for him.

'I gather from Mary, that Bobbie wants to be a crime reporter,' said Agatha, addressing Flynn.

'So she tells me,' growled Flynn.

'You seem unsympathetic to the idea,' replied Agatha icily.

'You noticed,' retorted Flynn.

'Men seem to think women incapable of anything, except homemaking. I wish her well in her ambition. I hope she does become a crime reporter if that is what she wishes.'

'Over my dead body,' replied Flynn, before finishing off his devilled egg.

'It hardly seems fair on her if you try to stop her being what she wants to be,' pointed out Agatha. 'Why do men want to hold us back? What are you afraid of?'

'Afraid of? What do you think Lady Frost? I'm afraid she'll get herself hurt, or worse. Do you have children, Lady Frost?'

Agatha was jolted by the question. She took a deep breath and replied, 'No. No, I was not so fortunate.'

'Well if you had, Lady Frost, then you'd know how much we worry about our kids.'

'I'm sure you do,' said Agatha. She went quiet for a few moments, recalling a moment, over forty years previously. She felt the stabbing pain in her stomach once more. The pain was unbearable. Tears formed in her eyes. The music of Wagner filled her mind. Then it stopped suddenly. She felt a hand on her arm. It was Flynn.

'Lady Frost, I'm sorry. I've offended you. I, I don't know what to say. I really don't. I'm a...'

Agatha finished the sentence for him, 'Father, Mr Flynn. Anything you feel is entirely understandable. I would merely say that at some point you must learn to trust your daughter. She strikes me, on short acquaintance, to be a smart and capable young woman.'

Flynn stared up at the end of the table, where Bobbie was engaged in conversation with Kit. She was all he had left now since Nancy's death. That and the job. They were his life, and he would fight until his dying breath to keep both. But the person he was looking at, speaking to the good-looking Englishman was not a child. It was a young woman.

He turned back to Agatha and grinned ruefully.

'You're probably right but allow an old man to be wrong.'

'You're not so old, Mr Flynn,' said Agatha. 'You said, she's all you have. May I take it that you lost Mrs Flynn?'

'Yes. I lost Nancy a couple of years ago,' replied Flynn, fighting hard to control his emotion. 'Lord Frost?'

Now it was Agatha's turn to fight back the tears, once more. She nodded and said, 'I lost Useless ten years ago. In Agadir.

He died just as the German gun boats were sailing into the harbour.'

Flynn looked at Agatha with sympathy, but then a thought struck him, 'Agadir? It seems to me there's more to you than meets the eye. And I mean to hear it.'

'How fascinating,' said Alastair smiling desperately. Those who knew Alastair, would have recognised the expression on his face. He looked like a man listening to a mother, listing the wonderful talents of her son.

'Then I tried for a part in Othello.'

'They should have chosen you, Ethel. You would have been marvellous Desdemona, I'm sure.'

'Who? Anyway, I do love your accent Alastair,' said Ethel. 'Then I went for a part in The Belle of New York.'

'Don't tell me, they overlooked you,' said Alastair, looking scandalised by the very idea that such talent was not being given a chance to shine.

'They did. It's all who you know. And a bit of you-know-what. So, I came back here and then, thanks to my sister, I found some theatre work,' answered Ethel.

Alastair seemed marginally more interested in this. He asked her if she had appeared on Broadway.'

'Oh yes, just chorus work but it pays well.'

'And you are still working with your sister? That must be nice for both of you?' said Alastair, finding his torpor returning.

'It was until she left a month ago. Some new man. He didn't like her on stage and what we were doing. Too exposed, he said.'

Well, if anything is designed to rekindle a man's interest in a conversation it is a young woman admitting she has a job which leaves her very exposed.

'What were you doing?'

'Do you know Ziegfeld Follies?'

Alastair had certainly heard of the Ziegfeld follies. Who hadn't heard of this long-running show? It had been running on Broadway for well over a decade and launched the careers of many famous stars.

'Are you a Ziegfeld Girl?' asked Alastair. She was certainly attractive enough to be one.

Ethel nodded enthusiastically, 'I sure am. I've been in the show for two years now.'

'How wonderful. You must have met some big stars,' said Alastair.

'I worked with Fanny Brice this year, you know,' said Ethel, proudly. Fanny Brice was one of the most famous performers in the country. 'Have you ever seen her, Alastair?'

Just at that moment Kit, who had been deep in conversation with Bobbie Flynn, overheard the conversation between his uncle and the young woman. Too late, he realised he had just taken a rather large sip of wine when his eyes met Alastair's. There was a look of glee in those eyes as he heard his uncle say, 'Oh I've come across Fanny many times.'

Everyone turned to Kit as he began coughing unexpectedly. He waved his arm up and down and stuttered, 'Something went down the wrong way. I shall be all right in a minute.'

12 8:15pm

Kit returned to the dining table, after a few minutes in the bathroom and assured everyone he was feeling better. He glared at Alastair as he said, 'I think an errant mushroom was my downfall.'

Alastair's eyes shone with good humour and his smile, only just, managed to avoid being triumphant. While Kit took his place, Amory tapped the side of his glass and rose to speak.

'I don't mean to make this formal but, I shall,' he said to some laughter. 'First of all, thank you for attending what is, probably, the only party of its sort in New York. It's like a cocktail, I guess: one-part murder mystery, one-part convivial conversation and one-part dancing.'

'You know that cocktails are illegal young man,' pointed out Flynn, who was still by no means sure that what he was doing was moral, never mind fun. He trusted Bobbie, but he sensed that, she too was feeling increasing qualms about the evening. Laughter greeted this response from Flynn including Amory.

'Now, now Inspector Flynn. Let's not bring the law into this, if we can avoid it, old fellow. I think we've had a nice hour chatting and getting to know one another. Now we've reached the part of the evening, before the dancing, where we can put on our deerstalker hats and share our views on the little mystery I created.'

Amory caught the eyes of Dick, who was glaring at him from the other end of the table. Agatha noted the moment the two men shared. That moment if she had been asked to describe it, was 'loathing'.

'Before someone raises it, like you Dick, for instance, I will admit that the events described in the short story are, somewhat, inspired by a real-life case.'

'Then why not tell us what happened?' asked Agatha. 'Clearly, Dick and Chester are perfectly aware of the events.'

'Well, I don't think they share the police's view of what happened,' replied Amory. 'Nor do I.'

'So what do you propose we do, Amory? Try you here and now?' asked Dick. His comment surprised everyone because, for the first time, he no longer seemed the drunk, that had parked himself on the sofa, but someone with a considerably sharper manner than hitherto displayed.

'Ever the lawyer,' smiled Amory. 'I hope you have a case, evidence, witnesses. I'm no lawyer, but I gather they work well in trials.'

'This is a show trial, then' said Dick, rising, a little unsteadily to his feet. 'The question I have in my mind, Amory, old pal, is why now? What is going on in the diabolical brain of yours?'

'Harsh, Dick. I'm complicated, I grant you. Diabolical? Well, perhaps just a little.' This appeared to silence Dick for the moment, so Amory forged ahead. He was keenly aware that the atmosphere in the room had chilled distinctly because of the comments made by Dick. He needed to regain the initiative, otherwise his plans would go awry.

'I think we should get started before the band reappear. Now I deliberately placed you with new people partly so that you could get to know folk and also because I want you to have already chatted with your partner-in-crime about the story. What I would like is for each of you to either ask me a question or offer a thought on what happened in the story.' Amory turned to Kit at this point and said, 'Perhaps I could ask you to start us off?'

Kit knew what he wanted to ask. It was far too early to offer a solution, particularly when several of the dinner party knew more about what had really happened.

'Very well Amory. I'm happy to get things going,' said Kit. He took a sip of wine and then continued, 'You started off with a quote from Shakespeare. *As You Like It*, if I remember correctly.'

'You do,' confirmed Amory.

'That being so, am I to assume that everyone present is in this story?'

'Most everyone is in the story.'

'But, if Mr West is to be believed, we are not all part of the real-life incident that inspired this story.'

'Correct.'

'One final question, before I let someone else cut in, so to speak, if we are most of us in the story of a real-life event, even if we were not part of that original event, then it suggests that the story is not quite finished.'

Amory's eyes lit up and, from the corner of his eye, Kit noted that Dick, at the end of the table, seemed to jerk to attention.

'I feel I may have done Englishmen a disservice in the story, Aston. A very big disservice indeed. Shall we hear from someone else before I respond? Now, I was going to hand over to the next in line but, if I may, Bobbie, I think I'd like to hear from Lady Frost. Unless I've missed my guess, you have struck me as every bit as gifted as your nephew.'

'I wouldn't go as far as to say that,' said Agatha who most certainly thought it.

'I would,' said Kit, Mary and Alastair in unison. This brought a ripple of laughter around the table from everyone, except Dick, who was now studying Agatha intently.

Agatha began to speak. The only sound in the apartment, aside from her voice, was the sound of a distant siren wailing far down below on the street and the patter of rain against the large windows. She turned her eyes towards Chester.

'Mr Lydgate. You work in the financial markets, I understand.'

'Yes, and please call me Chester. Everyone else does, Lady Frost.'

'Very well, Chester. May I ask, how long you have held your present position?'

Kit smiled at his aunt. He could see where this was heading, and it was something he had been curious about himself.'

'Well, around two years I suppose, why do you ask?'

Agatha held a finger up, as if to indicate that she would respond in a moment or two. She turned to Dick West. There was a smile on the young man's face and, if Kit was not mistaken, a recognition of where his aunt was taking this line of inquiry.

'Two years also before you ask.'

'Thank you, that clears up something I was wondering about. Now, to return to the story for a moment. The three boys were close friends, and it appears they were based on the three of you, if I'm not mistaken.'

'I won't deny it,' confirmed Amory. He too was smiling, but there was something else on his face. There was fear in his eyes now. It was clear he had not expected his English guests to be quite so perceptive. It was as if he was rapidly having to recalibrate his original model.

'If you don't mind me saying,' said Agatha, who paused long enough to glare at Alastair, who had just struck a match for his cheroot. He smiled back unapologetically. 'If you don't mind me saying, there appeared to be a distinct atmosphere between you young men. I would suggest that things are not as they once were between you. In fact, I would go as far to say, I sense a degree of hostility.'

'I wouldn't go that far,' said Chester. 'I see Amory from time to time.'

'I would,' laughed Dick, now beginning to enjoy himself.

'Why is that?' asked Agatha. She was the picture of an innocent befuddled old aunt. Kit knew she was anything but.

'Well, we sort of went our separate ways, I suppose,' said Chester.

'Were you and Mr West in France?' asked Agatha to Chester.

'Why yes,' spluttered Chester, 'How on earth did you know?'

'Oh, just a lucky guess, Chester. I shall assume that Mr Beaufort like Archie in the story chose not to go to the War,' replied Agatha, reaching for a sustaining drink of wine. Man and aunts do not live by bread alone.

Dick nodded in approval to Agatha as she made a gesture which suggested that she was relinquishing control.

In Kit's view, Amory appeared to have regained his composure. He thanked Agatha and then turned to Mary.

'Your husband and aunt are quite a hard act to follow. Yet I suspect, Mrs Aston, you will be equal to the challenge.'

Bobbie regarded Mary intently. Her short acquaintance with Mary had given her the very real impression that she was, not just very pretty, but exceptionally smart. She was curious to see how she would respond under the glare of the spotlight that Amory had cast on her. Of Amory she was becoming increasingly less enamoured. There was a darkness there, that she had not perceived before. Pushing Mary forward in such a manner struck her as particularly ungallant and yet all too typical of her friend.

'Yes, just the one question, for now, but it has not been covered yet and I think it's high time that we did.'

Bobbie held her breath. Her eyes were fixed on Mary now. She could see that Mary's eyes were wide, the pupils dilated. Unless she was mistaken, Mary seemed to be having trouble breathing. Then Bobbie recognised it for what it was.

Anger.

Bobbie could sense the anger, radiating from the young woman, and she was feeling it too.

'Please go on,' said Amory gently. He felt that Mary was like a bomb about to explode.

Mary began to speak, in a voice that was tight with emotion.

'We have established that the story is, to all intents and purposes, a true one.' A few heads nodded at this. 'That being so,' continued Mary, 'would you mind if we gave Helen du Bois the dignity of, at least, using her real name?'

13 8:15pm

The Troopers stared in satisfaction at the empty plates. Two courses had been provided and two courses had been dispatched quickly. Fritz passed around his hip flask, and they all took a swig. This was a risk as Fritz was known to favour a fairly robust liquor that could probably corrode iron.

The four men's eyes watered, and not from nostalgia, after they had each consumed a mouthful.

'Where do you get this stuff?' asked Lanky, wiping his mouth and grimacing. He raised his hand to stop Fritz, who was about to tell him. Fritz could be very literal. 'I don't want to know,' laughed Lanky.

Fritz laughed too but could not quite understand why Lanky had asked him in the first place. This seemed to be a staple of American humour. He hoped one day that he would be able to understand it. The British were worse. They didn't even tell you when they were making fun of you. At least you knew where you stood in his new homeland. In this regard, it was just like home.

Tommy had been quiet for much of the dinner and felt a nudge in his ribs from Lanky.

'What's eating you?'

'You know, things,' replied Tommy. Then a thought struck him. 'What did you make of that story by Mr Beaufort?'

Lanky's eyes lit up. He said, 'Hey, I meant to ask you too. Wasn't that something? I mean it was just like...'

'Yeah, that's what I was thinking it was just like that time, you remember. Poor girl. I'll never forget her.'

'Yeah man, she was hot stuff. Such a pity,' agreed Lanky. Any further discussion on the subject was interrupted by their drummer Arnie Nichols.

'Look over there,' said Arnie. 'Have you seen the piano?'

They all looked. There, unquestionably, under a cotton cover, was a piano.

'What do you say we give it a try?' said Tommy. 'Fritz, your fingers nimble?' In response, Fritz moved his fingers like he was playing an invisible piano. 'Let's see if we can liven this place up.'

The restaurant had very few people in it just then. It would be more crowded soon as folk arrived for the new year celebrations. Tommy went over to the *maître d'* and asked if they could play the piano. A quick scan of the empty restaurant was met with a shrug.

'Most of the tables are booked from nine.'

'We'll be gone by then,' confirmed Tommy. He nodded over to his three bandmates, and they quickly moved over to the piano and removed the cover. Underneath was a beautiful, black, baby grand piano.

'It's no Steinway,' said Fritz who was being serious. The others laughed at this, and he looked momentarily confused by their reaction before he realised he'd just told a joke. He sat down trying to analyse what had just happened. He'd said something that was true but was also funny. Perhaps it was the way he'd said it. He thought about it more as he played a few notes on the piano. It had been tuned and sounded as good as it looked. As he played *My Melancholy Baby* all he could think was if I say "it's no" before I say something true, people will laugh. How easy is this?

A few of the folk in the restaurant began to shout out requests. Tommy looked at his bandmates.

'What do you reckon?'

Fritz began to play the song a little louder and the others began to sing close harmony to this. Even the waiting staff stopped to listen, and a few kitchen hands came out to listen.

The end of the song was greeted with wild acclaim before the *maître d'*, with a grin splitting his face, ordered the staff back to work. One of the tables booed him, which provoked laughter all around and few hand claps emanating from the kitchen, which drew even more amusement.

No longer under an obligation to play for the audience, Tommy extracted from his pocket the lyrics to the song he'd written.

'Here you are Fritz, I finished it earlier,' said Tommy, while the band crowded round to look at it.

Fritz read through the finished lyrics.

Blue Nights

So you left without a goodbye.
You've broken my heart,
with nary a sigh.
You say it's a new start,
and I want to die.

Those blue nights
they're closing in.

Mem'ries of those fights,
and what might've been.

Won't you come back dear right away?
No questions asked dear,
I want you to stay.
There'll be nothing to fear.
now, we'll find our way.

We'll make it work, dear.
Just wait and see.

Those blue nights...(repeat)

'Very good,' said Lanky. He smiled sympathetically and put his hand on Tommy's shoulder saying, 'Did you have anyone in mind?'

Tommy smiled sadly and shook his head. Even writing those lines had felt like a punch in the gut from Dempsey.

After fifteen minutes playing around with the song, the band decided to call it a day. They would soon be required to go up to the apartment once more. Fritz put the paper containing the lyrics in his pocket and they rose from the piano to return to their table. The *maître d'* was waiting for them.

Arnie tapped Tommy on the arm as they walked back to their table.

'Hey Tommy, I hope everything works out with Dorothy.'

'Thanks. I don't know what to say anymore. Kids.'

'Yeah, kids.'

They reached their table. The *maître d'* was smiling when they arrived.

'You guys are good. A distraction, but good.'

'I think we made you a little unpopular with your staff,' laughed Tommy nodding towards the kitchen.

'Don't worry, I got to that point a long time ago. I'm not sure if you knew, but Mr Beaufort has taken care of your bill.'

'That's great,' said Lanky, 'but I wish you'd told us earlier, I'd have eaten more.'

14 8:30pm

An apartment in Manhattan: 31st December 1921

She sat by the window of her third-floor apartment and stared out. The New York streets shimmered in the rain, as cars, seemingly inspired by mock Tudor architecture, splashed passers-by. This made her smile, before a feeling of guilt would set in, as her sympathies switched to the unfortunate people whose big night might conceivably be ruined by the soaking. Yet, the process repeated itself every few minutes, as people would stand on the sidewalk near the large puddle, that seemed like a target for the big cars to drive through.

A part of her thought that she should go down and warn people. She didn't have the energy. Besides, he'd told her to stay there and wait for him. She turned and looked at the photograph of the man. He was so good-looking. How had she ever managed to meet someone like this. Rich, caring, with looks that would have made Douglas Fairbanks grind his teeth in jealousy.

She'd moved into the apartment only a few weeks previously. Just before Christmas. It was his present to her, and she had been astonished. It was a pity that he chose then. She wanted to spend Christmas with her family, yet she knew they wouldn't have approved. They weren't married, her mom would say. Her father was not quite so religious, but he was a jealous sort. He'd have opposed this too and he'd have tried to take out his anger on him.

She'd made her choice though. Once they were married her family would understand. And then they would meet him. To know *him* was truly to love him. Mom would fall for those long eyelashes and smile. Dad would be more practical. He would see how wealthy this man she loved was and forgive everything.

Another couple were splashed on the sidewalk. She put her hand up to her mouth to stifle the laughter, as if by doing so, she would be absolved of any accusation of malice. She felt guilty again though. Tears began to fall from her eyes. She *was* malicious and spiteful. The way she laughed at those poor couples on the street, facing a miserable night because they were wet. Perhaps one would blame the other. Perhaps they would be angry at one another, they would argue and separate.

How awful she was for having laughed at them. How could *he* ever love someone so full of malice? She rose from her seat and walked over to a full-length mirror and looked at herself. She was still quite young. Pretty enough. Then she looked at what he'd asked her to wear. It seemed a strange request, but she'd done as he'd asked. There wasn't much of it. Just looking at herself made her feel cold.

She went over to a chair with her coat draped over the back. She lifted it and put it on. When he came to the apartment she would be ready. She smiled as she thought of what he would say when he saw that she'd worn what he asked. She smiled at the thought of what he might do. Feeling a little warmer with the coat on, she returned to her chair and sat down.

Suddenly something landed on her lap.

'Hello Coco,' said the young woman. The black and white cat glanced up at her for a moment before slowly curling into a ball in her lap. She began to stroke her feline friend behind the ear. This was greeted, as it always was, with loud purring that seemed to fill the whole of the small apartment with its good-natured contentment. Coco's presence brought some sense of perspective to the young woman. She felt better about herself now.

Coco had been the second present from him. He knew she would be lonely. He was thoughtful like that. Coco had arrived on Christmas Day. She's perfect, she said. I love her. I love you.

She remembered everything about that morning. It had been so perfect and then he'd had to go. She felt bereft. But later that evening he had returned and stayed Christmas night. She cast her eyes around the apartment. It was like something from a moving picture. It just felt so glamorous. Once her family saw where she was living, they would understand. They would accept the situation. He always said that marriage is so conventional. He didn't want that for them.

It all sounded so daring. He made everything seem like a wonderful adventure. As if they were characters in a wonderful romantic novel. As if to prove the point, she saw another couple on the sidewalk, almost being soaked by a passing car. Couldn't they see the large puddle? Sometimes you have to stop blaming the other person and take a little responsibility yourself.

'You wouldn't go near the puddle, would you, Coco?' said the young woman. The cat jerked its head upwards as she stroked it and purred while she cried tears of happiness, of loneliness and of fear.

Her eyes glanced towards the object sitting, gleaming, on the table by the window.

She felt a chill descend over her, that even her coat could not protect her against.

15 8:45pm

Bobbie stared across at the young Englishwoman she had just met that night, for the first time. She knew at that moment that she wanted her to be a friend for life. The question Mary had asked had detonated like a bomb.

Amory nodded to Mary and was about to reply, but Dick beat him to the punch.

'Her name was Colette,' said Dick. His voice was a little slurred as he continued, or perhaps it was emotion. 'Colette Andrews. She was twenty and she died on New Year's Eve 1917. Suicide, they said. She took one of Amory's pistols and shot herself. No one knew why she would do such a thing. I mean she had everything to live for. Beautiful, rich, smart. She had the keys to the kingdom all right, yet she took her own life.'

'She was little highly strung, Dick,' pointed out Chester. 'I mean, I never understood half of what she was saying. And then there was all those poses she struck. She seemed to think there was a moving picture camera on her all the time, you know. Always putting her hands to her mouth like they do in the pictures. I wasn't sure if I was with Colette or Mary Pickford.'

'Where did all of this happen?' asked Bobbie, leaning forward like a cop at an interview.

'At Princeton,' replied Chester. 'We were all out together. We knew it would be the last time.'

'Why was that?' asked Bobbie.

There was a moment's silence and then Kit filled it.

'You were going off to the War, weren't you?' said Kit.

'We were,' said Dick. There was something pointed in what he was saying, or perhaps it was just the way he was looking at Amory.

'You were,' agreed Amory. 'Perhaps you should have listened to me, rather than your conscience.'

'I killed my conscience, and a great deal else besides, in France,' retorted Dick. There was neither anger nor pride in his words, but nor was there sadness. Kit understood why. Whatever Dick was now, he was no hypocrite. He'd killed people, probably many and did so because the alternative would have meant his own death or those of his comrades. It was an easy choice and the more Kit thought about it the more horror he felt at what they'd been asked to do. A lot of old men had pit two armies of young men and asked the unaskable. As if to emphasise Dick's point, rain pattered against the window of Amory's apartment, like machine gun fire.

'The weather understands me, even if none of you do,' said Dick bitterly.

Just as the party seemed as if it would be derailed by the wound that had been ripped open by Dick's comments, Freddy opened the door to the returning band. The table turned to look at them, which made Tommy and the other band members self-conscious.

'What do you think, Bobbie? The daughter of a police inspector. Prospective crime reporter. The apple doesn't fall very far from the tree methinks.' asked Amory, fixing his eyes on Bobbie. 'It would be good to have a professional opinion.'

Bobbie Flynn glowered at Amory. Over the course of the evening, she had slowly taken a dislike to both him and Dick West. She quite liked Chester and the English folk, otherwise she would have taken her leave. Now, she wanted to stay, because she was beginning to suspect that something else was at play. Had a real-life murder taken place at Princeton, all those years ago? She took a deep breath and addressed the table as much as Amory.

'There is precious little to go on with just your story. I think if I questioned Mr West and Mr Lydgate, I might find out a lot more about what happened. Then there is the evidence of the room itself. I would want to see photographs of the room. I would want to question her friends, Princeton staff who were on duty that night. In short, I would want everything that is not normally available in a novel or, as in this case, a short story.'

'How professional of you,' said Amory. 'You should be in the police.'

Coming from him, it sounded like the insult he'd intended. He ignored the sharp look that Bobbie Flynn and her father gave him. Amory's eyes flicked towards Laura, who had not said very much all evening.

Kit regarded her also. She was, unquestionably, very attractive, albeit with an unfortunate penchant for eye make-up and hair-colour from a bottle. To Kit's eyes she needed neither. Somewhere underneath was probably a beautiful young woman who was selling herself a little cheaply. He wondered why this should be.

'Sorry to burst your balloon, Amory, but I didn't read the story. I know what you're like. When I saw it was by you, I thought I'd give it a miss. Life's too short honey, and you took up way too much of mine as it is.'

'It wasn't that long, Laura,' said Amory. He wasn't being defensive. There was more than a hint of regret in his tone. Perhaps, thought Kit, this one had not gone Amory's way.

'It was long enough,' said Laura and glanced nervously in Dick's direction. He was staring at his drink, as if deciding what he would do. He did what he usually did. He took a slug from the glass to drain the remaining contents and reached for the wine bottle. It seemed as if every woman he showed an interest in, Amory had been with her first.

'Does no one want to know what I think?' trilled Ethel, blithely unaware of the tension that was slowly constricting the table like a tourniquet.

Alastair resisted the temptation to speak on behalf of the whole table in saying "not really", and said, instead, 'Of course, Ethel, I'm sure Amory, like the rest of us, is on tenterhooks for your thoughts.'

Ethel grinned at Alastair and said, 'You're a real gentleman.' Alastair felt immediately ashamed for what he'd said and tried to avoid the dagger-like look coming from Agatha.

'Please my dear,' said Alastair gently. 'The stage is yours once more.'

Ethel smiled at the reference to her real-life job and then launched into her thoughts.

'I don't know about Helen or Colette, but it seems to me, she was real unhappy. You know a girl doesn't go to one fella and then another like that, unless she doesn't like herself very much. That's what I think.'

This was unquestionably more interesting and acute than anyone would have suspected from this young woman.

Mary was equally guilty of this but, ever the woman, would not admit she was wrong. She nodded her head to this and asked, 'Do you think she was trying to find proof that she was somehow worthy by dating men who worshipped her beauty?'

'Yes, Mary, that's what I think. You know we girls don't have the same opportunities as you boys,' pointed out Ethel, to which, Agatha and Mary said "hear, hear" in unison. Ethel continued, 'Some of us knew we would have to work for a living. To survive. Mary, I don't mean to pick on you because I can tell straightaway you're a sweet girl. Let me tell you Mary, you're more than that. You're a beauty too. But here's the thing, Mary, that's the least interesting thing about you.'

Kit was nodding to this and, now, feeling thoroughly ashamed at misreading the young woman.

'You got brains. I can see that. Brains to burn and you've married a lord. My goodness, what I would give to marry someone like him. But you know what Mary? You could have been a lawyer or a doctor or an architect. You have something. I see you, Bobbie, and I see you, Laura. You gals have something too. Yet even you can't be what you could be, you know what I mean? Well, I got to think that, maybe, Helen du Bois was like that. She had beauty and she had brains and she knew that her life would be married to some guy that was rich and clever at making money, but not smart like her. Then she meets this guy Archie, and he gets her. He really does. But something happens between them. I don't know, they fall out. They argue. She catches him with another girl and then she thinks – well, that's it. That was my shot. Nothing can be the same again. That's what I think.'

A stunned silence followed briefly. It was Dick who was the first to speak. He said, 'I think Colette's education consisted of reading romance novels and English poetry. She was an actress in all but employment. She talked the most outrageous nonsense.'

Ethel's face fell slightly at this.

Then Dick finished with this remark, 'And she was smarter than any of us. Even you, Amory. Well done, Ethel.' He raised his glass to the young woman and then realised it was empty. The wine bottle was empty too, so he took a hip flask from his breast pocket and poured colourless liquid into the glass before raising it at long last.

Ethel perked up at this. Then she felt a hand close over hers. Alastair winked at her and said in a low voice, 'Well done my dear. Bullseye.'

Ethel grinned proudly and decided to quit at that point. She was a take-the-chips-off the table kinda gal and she wasn't about to push her luck further that night if she could help it.

'You're right, Dick. You too Ethel. She was the most clear-eyed of us all and the bravest. She knew that youth was pure, and that experience and wisdom only resulted in the annihilation of curiosity. Rather than surrender to the slow diminution of her soul, she chose the most glorious way of showing her contempt for the futility of life,' said Amory.

'Balderdash,' said Agatha, which had Kit almost cheering her. 'You conflate pleasure with happiness, stupidity with purity and, worst of all, you make her death seem a glorious gesture of personal independence when, in fact, it was a waste. A giant waste of a young life, a life that had not had the chance to grow up.'

Silence fell once more on the room. Agatha, realising that she was partly responsible for dampening the mood, perked up. Observing the band beginning to play a soft lilting melody, she stood up and addressed the table.

'Well, I don't know about you, but I think I could do with a dance to work off some of that lovely food before dessert. Who's game?' said Agatha, looking eagerly around the table. Amory was on his feet in a moment. He walked over to Agatha and bowed.

'Lady Frost, may I have the honour of this dance?'

The Troopers saw the arrival of a septuagenarian and the Zeus onto the space in front of them. Agatha turned to the band members and, with a stage whisper, said, 'Put some life into it boys. I might be old but I'm not quite dead yet.'

Tommy grinned at Agatha and then nodded to the boys. Arnie was laughing behind the drums. He upped the pace, which drove Fritz and Lanky to do likewise. They embarked on a ragtime number.

'Bravo, Lady Frost,' said Amory.

'Keep up, Mr Beaufort.'

'Yes sir,' replied Amory, laughing.

Inspector Flynn rose from the table and smiled to the other guests.

'I guess this is my cue to leave you, for the moment. I need to go and see some of my men. With any luck I'll be back for midnight.'

The table chorused their goodbyes and Flynn made his way, past the unusual dancing pair, to the door. Soon Kit and Mary joined the dance floor, followed by Bobbie Flynn, who asked a delighted Alastair to be her partner.

'You're very kind young lady. I'll try and avoid your toes,' said Alastair.

Bobbie nodded towards Agatha and said, 'If you dance anything like your sister, it's me that'll have to up her game.'

Ethel was not someone to sit out a dance and yanked Chester onto the floor, leaving only Laura Lyons, staring glumly at the floor, ignoring Dick entirely.

16 9:30pm

Midtown Precinct North: 31st December 1921

Police Inspector Flynn's second stop of his tour, of Manhattan precincts, was the Midtown Precinct on West 54th Street. They were busier than normal. This was typical of New Year's Eve. It was all the usual things that happened at a weekend, only more so. For some reason because folk were celebrating, they let their guard down. Doors and windows were left open, despite the cold, folk were too drunk to notice they were being robbed. Houses were broken into, bags snatched, pockets picked. Even with Prohibition, alcohol was freely available, and more people were drinking, many who did not normally imbibe.

Yes, New Year's Eve could be a royal pain in the rear and Flynn was seeing this first hand. He walked past one overworked desk sergeant called Moran. He received a nod and nothing more. Flynn would not have expected him to stop what he was doing just to acknowledge the arrival of a senior policeman. He'd once been that desk sergeant. Nothing worse than visits from on high, from martinets expecting the world to roll out a red carpet.

He went upstairs to see the detectives. The office was painted a light green that reminded him of the results of his last hangover the day after "Thirsty Thursday" when Prohibition became law. He wasn't the only one hangover-sick the next morning of Friday 16th January 1920.

'Who's in charge?' asked Flynn walking into the office. No one stood. Flynn smiled to himself at this. They looked exhausted already and their night still had another few hours before the next shift came in. The captain's office was empty, and this was not a good sign.

'It's O'Riordan, but he called in sick earlier.'

Flynn resisted the temptation to raise one eyebrow and say "really?'. This wasn't the time to question one of his captains, but he would certainly be checking up on the man who would leave his men without senior cover on a night like this. He stared down at the young man who'd informed of O'Riordan's illness. There was something familiar about him. The young man rose to his feet as if he'd woken up as to who Flynn was.

'Sit down,' said Flynn in a manner that suggested he was profoundly unworried by the lack of formality. 'You're Detective...?'

'Nolan, sir.'

'Nolan?' said Flynn. He remembered the name now. He'd been involved in a few murder cases over the last year that had resulted in convictions. His reputation was growing. Flynn knew about him all right. A highflyer. There had been many over the years. Once upon a time he'd been one. Not many stayed the course. Distractions were many, strong characters few.

'You don't look Irish,' said Flynn staring at the six-foot young man with dark curly hair and darker eyes.

'My mom's Italian.'

'Italian Irish? That's a cocktail and a half.'

'So my dad says,' replied Nolan, a half-smile in his eyes, his mouth serious. He took his seat. He'd been typing a report.

'What's that?' asked Flynn, nodding towards the report.

'A robbery earlier.'

'Which was it? Window open or drunk and asleep.'

'You can write this one if you want,' said Nolan glumly.

'Been there son. I rose to the top on one crummy report after another.'

'Thanks for the pep talk,' said Nolan resuming his typing which made Flynn smile.

''I'd put a comma before "and" if it were me,' said Flynn, now beginning to enjoy himself.

'I love punctuation pedanticism. You should be a book reviewer,' came the sour reply and Flynn had to stifle his laughter.

The phone was ringing in the captain's office. Flynn looked around at the other men. Two were on the telephone. They were men Flynn had known for years. Each was in his forties. Both could do with losing a pound or two. Neither would make captain, neither wanted the responsibility. Nolan would almost certainly do so if he didn't get himself killed first. The young ones could be headstrong. Take risks that were unnecessary. If they survived long enough, they would learn. Or fall by the wayside in other ways.

In a few strides, Flynn was in the office and picked up the phone.

'Yes?' he barked.

'O'Riordan, is that you? Where the hell have you been? There's cops everywhere here.'

Flynn was astonished by this. He kept silent, waiting to see what else might be said.

'O'Riordan?'

'Yes?'

'Who is this?'

Flynn felt like asking the same question. He needed to say something so that he could hear more.

'Go on,' he barked into the phone. He tried to sound like O'Riordan, but he was no impersonator.

'Who is this?' asked the voice on the other end of the line. Then the line went dead.

Flynn sat down to ponder on what he'd just heard. The pondering left him distinctly uneasy. However, he'd been a cop too long to jump to conclusions, without having more evidence. His eyes wandered back into the squad room. All three men were on the phone now. Nolan was typing while speaking.

Flynn's eyes scanned the squad room. The paint was peeling off the walls and one corner looked suspiciously damp. He would love to have given them a better place to work. A shiny new office. But there was no money in the budget for such niceties. They needed more men rather than nice looking squad rooms.

He rose slowly to his feet and made his decision. Rather than touring round the other two precincts he'd planned to go to, he'd stay here and see if he could be of any use. He much preferred being on the ground than in meetings with politicians or managing over-worked captains, over-paid defence lawyers and underpaid public prosecutors. He was at his best with his men.

Standing up from the desk, he walked over to the window. He could see a halo of light a few blocks away. This was Broadway. It was a bitter night. Maybe it might discourage some of the usual felonies that could be expected on New Year's Eve, but he doubted it.

'Hey Harry,' said Flynn addressing the sergeant who had just put his phone down. 'What's new?' The Harry in question was a big sergeant named Harrigan.

'Happy New Year, sir,' said Harrigan. This was said sarcastically which made Flynn smile. 'Are you modelling the new uniform, sir?'

Flynn glanced down at his dinner suit and laughed. He replied, 'I am. You'll have one soon.'

Harrigan patted a rather large stomach and said, 'Hope they have enough material.'

Flynn grinned and then said, 'Happy New Year to you too by the way. Still dealing with master criminals out there?'

Harrigan shook his head and smiled, 'One guy tonight made me laugh. He tells me he bought some liquor from a guy in the street. Just as he hands the money over, a cop comes by. Arrests the guy selling the liquor. They go off and the guy samples his drink.'

'Water?'

Harrigan laughed out loud and nodded saying, 'Water.'

'How many times has this guy been "arrested" tonight?' asked Flynn, 'We should inform folk more about this fake cop scam.

'Three times already. We have a guy looking for him, but what with the weather...' Harrigan left the rest of the sentence unspoken.

Flynn nodded at this and shrugged. 'Yeah, I'd say they'll have made fifty bucks already. They'll call it a night. No point in risking a cold and they'll know that we know they're out there.'

'That's what I figured. Who knows?'

'Indeed. We may get lucky. I just hope the weather stays like this. No offence to the revellers, but it would sure make our life easier for once,' observed Flynn. 'Now, where can I get some decent coffee?'

'You're in the wrong place for that, sir,' laughed Harrigan.

Flynn looked out the window at lights shimmering on the New York Street. This wasn't a night to be going out on. He'd risk a coffee here. Meanwhile the phones were ringing again. Fleischer, the other detective on duty, swore out loud at the phone and then apologised, remembering that Flynn was in the squad room. Flynn did not turn around from the window. He just waved his hand in a gesture that meant, "forget it".

He couldn't blame the men for blowing off steam from time to time. He felt like doing it himself. How many New Year's Eves had he had with Nancy? Nowhere near enough. Since her death he always chose duty on New Year's Eve. He couldn't bear being alone in the apartment without her and now that Bobbie was out and about. He hoped she was happy. He hoped she would meet someone worthy of her.

What else was there for him to hope for now? Grandkids? He doubted his daughter was anywhere near being a mom. He doubted he was anywhere near ready to be a grandad. Yet, every so often, he would find himself looking at families with young children in the park and grandparents. He knew he wanted this someday.

The shrill tones of the phone in the office chased such thoughts away. He had work to do.

17 9:30pm

The arrival of dessert, as announced by Freddy, signalled the end of a vigorous hour of dancing that only Dick sat out. Laura, following some persuasion from Chester and Ethel, joined the others and proved to be a more than capable addition. Agatha's face was a little flushed after barely taking a break for a full half hour. She had enjoyed every second on the floor. When the music ceased, she wandered over with Kit and Mary to say thank you to the band.

'Well, you chaps certainly know how to play. I've no idea what I was dancing there, but I certainly enjoyed it,' said Agatha picking up some sheet music and using it as a fan. This raised a smile with Fritz.

Tommy piped up, 'That was a quickstep. You did pretty good there lady.'

'Quickstep? I must remember that one,' said Agatha. Kit nodded to the band while Mary smiled to them. They all smiled back at her and ignored Kit. This was noted by Mary who gave him a look of undisguised triumph. Mary left Kit for a moment and took Agatha's arm and led her away from anyone who could listen.

'So, what did you learn from Amory.'

'Nothing that added to the story,' said Agatha, but she seemed troubled. Mary could see this in her eyes, and she frowned.

'But?'

'I'm not sure. It felt to me as if he were dropping hints about something else.'

'You mean the story that we read is not actually the one we are meant to be solving.'

Agatha turned to Mary. She seemed more than troubled now.

'That's exactly what I mean.'

Dessert consisted of cupcakes in the design of either a tuxedo or flapper dress adorned with silver sugar pearls, surrounded by a brandy cream. Like the previous courses, it was delicious. Whatever reservations Kit was developing about the host, he certainly knew how to throw a party. The food had been excellent, and the music, as played by the Troopers, was proving to be a hit with everyone, save for Dick.

Freddy brought some dessert over to the band after the table had been served and some dessert wine. Kit, meanwhile, shifted his eyes towards the end of the table and found that Dick was looking back at him.

'How are things in England since the War, your lordship?'

There was more than a hint of a sneer in how he said this, but Kit ignored it. Kit smiled and replied, 'Please call me Kit. I hate formality. Or perhaps that's what you called the chap at Princeton.'

'I didn't do much of anything. I mostly ignored him,' replied Dick.

'Why was that?' asked Kit, genuinely curious.

'I had the feeling he was in the States to avoid doing his duty,' replied Dick.

'Ah one of those,' said Kit.

'One of those,' repeated Dick. 'Maybe, if a few more of his like had fought, you wouldn't have needed us to come over and bail you out.'

Kit was surprised by this. The bitterness was now out in the open. He thought about how to respond. On the one hand, Dick had come over and fought, with Chester, in a conflict that had damaged everyone who had participated. One could argue it had not been his fight. But he'd done his bit. He couldn't ignore this.

He remained silent for a few moments as the eyes of the table fell upon him.

'My country will always be grateful for the support you gave us. It made the crucial difference in the end.'

'We won it for you, you mean.'

'Dick that's not fair,' said Chester. 'A lot of good men died fighting the Hun, most of them were not American.'

'Most of them were not sitting in castles either, surrounded by servants eating fowl,' responded Dick. He seemed unwilling to let up from accusing Kit of cowardice. From the corner of his eye, Kit saw Mary's face growing hotter than a Mexican chilli. Of more immediate concern was the fact her hand was on a side plate. Kit could just imagine that same plate flying across the table and rearranging Dick's sour, albeit good looking features. He caught her eye and shook his head.

Mary seemed none too pleased, to be denied the opportunity to test her plate throwing abilities, but she relented.

Bobbie Flynn who'd seen the exchange between Kit and Mary was incensed, though. She rose to her feet and pointed at Dick threateningly.

'I don't know who you think you are mister, but your manner all evening has been rude and ungentlemanly. And to cap it all you make disgraceful insinuations against one of Amory's guests; someone who fought with valour and at no little cost to himself, against the Germans. You should be ashamed of yourself.' Bobbie was almost shaking with rage. Mary smiled at her, but Bobbie could see the tears in her eyes.

Bobbie's anger took the wind out of Dick's sails. His face coloured and, for once, uncertainty spread across his face. He fixed his eyes on Amory who had a strange smile on his face. And Amory was not going to pass up an opportunity like this.

'Yes Dick, Captain Christopher Aston was fighting for his country while we were foxtrotting around Princeton. What do you have to say to that?'

To add to Dick's misery Laura began to clap ironically at her date. Dick's head jerked around to her, hatred streaming from his eyes like lava.

'Maybe you should go back to Amory if you feel like that,' snarled Dick. He stood up and walked away from the table. He slumped down on the sofa in what the rest of the table correctly interpreted to be a sulk.

Kit decided that, as he had inadvertently been the cause of the latest crisis, then he should be in some way the manner by which it was ended. He rose from the table and sat down beside Dick. He handed Dick some wine. The young American stared at it for a moment and then said truthfully, 'I've probably had one too many of those, don't you think?'

This was certainly true, but Kit decided to take his uncle's advice culled from baseball. You don't have to swing at every pitch. Dick's eyes flicked towards Kit. Then in a rather embarrassed voice he said, 'You must think me a perfect chump.'

'Honestly?' replied Kit, maintaining a straight face for a moment, before breaking into a smile.

'I'm sorry,' said Dick. 'What I said was inexcusable. I hope you'll forgive me.'

'Nonsense,' said Kit. 'I'm pretty sure I can extract more feelings of guilt from you if I try.'

Dick chuckled at this before saying, 'Well, I'd deserve it.'

'When did you reach the War?'

'Around April,' said Dick, his eyes staring sightlessly into the distance. 'I had no idea,' he continued before his voice trailed off.

'No,' agreed Kit. 'You had to be there.'

Dick turned to Kit, a frown on his face.

'If you don't mind me asking, and please don't take this the wrong way, but why wouldn't I have heard of you. I mean a lord fighting at the front.'

'My war ended a few months before you arrived,' replied Kit.

'What happened?' asked Dick, genuinely curious.

Kit reached down and gave the lower part of his leg a rap. It made a hollow wooden sound. Dick's mouth all but fell open. Finally, he was able to speak.

'I'm so sorry. I really am an ass.'

'Don't worry. It's how I met Mary,' said Kit before explaining how she had nursed at the front. Dick glanced back towards Mary, whose expression suggested that she was still considering the manner in which she would kill him. He shook his head in shame. Just as he was about to apologise once more, Kit held his hand up and gently shook his head. The matter was over as far as he was concerned. Dick nodded gratefully and reached over to his wine.

'I almost wish I'd been wounded. Lord knows, I tried hard enough. One last sip. Bottoms up.'

'While we're here,' said Kit. 'Would you mind telling me what the devil is going on here tonight? Perhaps start with the death of Miss Andrews.'

Just then Amory rose from the table. Silence had fallen over the room as Kit spoke with Dick. This had somewhat moved attention away from him and that was never going to be a situation he would welcome for long.

'If you'll excuse me for a few minutes, I have some business to attend to, but please, continue to enjoy yourselves and if we have any new theories on the events in my story, then please don't keep them to yourself.'

Kit watched Amory leave the table and ascend the stairs unsteadily to his bedroom. He seemed unwell or perhaps the alcohol was beginning to take effect. After he had disappeared, conversation resumed at the table. Mary rose from her seat and came over. She stood over Dick in a rather threatening manner.

'Is your wife capable of murder?' asked Dick.

'Where my husband is concerned, you may count on it,' said Mary sharply. Her eyes narrowed and they shifted between Kit and Dick.

'Before you deliver a richly deserved *coup de grace* to my bean, might I point out that I have apologised to your husband unreservedly and I would like to do so with you,' said Dick.

Mary was silent for a moment. Her eyes bored into Dick's. Then, after a few seconds she said, 'Well, get on with it then. Apologise.' Dick's eyes widened in a rather amused but horrified way. Just as he was about to prostrate himself in contrition before the remorseless cruelty of female mercy, Mary grinned and wagged her finger.

'Don't do it again.'

'I shan't, I promise, sir,' said Dick offering a salute.

Mary responded to the salute like a senior officer on parade, which is to say she nodded and moved onto the topic that she had come over to discuss.

'If you think you're going to tell my husband what this is all about, and not include the rest of us, then you'll be back in the doghouse before you can say "Babe Ruth", or something American like that.'

'I think I've fallen in love,' said Dick before turning to Kit and saying, 'I hope you don't mind?'

'There's a long line of people, I'm afraid. Anyway, you were about to say?'

They heard the sound of Amory's bedroom door shutting which caused everyone to stop talking momentarily. Then Dick said, 'Well, I guess that's my cue. The break with Amory started long before Colette died. Then, well, once Chester and I decided to go over, things changed. He became worse. I remember he took up a collection for French war orphans and then spent the money on cocaine. I think we cordially loathed one another by this point. However, we were still together I suppose, New Year's Eve was upon us, and we were to go to war after.'

Dick shook his head sadly as he recalled the night. He took another sip of his drink and then began to recount his memory of what had happened.

18

Iroquois Club, Princeton: 31st December 1917

'There was a band playing ragtime and we were dressed like Cowboys. No, Amory was dressed like he was in the 7th Cavalry. The girls were dressed like Minnehaha. This was the Iroquois Club, and it was pretty wild. Princeton was pretty wild in those days, and I guess we knew we were going to war, so it was even worse than usual. The Iroquois Club was every bit as vulgar as you may imagine. The walls were decorated with paintings of braves that would have licked Jack Dempsey one hand tied behind their back, beautiful squaws wearing next to nothing. There were buckskins on the wall, headdresses worn by the waiters and the tables were underneath cotton sheets that were meant to look like wigwams.'

'The club was hot, stuffed full of people drinking, dancing, and smoking, when Amory, Chester and I arrived. We were with Rupert Brooke, that was our nickname for the man Amory called Fauntleroy in the story. We were to meet Colette there. Chester and I were pretty drunk. Amory was in an even funnier mood than normal. Abstinence only made him seem more aloof, artistic and argumentative.'

'Once we'd signed up for officer training, his attitude towards us seemed to change. It was as if he were anticipating us looking down on him for refusing to do as we had. We would never have done that. He made his choice. We made ours. It was that simple. But not with Amory. He wanted to turn it into one almighty drama. About him, as usual.'

'Anyway, there was already an atmosphere when Colette arrived. And boy did she make an entrance but, even then, I knew something was up. She came up to the table soaking wet. It had been raining. She was wearing a raincoat, but she was barefoot. I thought that seemed a bit odd. In fact, there was a look on her face I can't describe. She seemed like a schoolboy who'd stolen some apples from the orchard. A few folk were gazing our direction now. Colette had that effect on people even when she was wearing an old mac. You just noticed her.'

'She started giggling. Then we saw why. She took off her hat and threw it on the table then she threw off her raincoat, in a manner that would have had a Burlesque girl nodding in approval.'

'It was as if the whole world stopped at that moment just as she'd meant it to.'

'She was wearing an Indian warrior's ribbed breastplate made from real bones on her chest. Around her waist she had a loincloth that was only just about decent. That was it. Nothing else. Amory stared at her with a strange smile. We all stared at her. Every last one of us. In fact, the whole room was looking at her at that moment. A few young freshmen started to applaud but were shushed by the others.'

'Then I said to Amory we'll be thrown out of here.'

'A few of the men were getting elbowed by their dates for staring at Colette. Then all hell broke loose.'

'A few men came over to us to complain very loudly. They didn't mean it of course. This was just a show for their girls.

They probably wanted to get a better look at Colette, and she was happy to give it to them. There was no shame in that gal. She walked onto the floor and started the dance Amory described. It was all very strange. People were booing her. She didn't care.'

'It didn't take long for the club owners to come over. They told us in no uncertain terms that Colette had to leave and put some clothes on. Amory started to argue with them. I think every guy in the club was blessing him at that point, as it gave them more time to stare at her. I think Amory knew this and so did the owners. The argument lasted a lot longer than it needed to. All the while Colette was dancing, until Chester went over and took her away from the floor.'

'Eventually a few gals got up to leave and that was enough for the owners. They started to get a little heavy. They said either we leave, or we would be thrown out. Had Colette not been there we'd have taken them up on their offer.'

'We left under our own steam. Chester draped the mac over her shoulders. She'd caused enough of a stir. Don't ever come back shouted the owners, but I thought they'd be round to us the next day to say forget about it. Come back any time.'

'Outside the rain had stopped. We trooped along the street. Colette was laughing, but we didn't find it so funny. There was no one going to let us in wearing the ridiculous costumes we were wearing.'

'Amory began to laugh like Colette. It was all so funny he said. Chester and I didn't much like any of this. Seeing her dressed, or undressed as she was, was too much of a reminder of what Amory had stolen.'

'We began to argue with him. Chester accused of him of planning this all along. Even Chester who never loses his temper was angry. We must have looked ridiculous, three cowboys standing in the middle of the street having an argument. Then Chester tells us to shut up. He says where's Colette?'

'We looked around and she was nowhere to be seen. Her raincoat was lying on the ground. Amory burst out laughing at this. He said where is she going dressed like that?'

'Chester and I were sobering up pretty quickly and we were thinking the same. Only neither of us found it funny. The best that would happen to her was that she would be arrested by a cop for indecency. We didn't want to consider the worst.'

'I said we'd better look for her. Amory didn't seem to understand, or care. So it was me and Chester. He went in one direction; I went in the other. The plan was to meet back at the apartment by midnight. Amory stood and gawped at us as we left. He seemed to have lost his senses.'

'I spoke to a few people who'd seen her. Of course, they remembered her. A few had tried to stop her, but she just laughed at them and gave them a kiss and ran off. She was laughing like a loon they said. They'd no idea where she was going to.'

'It was near midnight. I could hear the firecrackers going off. Some folks just can't wait. When it started raining, I thought it was time to go back.'

'I saw the cops in the distance. A lot of them. They were stopping people from entering the building. I asked them what had happened. They told me a girl had killed herself.'

'I knew immediately it was Colette. Don't ask me how. I just *knew*. They wouldn't let me in until I saw Amory, he was with a detective. Then they let me through. Chester was crying. I went over to him and asked him what had happened. He said she'd killed herself. Killed herself using one of the pistols that Amory had bought.'

'And I said no, she hadn't killed herself.'

'It was Amory.'

19 9:45pm

She looked at the clock on the wall. Was he going to come tonight or not? He said he would, but then again, sometimes he broke his promises. Like when he whispered to her that he wanted to be with her for all eternity. She was romantic enough to want this too, but somehow she could not quite believe him. Then when he told her how this would happen she was shocked. The object, gleaming malevolently on the table, reminded her of what he had said. She shuddered a little.

Promise me you will, he had said. I will. Even if I am not there, promise me you will. I will, I promise.

Midnight.

On the twelfth ring of Christ Church, he said.

Tears formed once more in her eyes, and she wondered if she was going mad. Then again, wasn't love a form of madness? To impute onto another, ideals that you knew you did not have, that you knew probably did not exist, outside of a romance novel, ideals that made no sense whatsoever. Yet she had given up everything to be with him.

The church bell struck.

He wasn't going to come. She knew it. From her pocket she extracted a letter he had written to her.

Letter? Instructions more like. In the letter he had told her to go to the chest of drawers. Inside the top drawer she would find the courage for what he wanted her to do. The bottle contained a drink used by the Comanche Indians. She remembered the first time she had tried it with him. He said it was made from peyote and mescal beans. That the Comanche and other plains Indians would drink this and then dance for many days before they fought their enemies.

She stood up and went over to the drawers. She did as he asked and opened the top drawer. The brown bottle was there. She unscrewed the lid and put her nose to the rim. It had a sweet smell. She took a sip. Yes, it was quite sweet, yet by the time it reached the back of her throat it was a little more bitter. On top of the drawers were two tins. She opened the first one up and dipped her index finger in. The substance was white and viscous.

She looked in the mirror and then brought her finger up to her cheek. She drew a line from the point where her eye met her nose down her cheek to the jaw. Then she repeated the process for the other side of her face. She became fascinated by the feather that was attached to the back of her headband. It seemed like a dagger silhouetted against the street lights outside her window.

She took another sip from the bottle. It made her feel warm inside. Her skin was burning now. She threw off the coat that was on her shoulders and set the bottle down. Turning around she saw the rain splash against the window, as if someone had thrown it from a bucket.

Outside she saw a bottle crashing on the ground onto the empty sidewalk. It shattered into a thousand pieces before being swept up in the torrential rain. A few people went past seemingly unaware of the glass they were crunching through.

Why would anyone want to be out on a night like that?

You could catch your death.

20 9:45pm

Silence.

Dick's eyes glazed over as the events, of four years ago, played out once more, as they had done almost every day since. His voice was barely a whisper as he uttered the damning accusation on Amory.

Kit turned towards Chester, who seemed to be overcome also, from the memory of what had happened.

'I'm sorry for your loss. It clearly was quite a shock for you both,' said Kit, speaking for everyone.

There was no need to ask Chester if this was how he'd remembered it. From the look on his face, it was clear that what Dick had described were exactly the events that led to the death of Colette.

'Yes,' said Chester at last. 'That's what happened.'

However, there were many details missing. Kit met Agatha's eyes and it was clear she was thinking the same.

'I'm sorry that you had to relive such an awful event, Mr West,' said Agatha. 'However, if you don't mind me saying, that's a serious accusation that you have levelled at Mr Beaufort. The fact that we are here tonight with him suggests that the inquest on the death of Miss Andrews did not agree with your assessment.'

Dick looked up at Agatha. She's a shrewd one, he thought. He nodded at this and said, 'Of course, you are quite right, Lady Frost. The inquest was a sham. They could not place anyone, except Colette, in the apartment, so they concluded it was suicide. They considered her rather bizarre behaviour which they put down to having taken drugs on that night. The jury was formed of middle-aged men. You could see they disapproved of her, her lifestyle, her personality. A feeble-minded, flighty young woman, high on drugs, who kills herself. It didn't take much for them to find death by misadventure.'

'So, no one else was seen near the apartment,' pressed Agatha, keen to stick with the detail of what they did know, rather than what they *supposed* had happened.

'No. We were all out looking for her and the man at the desk did not see anyone go up to the rooms from the entrance.'

'I see,' said Agatha. 'So there was no way for anyone to go into the room, unless they were already in the building?'

Dick thought about that for a minute. Then he said, 'Not quite.'

'Fire escape?' prompted Kit.

'Correct. Someone could have used the fire escape to reach the room, but they would have been seen. We were on the third floor, and they would have to have passed several rooms. Yet, no one noticed anything.'

'But it was theoretically possible for someone to go up to the rooms?' suggested Kit.

'It was,' said Dick, but he seemed unconvinced.

'Then how would Amory have reached the room?' mused Agatha.

Dick thought for a moment before saying, 'I think he was already there. I think he went there directly and managed to enter when the man on the desk was distracted or had left it for a second.'

'Of course, the man on the desk was never going to admit to having left the desk for as much as one second,' said Agatha drily.

'You read the report?' replied Dick sourly.

'But then how would Amory have left the room?' asked Mary.

Dick sighed and shrugged his shoulders. All he could think to say to this was, 'Well, he did.'

It seemed as if it was safe to ask more questions now. Bobbie Flynn had been listening intently to all that had been said. She asked Chester, 'When did you, Amory and Mr West reach the apartment?'

Mary smiled over to Bobbie. This was going to be her next question.

'I was the first to get back,' said Chester. 'It was just after midnight because I heard the firecrackers going off and I realised I'd missed the new year. I went up to the room as we agreed and saw Colette lying there, the houseboy, Francis, was outside. He said he'd heard a bang. I told him it was the firecrackers and not to worry. Of course, when I opened the door, there she was.'

'You found her?' asked Bobbie.

'Yes. Of course, I saw she was dead. It was awful. The gun was in her hand. I shut the door immediately. Francis was screaming the place down. I felt like doing the same. We were calling the police when Amory returned.'

'What time was this?' asked Agatha.

'I think around ten after midnight. The police were along in a matter of minutes and Dick came soon after them.'

'What else do you remember about that night.'

Chester shook his head and could only think to say, 'It began raining again.'

'When?' asked Kit.

Dick and Chester both turned to Kit in surprise. Then they looked at one another.

'It was raining when I came back to the rooms,' said Chester.

'Heavily?' asked Kit.

'Yes, I suppose it was,' said Dick frowning.

Kit glanced towards Agatha and then Mary. He said, 'I imagine you were both pretty much soaked through.'

'We were,' confirmed Chester and shivered, involuntarily, at the memory.

'Two more questions,' said Kit. 'Firstly, you said that the houseboy, Francis, was screaming the house down. Were there many people in the rooms? Did they come out onto the corridor?'

'Yes,' said Chester. His brow was deeply furrowed. 'That's what happened. The place was in uproar and the some of the boys wanted to see the body. I had to hold them back. Then they realised I was serious.'

'When you found the body, Chester, did you check the rest of the room, or did you return to the corridor?'

'I didn't check the room. Colette was clearly dead. That wound. No one could have survived.'

Kit nodded and continued the story, as he understood it, 'So you closed the door, began to calm Francis down, which is when the other students appeared and tried to gain entry to the room. You stopped them and then you went downstairs to phone for the police.'

'Yes,' said Chester somewhat surprised. 'That's exactly as it happened.'

'How long did you take to do that?' asked Agatha.

'I don't know. It couldn't have been more than a few minutes. No more than four minutes.'

'Then you returned to the room. You stayed outside?' asked Agatha.

'Yes. We all did.'

'Then Amory appeared,' asked Kit. 'Last question from me. Was Amory soaking wet as you had been and Dick too?'

Chester's eyes widened.

'No. No, he was quite dry.'

All eyes turned from Chester to Kit. He turned to Dick and said, 'I have a feeling about this. I'm not saying he killed her, but it seems to me, that one possible explanation about why he would be dry is that he was in the room when you arrived, Chester. I think that, with all of the commotion, he had an opportunity to leave the room via the fire escape, without being seen by the people in the rooms. Then he could have run around the side of the building and enter in full view at the time you saw him.'

'I think perhaps Amory needs to explain his movements,' said Agatha, glancing up to the room.

All eyes shifted up the stairs to Amory's room. Freddy was standing outside it.

'Freddy, would you mind asking Mr Beaufort to join us?' asked Bobbie.

Freddy knocked on the door. There was no response. He knocked again. This time a little more insistently. Still there was no response.

Freddy glanced down to the party guests and shrugged in a what-do-I-do-now manner. Dick did not answer directly. Instead, he rose to his feet and jogged up the stairs to join Freddy. He banged on the door nearly taking it off its hinges.

'Amory. We need to speak to you. Open the door!' he shouted angrily. It seemed to Kit that, if Amory did appear, then Dick was more than capable of a little murder himself. He started for the stairs, followed by Chester who seemed to have the same idea as Kit.

'Something is wrong here,' said Kit when he reached the room.

'Well, why don't we find out what exactly,' said Dick. Kit had to admire how the cousins from across the Atlantic didn't stand on ceremony. In England, they might have debated over a cup of tea what to do next. Dick, with the help of the burly Chester got to work on battering the door down. Despite being a solid oak door, it never stood a chance, against a combined four hundred pounds of angry American manhood.

The door burst open, and they all stared in amazement at what they saw in the room.

21 9:45pm

Midtown Precinct North: 31st December 1921

Flynn stared out at the rain, from Captain O'Riordan's office and offered a silent prayer of thanks. The number of phone calls through to the squad room had died down as the rain grew heavier. Some nights it just wasn't worth it to make trouble. Fleischman had gone off duty. He'd offered to stay, but Flynn knew he was a family man. They would manage as they were. He turned his attention to Nolan and wondered if he had a family or, at least, a sweetheart who would be alone tonight because people like him were protecting and serving.

Flynn left the office to go over to Harrigan who was contentedly smoking a cigar. He slumped down in the seat in front of the sergeant's desk.

'Got another one of those, Harry?' said Flynn pointing to the cigar.

Harrigan grinned and took one from his inside breast pocket and handed it to the inspector. Flynn surveyed the cigar and glanced sideways at Harrigan.

'The Chief has cigars just like these, Harry.'

'He did,' said Harrigan with a wink. 'Not all of them reach his desk.'

Flynn shook his head and said, 'Crime is getting worse in this city.'

'Sure is,' agreed Harrigan, gleefully, as he lit Flynn's cigar.

'How's the family?' asked Flynn. He remembered that Harrigan had a couple of grown-up sons.

'Both boys in college. Imagine that sir,' said Harrigan proudly. 'One's training to be a teacher, the other is doing law.'

'A lawyer?' scowled Flynn. 'How could you Harry?'

Harrigan put up two large paws and shook his head. He said, 'I blame Molly. She said to him don't be like your dad.' Harrigan sat back and patted his large stomach. 'I don't know what she means.'

'Can't imagine,' grinned Flynn. Then he turned to Nolan who was sitting a few feet away at his desk. 'What about you kid? Got anyone waiting for you when you finish?'

'Zelda,' said Nolan.

'Zelda?' replied Flynn querulously. 'Unusual name for a woman.'

'Zelda is a black cat with a white streak here,' said Nolan pointing to the area around his mouth.

'How does she like new year?'

'Hates it. Lots of folk let off firecrackers. Scares the hell out of her, poor thing.' Nolan nodded towards Flynn's tuxedo. 'Do you mind me asking sir, why you're dressed up like a swell?'

'This?' said Flynn, brushing some fluff off the lapel of his jacket. 'I'm meant to be at a party tonight but thought I'd visit a few precincts first. Once I saw you were short-handed I decided to stay. It wasn't much of a party anyway. Didn't much like the host.'

'Will you skip it for the rest of the night?'

'No, I'll certainly be going back to it. My daughter was invited by the host. I'm not sure I want her staying any longer than is necessary. There's a lord and lady at the party too. Wasn't all bad, but I just didn't like the guy at all. Something strange about him.'

'Do you want me to run a check on him?' asked Nolan. 'There's not much else happening at the moment. Seems the weather is doing us a favour.'

'Yeah, seems so,' agreed Flynn. 'Yes, could you just make a few calls?' Flynn wrote down a few details about Amory and left Nolan to do the checking while he returned to O'Riordan's office. Something about Amory worried him. His manner was friendly enough but there was a distance in his eyes, or perhaps absence. If he didn't know better, he would have put that down to narcotics.

Yet, seeing Amory dressed so elegantly, in such a swanky apartment, with guests who were of a very high social rank, it didn't square with this sense that he had about their unusual host. Yet the feeling that something was wrong persisted. Had Amory been wearing a cheap suit and living downtown, he'd have had a very different view of what his senses were telling him.

The truth was, he wanted Bobbie away from him. Perhaps it was an old man's jealousy of a potential suitor for his daughter, but Flynn knew it was not only this. Despite the outward cordiality of Amory, his obvious good manners and extreme courteousness, Flynn could not forget those eyes. They were a strikingly clear blue and seemed empty of any feeling. Not dead, but like those of someone who cared not a jot for what people felt. They represented a paradox about the man.

Then there was the short story. It had seemed like an unusual, perhaps even entertaining, gimmick for a party. Now, having met the man and his friends, it struck Flynn that there was perhaps a more sinister narrative. He was glad that Nolan was checking on Amory and what had happened at Princeton. He had told Nolan not to worry about traffic violations, but to concentrate instead on digging up more about the story of Helen du Bois or whatever her real name was.

A few minutes later, Nolan appeared at the door of the office.

'Has something come in?' asked Flynn urgently.

Rain splattered the window which appeared to answer Flynn's question on the lack of crime in the immediate precinct.

'No, just some pockets no longer have a wallet. One old lady phoned in that her Chihuahua was nearly dognapped.

'Go on,' said Flynn, who wasn't sure if he really wanted him to.

'She took the dog out for a walk,' explained Nolan.

Flynn glanced towards the window and foul weather outside. Noland grinned and shrugged.

'I don't know why, either. Anyway, the dog was in the bag,' continued Nolan.

'You mean it wasn't even walking?' said Flynn in an exasperated voice. Now he knew he didn't want to hear any more.

'It gets better.'

'It won't,' growled Flynn.

'No, it won't,' laughed Nolan. 'Anyways, the snatcher grabs the bag, dog and all, and he's off to the races. Except the old lady gives chase. Apparently, she was the fifty-yard dash champion at her school in 1522 or something. Now she's giving forty years minimum and twenty yards, but she says she's keeping up with him all the way down Broadway. When the snatcher reaches the corner of 51st and Broadway, doesn't he only get splashed, and I mean completely drenched, by a car passing the sidewalk. The snatcher drops the bag and the dog, gives it up as a bad job and he was last seen sprinting through Central Park.'

Even Flynn was laughing by this point.

'Anyway, that's not why I came to see you. It's about this guy Amory. They remember him all right at Princeton and the girl that killed herself. It was a strange one. No one liked the smell of it, but nothing could be proved.'

Flynn's face hardened when he heard this.

'Go on,' said Flynn.

Just then they heard Harrigan shouting from the squad room, 'Hey sir, there's a call for you.' He motioned Flynn to come towards him.

'Can't it wait, Harry?' shouted Flynn irritably.

'No, it won't wait,' called Harrigan. 'It's Bobbie. She says there's been a death at the party you were at earlier. She says it's for real.'

A distant bell pealed to tell them it was two hours until midnight.

22 10:00pm

Hotel des Artistes, New York: 31st December 1921

Dick was first through the door followed by Chester. They stared in shocked silence at the sight of Amory's body sprawled on the ground. In his hand was a revolver just like the one that had killed Colette Andrews. If the sight, of the seemingly lifeless Amory, was enough to astound them, the décor in the rest of the room had an equally dramatic impact.

Two of the walls were decorated with photographs of Colette Andrews. The third wall had various paraphernalia of the old west, including a photograph of Sitting Bull, a headdress, tomahawks, a Winchester 73 and an old Mathew Brady photograph of General George Armstrong Custer and a poster for Buffalo Bill's Wild West show at Ambrose Park. There was another photograph over Amory's bed, rather like a religious icon, only this showed a Native American wearing a hat. Kit wondered who this might be to have such a prime position above the bed post at the head of the bed. On the opposite wall was the Frederic Remington nocturne Amory had mentioned. It showed some cowhands warming their hands on a fire at night.

Lying on Amory's bed was a US Cavalry costume which, to Dick's eyes, was identical to the one he had worn on the night that Colette died. By the time he had taken all of this in, more people had entered the room.

'The ladies mustn't enter,' shouted Chester, gallantly and, like most men, was roundly ignored by the fragile flowers that men mistakenly believe women to be.

Bobbie was the first of the ladies to see Amory. She was about to go towards him when Dick stood in her way.

'You shouldn't,' said Dick.

'What if he's alive,' cried Bobbie, although, to be fair, he looked a goner. Alastair, still smoking a cheroot, wandered over, knelt down and deftly put his fingers on the carotid.

'No, I'm afraid he's dead,' said Alastair. 'I'm sorry Miss Flynn, but Dick is right. It might be best if you do not see...'

Bobbie brushed past Dick and knelt down beside Amory. Alastair shrugged and left the rest if the sentence unsaid.

'I don't see any wound,' noted Bobbie.

Alastair was impressed by the self-control and awareness displayed by the young woman. Kit was now beside her and crouched down to look at the gun.

'There's no smell of cordite,' he observed. 'I don't think the gun was fired, which probably explains why we didn't hear anything down below.' Quickly, he looked around the room. Aside from the old west paraphernalia, there were also quite a few pots with flowers. His eyes alighted on a pot containing colourful flowers, like ones delivered earlier, which he could not put a name to. They were on top of a tall chest of drawers. Beside the flowers was a small metal jug which presumably had water in it. Mary was near the drawers, and she saw Kit staring at the flowers. She saw Kit's eyes widen and she stepped away from them.

The pansies were dead. This was not unusual, yet Kit was certain that these were the ones he had seen delivered earlier that day. He walked over to them. There was no distinct odour beyond the fragrance he would have expected from any type of flower.

'Where is Freddy?' asked Kit.

Freddy was outside being comforted by Agatha. The sound of his sobbing was audible in the room and just then there was a wave of sympathy towards Amory's manservant. Whatever misgivings Kit may have had about Amory, and he had many, it was clear that Freddy was deeply distressed by seeing the dead body of his employer.

Kit put his hand on Freddy's shoulder and looked him in the eyes.

'I'm sorry for your loss Freddy. This must be a terrible shock, I know.'

Unable to speak, Freddy nodded mutely. The grief on his face was genuine. Kit steeled himself to ask some questions.

'Freddy, are these the flowers that were delivered earlier today? Around the time Amory came to call on Mary and myself?'

Freddy nodded that they were. Kit fixed his attention on the flowers once more. To his untrained eye they looked as if they were either dead or dying. Then a thought occurred to him.

'Everyone, I think we should leave the room. I'm not sure, but there may be a chance that poison is involved and it could be that the flowers have been contaminated.'

Dick and Chester were too astonished to argue. They moved away from the body. Bobbie, however, was curious and came over to see the plants for herself.

'I wouldn't Miss Flynn,' said Kit, seeing her eyeing the watering can.

'My father's a cop, remember?' she replied. 'Don't worry, I'm not going to touch anything. Do you think that the watering can has poison in it?'

Kit turned to the can and then looked at the flowers. He replied, 'We'll leave that for the police, but it does beg an interesting question. If it's the watering can, then conceivably, it was one of us who put the poison there. An outside chance, but possible. I saw these plants delivered earlier. Whoever sent them may have infused them all with something that was gaseous and might have worked separately from any poison in the watering can. Anyway, we'll leave that for the police.' He looked unhappy, as he said this, which made Bobbie think that he did not quite believe it himself.

Bobbie took one last look around the room, as if she were committing everything to memory. She reminded Kit of Mary, or Agatha. He sensed that the case would be well underway long before the police arrived.

'I'll call my father,' said Bobbie. 'He's going round some of the precincts and said he would be back by midnight. He'll have to come earlier. He'll know what to do.'

As Kit was about to leave the room, he saw a small box sitting on top of the chest of drawers. It was open. Kit looked in. The box contained bullets. What he saw surprised him. Quickly he knelt down to check the gun. Using a pencil, he checked if it was loaded. Each chamber was empty. Agatha was in the room and looked at what he was doing. She quickly scanned the room, as if trying to create a picture in her mind of everything she saw. Her eyes fixed on another object sitting glinting on top of a small bookcase. She exchanged glances with Kit and then left the room.

Kit followed Bobbie out of the room and shut the door behind him. Everyone was standing, back on the ground floor of the apartment. Kit came down the stairs behind Bobbie. Just as he was about to speak, Bobbie announced to everyone, 'I'm going to call my father. He's at one of the local precincts.'

Kit reached the bottom of the stairs and watched Bobbie go off to the telephone. Mary glanced at Kit, wryly, and said, 'Looks like she's stolen some of your thunder, darling.' There was little by way of sympathy in her voice, only amusement.

Kit smiled at this and replied, 'It looks like we have a surfeit of amateur detectives here.' There seemed nothing else to do but to return to their seats and wait for the arrival of the police. Bobbie's first two attempts at tracking her father down failed, but it was third time lucky, and the dinner party guests listened in, as she quickly explained the situation at the apartment. When she came off the phone, she went over to the group who now included the band whose show was most definitely over.

'OK, my dad's on his way over now. I think I must warn you that we may be in for a long night,' said Bobbie. She turned to the band and said, 'Do any of you have telephones at home? You may need to call your family to explain the situation.'

Mary continued to smile at seeing her new friend take command of the situation. She was delighted to see a young woman show leadership. A quick glance at Dick and Chester confirmed they rather liked what they were seeing too. Bobbie was very attractive anyway and, to Mary's eyes, never more so when demonstrating such a cool head.

Behind Dick, Laura was weeping on Ethel's shoulder. It made Mary wonder what she and Amory had been to one another in the past. Amory certainly knew her and from what she knew of him, Mary suspected he and Laura had been more than just friends. She saw Dick turn around and look at Laura crying openly. Then he turned back to hear the band members confirm that none had a telephone.

Tommy spoke up at this point. He addressed Bobbie as she seemed to be leading matters in the room.

'Lanky, sorry John and I couldn't help but overhear the story that the young man related earlier about the death of that young woman. Well, this is quite something you see, as me and Lanky were there that night. We were in a band, and we played that club. We both remember seeing the young woman.'

This was quite a shock to everyone. Bobbie thanked Tommy for coming forward before adding, 'I'm afraid that this is another reason why you're in for a long night. You and Lanky, will be key witnesses.'

Agatha wondered if it made them suspects, but it seemed only a remote possibility. The police would have to deal with this as there may be other connections of which she was not aware. First things first, they had to tell the bandmembers' families that they would be delayed in coming home.

'Perhaps we can organise a telegram to go to each of their addresses,' suggested Agatha. 'I wouldn't be specific as to the cause otherwise we will have a deluge of news reporters, but something that says they will be delayed and not to worry, might be an idea.'

Everyone nodded at this, eminently sensible, idea. Mary offered to help Bobbie on this, and they collected addresses while Agatha scribbled a message that was suitably vague to be sent to the families.

'Who should go to the reception?' asked Chester. 'I don't mind.'

'It might be better if Miss Flynn goes,' suggested Kit. 'I think the police will have to treat the death as suspicious. In which case, I suspect, and I don't mean to imply bias on your father's part, but Miss Flynn may be under less intense scrutiny initially, at least until someone else takes over the case.'

'What do you mean?' asked Bobbie a little defensively. 'My dad is more than capable of handling this case.' Kit raised his eyebrows but did not reply. There was something on his face that gave Bobbie pause to consider what she'd said further. Then she grinned, 'Perhaps that might be construed as a conflict of interest.'

'It might,' suggested Kit. 'Of course, if he clears the case up before there is an opportunity to bring someone else in, then that might change things.'

'Or if we clear the case up,' replied Bobbie, a hint of her defiance returning. She glanced towards Mary, who had her arms folded and was smiling broadly. She noted how Mary then looked sideways to her husband in amusement. She might have interpreted this as mockery, yet she didn't think that this was the case with Mary. If anything, she seemed to be gently chiding her husband. In fact, she was sure of it.

She wondered why.

The two young woman went over to the band members and captured their addresses. Most of them lived in and around Harlem. After they had collected the addresses, they brought them over to Agatha who showed them the note she had written.

We are staying for another few hours at the apartment by popular demand. They said they would pay us for our time.

'I'll pay them for the extra hours,' offered Agatha. 'It's only fair.'

'That's very kind of you Lady Frost. I'll take the note down now, said Bobbie, taking the message from Agatha. 'By the way, I meant to ask you, have you ever been involved in a murder case before?'

'Yes,' replied Mary and Agatha in unison. They looked at one another. Mary smiled, but Agatha was more serious.

'Before you misinterpret what we meant, Miss Flynn, let me explain,' said Agatha.

For the next few minutes, Bobbie listened in astonishment as Agatha, with occasional interjections from Mary, explained just how familiar she, Mary and Kit were with murder.

'Good lord, I'd love to write about this for my paper,' said Bobbie.

'Aside from your newspaper being unlikely to accept such an article from you, a mere woman,' said Agatha bitterly, 'I think that Mary and I would prefer that our role in these affairs is not well known. We will, however, be happy to assist your father in his inquiries and I would strongly urge that you include Christopher in this. Though I would never tell him this myself, he has a remarkable ability to make leaps that I am no longer able to.'

'Nonsense Aunt Agatha,' said Mary, taking her hand.

Agatha smiled at Mary and felt a wave of emotion towards the young woman, who was more daughter to her than she could ever have imagined. If only Useless had met her, she thought. He would have adored her, as she did. Yet, the truth was, she was in her seventies now. Her faculties remained unimpaired, and she felt as strong as ever, but the reality was probably not so far from what Amory had said earlier. However much it was painful to admit, she was not as young as she once was. Life did that to you. You can barely see yourself age, yet you know it's happening. The physical changes are most obvious, yet the light was fading too. She didn't want to think about it, but it was.

While Bobbie left to send the telegram to the bandmembers' families, Mary and Agatha took Kit and Alastair aside. It must be said that any grief that Alastair felt towards the passing of their host, was being kept remarkably in check as he smoked his cheroot. He seemed almost put out to be asked to join the others to discuss what had happened.

'What do think?' asked Agatha to Kit.

Kit thought for a few moments, then said, 'I think this is one of the strangest things I have ever encountered. There's more going on here than what we think. This story has me worried, but I can't think why.'

'So, you think it's murder,' said Agatha, cutting to the chase.

Kit nodded, 'It's murder all right. I just can't help but feel that the murderer beat Amory to the punch, though.'

23 10:15pm

Bobbie Flynn had just despatched the telegrams when she saw her father, with a uniformed officer and one other plain clothes detective, arriving at the entrance to Hotel des Artistes. He was still wearing his dinner suit. Bobbie waved to him as he came through the doors. His face was grim but softened when he saw his daughter.

'Thank goodness you're all right.' Then he turned and gestured to the other policemen. 'Gentlemen, this is my daughter, Bobbie. Bobbie, meet Detective Nolan and officer Mulcahy. They'll help take statements.'

Bobbie and Nolan eyed one another warily. He seemed a little arrogant to her and she determined, there and then, to address herself only to her father. They headed towards the large elevator. On the way, Bobbie quickly summarised the events of the evening.

Arriving at their floor they burst through the door like a crowd at Macy's New Year sales. Flynn took in the scene before him. The band were gathered around the piano. They seemed to be working on something. Meanwhile, the dinner guests he'd met earlier were sitting at the table. Flynn noted that all of the alcohol had not been removed. This had been at Alastair's suggestion. He pointed out that it would not look good if evidence were removed, even if it put them all in a bad light.

'Where is the body?' asked Flynn.

Bobbie said, 'Follow me.' As they walked up the stairs, Bobbie turned to her father and said, 'Before you go in, can I have a quick word with you? I'm sure Captain Nolan...'

'Detective,' snapped Nolan.

'I'm sure your subordinate can deal with things for a few minutes.'

Flynn half-smiled at her daughter's dismissal of the young detective, but his face became more serious as he turned to Nolan.

'I'll join you in a moment,' said Flynn. Nolan glared at Bobbie before heading up the stairs to the bedroom while Bobbie took her father over to one side and explained what had been going on, in the lead up to the discovery. This included mentioning about their rather unusual English guests. This met with short shrift from Flynn.

'They may have solved a country house murder, but I'll be darned if they think they're getting involved with this. As far as I'm concerned, they are suspects.'

'Am I a suspect?' replied Bobbie in surprise. She studied her father who, it must be said, was not beyond fibbing to his daughter, just to see her reaction. This time he seemed in earnest.

Flynn regarded his daughter coolly, before growling, 'Young lady, if a murder really has taken place here, it may surprise you to learn that, not only are you a suspect, an important one at that, given you were his date tonight, but I am one also.'

This left Bobbie stunned. She watched him ascend the stairs and then she went over to join the others. Kit smiled at her when she came to join them.

'I wonder if your father has pointed out that we are all suspects, including him.'

Bobbie glanced in surprise at Kit and then grinned ruefully.

'I suppose that does make sense. Seems strange to be suspected by your own father who, it turns out, is likely to be questioned himself although I can't think why.'

'Jealous father?' offered Alastair, from behind his cheroot. He was smiling as he said this and then he added, 'Although I doubt he'll attempt to beat a confession out of you.'

Even Bobbie had to laugh at this.

'I'm sure one of the sergeants will do the honours,' added Alastair.

'I knew most of them when they were officers. I call most of them uncle,' pointed out Bobbie, grinning.

They all went over to the table and sat down. Freddy, unsure of what to do, sat alone smoking a cigarette. The only sound in the apartment was Fritz playing the piano with Tommy standing by him. The other two band members were sitting chatting separately. They were obviously not part of the song writing team.

As they sat in sullen silence, Agatha spoke to the rest of the table.

'I suspect that we are going to be spending a considerable portion of the rest of the evening here. I hope the rest of 1922 is a little bit better than how it's going to start. Anyway, I was going to suggest that we organise some teas and coffees.'

Overhearing this, Freddy leapt to his feet and made for the table.

'Forgive me, I will contact the restaurant,' he said, glad to be able to do something useful.

Kit stood up as he saw Freddy approach. The eyes of the manservant were bloodshot with grief. Kit put his hand on Freddy's shoulder. He said, 'Sit down and let me. I think you've been through an awful lot tonight.'

Freddy shook his head. He could not countenance the idea of not doing his job. He replied, 'Please sir, this is my job.' He left them to make the order.

'So what happens now?' asked Chester.

'Don't you remember?' asked Dick sourly. Then, realising that what he said had been snappier than he'd intended, he added, 'Sorry, old man. I suppose I'm still a bit shocked about what's happened.'

Laura glared at him sullenly, 'Are you sure? You don't seem all that saddened by what's happened.'

Dick's face reddened slightly, but his reply was calm, 'He was once my friend. Long before you apparently knew him.'

'What's going to happen now?' asked Ethel.

Kit answered for everyone, 'They will take each of us aside and ask us a series of questions. This will be our witness statement. Then they will look at the statements to see where there are omissions, differences of opinion and observations that might shed light on what happened.'

'Is one of us a murderer?' asked Ethel, while tying and untying her napkin as if to keep her hands from shaking.

'It's too early to say,' replied Kit gently.

Nothing on the faces of Dick, Chester or Laura suggested they agreed with that view, but they said nothing. It was clear Ethel was feeling greater anxiety than the others. Her mascara was stained around her eyes. Mary took her hand and suggested that they go to the bathroom to freshen up while they waited for the teas and coffees to arrive. The idea was gratefully accepted. Bobbie and Laura also decided to join them.

Alastair watched the four ladies head towards the bathroom and said, 'I can't say I've ever gone to the bathroom with a gentleman friend.'

This raised a few smiles at the table, from all except Agatha. Alastair noted his sister's reaction and duly ignored it.

'Have you ever spent time in a police cell?' asked Alastair, genially.

'Not in America,' replied Kit. 'I presume you have Uncle Alastair.'

Chester and Dick both chuckled at this. Alastair leaned back in his chair and stretched his long legs out.

'Twice, I think. Once in New Orleans and once in San Francisco.'

'What for?' asked Chester, who was genuinely intrigued.

'The first time, the police in Louisiana were taking their periodically dim view of gambling. The second time, they took an even dimmer view of my being drunk and disorderly. I thought that one was a tad unlucky. The gentlemen I was with was the troublemaker.'

'You were in a jail cell in France, earlier in the year,' pointed out Kit.

'Oh yes, you're right. Not in America, though.'

'What was that for?' asked Dick, taking a light from Alastair for his cigarette.

'Oh, that one was for murder.'

Dick stopped and stared at Kit's uncle, to see if he was joking. It was apparent that he was in deadly earnest.

'I trust this was a wrongful arrest,' said Chester, a trifle nervously.

'Who knows Chester? Who knows?' replied Alastair with a gleeful grin.

Dick began laughing at this, which brought a reproachful look from the policeman upstairs who had been listening in on the conversation. Alastair glanced up at his and saluted before saying in a stage whisper to the others, 'I could be in for spell in sing-sing by the looks of things. They'll never take me alive.'

Inside the room, Flynn watched Nolan at work, curious to see if the good reports he'd heard were justified. Getting down on his hands and knees, Nolan's first action was to check that the body was in fact deceased. Never a bad idea. Having the corpse suddenly wake up in the ambulance had not been unknown and was definitely a fast route to pounding the streets once more.

'Dead?' asked Flynn, reaching for a cigar before realising his last one had been filched from the Chief of Police by Harrigan. He smiled but felt frustrated at not having anything to smoke.

'He won't be dancing any time soon,' said Nolan, his eyes still on the corpse. He checked the neck and body to see if there were any obvious signs of violence. There were none. Then he looked in Amory's hand.

'No bullets in the chambers,' said Nolan. He glanced up at the uniformed man and with his eyes indicated for him to make a quick check if there were any bullets in any of the drawers. Nolan got to his feet just as the policeman indicated a box sitting on top of the chest of drawers.

It was full save for one bullet.

Mary and the other younger ladies returned to the table and sat down.

'Any arrests?' asked Mary.

'Alastair's just confessed,' said Agatha. 'I think they'll go for the electric chair.'

'He looks the criminal type,' agreed Mary before grinning at Bobbie Flynn who looked a little alarmed by the conversation. Then Bobbie smiled and shook her head.

'I think your English sense of humour is going to take a little getting used to,' smiled Bobbie.

'You'll have plenty of time tonight, my dear,' said Alastair puffing contentedly on his cheroot.

Mary looked at Kit who was staring out of the window overlooking Central Park. She nudged him on the elbow.

'So, Bloodhound. You're quiet,' said Mary in a gently mocking tone. 'What's going on in that beautiful head of yours?'

'I was wondering about that bullet,' mused Kit.

Mary's eyes narrowed. She said, 'What bullet?'

'The missing one in the box on top of the chest of drawers,' said Kit turning to Mary. He saw Bobbie Flynn glance sideways towards them. 'I wonder who it was meant for?'

24

Detective Nolan looked over at Flynn and said, 'So all of these folk are here at this party to discuss a murder story and then dance a Quickstep?' He did not sound too impressed and listening to him, nor was Flynn. He bitterly regretted the moment of weakness, that had seen him agree to joining her at the party.

'It wasn't my idea to come to this darn party, trust me. I spend enough time dealing with dead bodies to want to do it at a party.'

'What do you make of it all, sir?' asked Nolan.

Flynn shook his head in frustration. What could he say? A party thrown by a charismatic, yet strange, young man who had written a short story that was, apparently, based on a real-life suicide with a couple of guests who were part of the original real-life story. It was not just strange; something did not add up. And he was now a *de facto* suspect.

'First of all, son, we should talk about the fact that I am on your list of suspects, and I cannot run this investigation. I've left a message for O'Riordan to come and take over.'

Flynn noted, and pretended to ignore, the look of distaste on Nolan's face at hearing this news. Something smelled about O'Riordan, but he had more immediate problems to deal with than a police captain potentially on the take.

'Shall I cuff you and take you downtown, sir,' grinned Nolan.

Flynn stopped himself smiling back, replying instead, 'You'll do what the evidence tells you to. I'll sit in on the interviews for all except Bobbie. Get Mulcahy here to take down the statements. Where the hell is Doc? Some police department and we can't find Schwartz anywhere,' said Flynn. Glancing up at the big, uniformed officer he said, 'I take it you can write?'

'I was going to be a poet, sir,' replied Mulcahy.

Nolan grinned at this, 'Weren't we all. OK, let's start with our English friends. You say they've dabbled in crime. This, I have to see. English amateur detectives. Sounds like a corny dime novel.'

'I happen to like those corny dime novels, as you call them. Some good writers in there,' said Flynn.

Nolan glanced up at Mulcahy and said, 'How about you, or maybe you write them in your spare time.'

'I'm with the Inspector, I like 'em.'

'You would,' said Nolan sourly. 'Which one is the lord?'

Kit joined Flynn, Nolan and Mulcahy in the second bedroom of the flat which was to be the interview room. The three policemen sat facing Kit which made him smile. Nolan opened the questioning.

'How did you know Mr Beaufort?'

'I didn't meet him until today,' replied Kit. He explained how he and Mary had arrived that day on the boat from England. 'I'm sure all of this is verifiable.'

The answer appeared to take the wind out of Nolan's sails a little. He wasn't sure what to make of the man before him. His father had been born in Ireland during the famine. His grandfather had taken the family over to America to escape the misery and starvation brought on by the potato blight. This created mixed feelings towards the English. On the one hand, he hated the Empire and everything about English imperialism yet, at the same time, he had served in France and saw first-hand the bravery of many English soldiers and officers.

'I gather you served during the War,' said Nolan, trying a different tack.

'Up until November 1917.'

'What happened?'

'The Germans basically knocked me out of it,' replied Kit, tapping on his prosthetic limb. He was gratified by the look of surprise on the young policeman's face. Then he added, 'It meant that it would not have been possible for me to have met Mr West and Mr Lydgate when they were over in 1918. Amory didn't serve, so I wouldn't have met him prior to this evening.'

Kit had neatly anticipated the next couple of questions from Nolan, which appeared to ruffle him further. Flynn and Mulcahy suppressed smiles at the exchange.

'Tell me about how you met Mr Beaufort and what you can recall about this evening,' said Nolan.

Kit explained how he and Mary had spent the day and what had happened that evening. He made the note-taking easy for Mulcahy by providing an estimate of the time of the key events. This, he suspected, would be the approach adopted for the subsequent interviews.

The initial interview came to an end five minutes later. Kit rose from his chair and went to the door.

'Can you send your wife up, please?' asked Flynn.

'Yes,' replied Kit. 'One thing I noticed, perhaps you may want to consider it.'

'Go on,' said Nolan.

'The missing bullet.'

Nolan was once more caught by surprise.

'What do you mean?' asked Flynn.

'The gun was empty,' answered Nolan, not taking his eyes off Kit, 'but one bullet was missing from the box on top of the drawers.'

Flynn looked from Nolan back to Kit and said irritably, 'I must be losing it. Off you go.'

A minute later Mary appeared at the door. Nolan felt a wave of envy, towards Kit, as Mary sat down. She was one of the most beautiful women he had ever set eyes on. Her voice, when she spoke, had a clarity of diction that he'd rarely encountered before. She succinctly verified much of what Kit had already said, about the events of the evening. Nolan was sorry to see her leave, a few minutes later, after providing her initial statement.

'Who should we get now?' asked Nolan, wondering when the father would send for his daughter.

'I would get the old broad and her brother,' said Flynn. 'There's next to no chance that she or he had anything to do with this, but they may be useful in supplying more of the details around how they, and the other two, came to be invited to this party.'

Agatha came into the room and sat upright in her seat. When dealing with young detectives, she invariably adopted a demeanour and a countenance that bordered, but never quite crossed-over into aggressiveness. A pair of steely blue eyes settled on Nolan, rather making him feel as if he was the suspect. Alastair, meanwhile, slumped down in the seat, stretched out his legs and put his arms behind his head. The beatific smile on his face suggested he was going to enjoy every second of the encounter. His eyes crinkled, as they met those of Flynn and the two elder statesmen shared a moment of anticipation for the interview ahead.

Nolan started off badly.

'Lady Frost, I gather that you have done a bit of detective work yourself in the past. Perhaps we can call upon your expertise in this matter,' said Nolan, his face neutral, his intent clearly not.

'Young man,' began Agatha, and Alastair's grin widened notably. 'Old I may be, but I am not so far into my dotage that I can't see when someone is mocking me. To answer your question, yes, I have been involved in a number of cases, most of them before you were born, all, but one, of which were brought to a successful conclusion. If you wish to call upon my help, then say so, but don't think, for a second, that I don't recognise when someone is patronizing me. Now, I have a question for you.'

Nolan was dumbstruck by this response. Flynn shifted in his seat and decided against providing any help to him. It was just far too entertaining, for him not to wish to see it continue. Nolan rallied his forces.

"What did you want to know?'

'Are you aware that there is a bullet missing?'

It was Flynn's turn to be dumbstruck. He said out loud, 'I really am losing it.'

'Yes,' replied Nolan, glancing at the older detective wryly, 'We are aware.'

'I wasn't,' admitted Flynn with a trace of irritation. 'Your nephew noticed.'

'Christopher is rather good you know. If you need help from anyone it's him. I wouldn't put myself alongside him,' said Agatha.

Alastair wiggled his hand at this point to suggest that he would.

'You would?' asked Flynn.

'One has to allow a little for age, of course,' said Alastair, 'But Agatha was every bit as good, in her day. If I were you two gentlemen, I would not ignore what they say, but it's up to you. You can ignore me entirely, of course.'

This brought a smile from Flynn, who had taken a liking to Alastair. Quite apart from the fact they were of a similar vintage, he had a similar take on life that amused him greatly.

'Now, I suppose you want us to provide a statement on how we knew Amory, what we saw this evening and when we saw it,' said Agatha.

'Yes,' said Nolan frowning. 'That's exactly what we want.'

Agatha turned to the uniformed man who she had noted was poised to start writing the notes from the interview, 'Officer...?'

'Mulcahy ma'am,' replied Mulcahy.

'Are you ready?' she asked. Upon receiving the nod, she launched into her statement pausing, only momentarily, when asked to clarify a point that she had made. Alastair contributed nothing beyond the odd chuckle and an "oh yes, I'd forgotten about that'.

When the statement drew to a close, Agatha turned to Flynn. She said, 'You may want to speak to Tommy and Lanky about this evening.'

Flynn looked confused at this. 'What do you mean,' he asked. 'Who are they?'

'Tommy is the trumpet player and Lanky is on double bass. They were both witnesses to what happened in the short story, or true story should I say, that Mr Beaufort wrote for this evening.'

'Thanks,' replied Flynn. 'I'll bear that in mind.' The thought of the short story having some influence on the death of Amory had been growing in his mind. Now, it seemed almost certain that many of the people here this evening had a connection to the death of the young woman in the story. His thoughts on this were broken as Agatha and Alastair rose to leave. Nolan and Flynn thanked them for their help.

As soon as the door closed, Flynn looked at Nolan in the eye and growled, 'Son, I don't want some "Redcoat" solving this case before we do. You hear me?'

Nolan grinned and nodded, 'I hear you.'

'Now, let's get the Americans up. We'll start with the two girls, Ethel, then Laura, then the two boys and the servant. We'll do Bobbie and me last.'

25

'I always wanted to be an actress,' began Ethel. Nolan and Flynn settled into their seats for the long haul. Thankfully, Nolan proved adept at moving Ethel along, from her digressions into her career, to keep her on subject.

'When did you first meet Amory?' asked Nolan, just before Ethel began shaping up to rant about the casting couches she faced in New York.

'I only met him tonight. He was so good-looking. It's such a waste,' said Ethel, providing the briefest reply so far in the interview.

'And Mr Lydgate? How long have you known him?' asked Flynn.

'Oh, Chester and I go way back. Maybe three weeks. I was in a bar, sorry, I meant restaurant, and I was crying, and he came over and was very nice. A real gent.'

'What had upset you?'

'My sister disappearing like that,' replied Ethel.

'Have you filed a missing person report?'

'Oh, we've heard from her. No, she just quit her job and went off with some guy she met at the theatre. She got me my job, or did I tell you that?'

'You did,' said Nolan. 'You didn't say that your sister had gone missing though, but just to clarify, you don't think this a police matter?'

'Aw no, she's done it before. She's a fool to herself where men are concerned. She never listens to me.'

'I'm sure she would benefit greatly,' interjected Flynn. 'Now can you tell us what you remember about this evening?'

Ethel related the events, as she remembered them, with only occasional digressions into the dependability issues of men. The story tallied with the others, that the policemen had already heard.

So far, it seemed that everyone had an identical view of what had happened over the evening, which was useful in eliminating suspects, but provided little by way of motive and opportunity. However, the order in which they had interviewed the suspects had been deliberate on the part of Flynn. He had started with the people he considered the most disinterested or had known Amory for the least amount of time. He would ask Mulcahy to deal with the band separately, as they fell into the same camp as the English guests but, until he heard differently, had less direct contact.

When the interview with Ethel was finished, Flynn suggested they take a break while Nolan familiarised himself with the story. It might help when it came to seeing Dick West and Chester Lydgate particularly. They were his chief suspects, if a murder had taken place, although even the houseboy, Freddy, should be considered, thought Flynn.

The question Flynn needed an answer to, was whether or not Amory had been murdered. Where was Doc? He cursed the fact it was New Year's Eve. This only complicated matters. He needed to have a sense of whether they had a crime scene.

Flynn was not a man to commit himself, without clear evidence, but he trusted his instincts. His instincts told him that someone had poisoned Amory. Nolan held the door open for Ethel and then he and Flynn followed the young woman out of the room. They were met by a scene down on the ground floor of the flat that shocked them.

While Ethel was with the policemen, conversation had stalled at the dinner table. The enormity of what had happened or, perhaps, the alcohol, was having its effect. The only noise in the apartment was the piano and one of the band singing snatches of a song. Kit was sitting with Mary and Bobbie, listening to the band. On a whim, he stood up and decided that he would like to see the song writing process first hand.

'Shall we?' he said to the two ladies.

'Good idea,' said Mary, rising from her seat also. Bobbie joined her and the three of them wandered down to the piano.

'I hope you don't mind,' said Kit. 'We were curious to see you in action.'

'I wish there was more action, sir,' said Tommy.

'Writing a song?' asked Mary, leaning over Tommy's shoulder to look at the lyric sheet.

'Yes, just something I thought of yesterday. Fritz usually puts music to it. I say usually...' he broke off to laugh at his writing partner.

'Give me a break Tommy, you need to change some of the words. They lack melody,' replied Fritz. Kit glanced down at Fritz and their eyes met. Then Fritz grinned ruefully and said, 'Yes, I'm one of the Boche.'

Kit smiled and shrugged at this, 'I'm glad it's over. Your countrymen put up some fight. It took a few of us to beat you.'

Fritz's face grew more serious at this. He replied, 'Unfortunately, there's quite a few people who don't think you won. We have many problems back home.'

Kit nodded, 'So I hear. I don't think the peace was particularly well thought out. I hope we don't regret this.'

Fritz held his hands up and said, 'Look, I'm an American now and glad to be here, but I can tell you, I know a lot of guys who don't think this is over. Me, I'm just going to write some songs and take care of my family.'

Tommy was half listening to the conversation, while crossing out some of the words on his original sheet. He sat back and decided to take a break from it. He noticed Kit reading the lyrics, so he handed it up to him and said, 'Any ideas?'

'I'll want ten percent if it's a hit,' said Kit.

'Three,' grinned Tommy.

'One percent and I won't take a penny more,' said Kit reading through the lyrics. He nodded as he read. Then he glanced towards Tommy, 'You lost your girl?'

'Daughter. I lost plenty of girls in my time, but this one hurts the most,' said Tommy.

'I'm sorry for your loss,' said Mary.

'Oh, it's not like that,' explained Tommy. 'We had an argument about some guy she was seeing. She left the house. The guy's a no-good louse, and that's just his good point.'

Putting another cigarette in his mouth he asked Mary and Bobbie, 'Do you ladies play?'

Mary glanced towards Bobbie who shook her head. Mary nodded before replying, 'Only pieces I've learned or with some music in front of me. I quite like singing. It's a little easier.'

Fritz rolled his fingers along the piano and said, 'We'd sure love to hear you.'

Mary reddened and replied, 'Only if Bobbie joins me.'

Bobbie grinned, replying, 'I'm game.'

'What'll it be?' asked Tommy, motioning the two other boys over.

'Do you know "*Poor Butterfly*"?' asked Bobbie. 'Amory liked it, I remember. It seems appropriate somehow. It works quite well with two voices.' She looked at Mary hopefully. Mary smiled and nodded back.

The rest of the dinner table came over and stood by the piano as Fritz began to play the melancholy melody, based on Puccini's tragic opera. Arnie and Lanky joined in and Mary began to sing with Bobbie, singing in duet. Laura's eyes began to fill with tears as she heard Mary's beautiful crystalline voice sing the popular song. Mary took Laura's hand as she sang.

When the song concluded, everyone burst into applause, including from the landing up above. Standing there looking down was Ethel, flanked by a bemused Inspector Flynn staring down at his daughter singing. Staring down, also, was Detective Nolan. Bobbie's face flushed red, and she looked away.

Ethel descended the stairs, followed by Flynn, while Nolan remained on the landing. Flynn frowned at his daughter as he passed her. He went to Alastair and said, 'Can you do me a favour and bring a copy of the story up from your apartment? I'd like Detective Nolan to read it.'

Alastair met the eyes of the policeman and replied, 'Perhaps you should accompany me Inspector Flynn just in case I should make a break for it.'

Flynn seemed confused, for a moment, then the light of understanding shone brightly in his eyes.

'You look the type. Good idea, I will accompany you down to the apartment. Your civic responsibility does you credit, sir.'

'As does his wine collection,' murmured Agatha as the two men passed her. 'On second thoughts, let me help you find it.'

Ethel made her way immediately over to Chester to be comforted. She was still upset following her time with the detectives. Mary went over to them and put her hand on the young woman's shoulder.

'Was it so bad?' she asked Ethel.

'No, they were nice, but I got to talking about my sister going and, well, I was a little overcome. I'm worried about her.'

Chester pulled her close and said, 'Tell you what my dear, when tonight is finished, we'll go find her, first thing tomorrow morning. I can't bear to see you unhappy.'

'Thanks Ches,' said Ethel 'but I don't want you to get hurt.'

'Ethel, I faced the worst the Boche could throw at me, some lout isn't going to worry me too much. I can handle myself.'

Mary smiled at Chester and patted his hand.

'Looks like you have a keeper there,' said Mary.

'He's too good for me,' laughed Ethel.

'We're too good for them,' corrected Mary which drew a smile from both Chester and Ethel. Kit, who was approaching them, overheard the remark and replied, 'So you keep telling me, darling,' said Kit.

26 11:15pm

Half an hour later, Nolan looked up from the sheet of paper, that both he and Flynn had been reading. He glanced again at the words "The End". Mulcahy who had also been reading the story shook his head and said, 'What was that about?'

Flynn glanced to the young detective and said, 'Any ideas?' Flynn was feeling considerably revived after fifteen minutes helping Agatha and Alastair finish off another bottle of wine they had started pre-party.

Nolan half-smiled, but then it turned into a scowl of irritation. The story had irritated him immensely. He thought about the apartment they were in. He could save for a lifetime and never afford such a place. Yet Amory had done no work, as far as he could gather, had limited talent as a writer, if the short story were any evidence, and he had avoided going to Europe except, probably, to do nothing more violent than ski.

Flynn grinned, 'You seem unimpressed.'

Nolan shrugged, 'I won't comment on its artistic merit, but you'll have seen, that some of the folk mentioned in this story are sitting downstairs now.'

'That was my feeling earlier this evening when I met them. To be fair to them, they said as much also.'

'So, Amory has basically told the story of Colette Andrews. I wonder how accurate it is or is he trying to absolve himself of blame?' asked Nolan. It was a rhetorical question and Flynn chose not to respond.

'Let's get the others up. We'll start with Miss Lyons. I'm not sure how she's connected to the story,' said Flynn, 'but I know she was seeing Amory, at one time.'

'Jealousy, because he's seeing your daughter?'

'He's not seeing my daughter as you put it,' growled Flynn in irritation and then stopped himself. 'At least I don't think it's so serious as that, but I'll let Bobbie tell you. I won't be in on that one. Yeah, maybe it was jealousy. Let's find out.'

It occurred to Flynn, now that he was sitting opposite Laura Lyons that, up close, and somewhere beneath the paint, was a beautiful young woman. When he had first seen her, earlier, he thought she seemed attractive but a little hard. Over the course of the evening and the tragic events that had occurred, the hardness had become more brittle. She seemed to him to be very close to breaking down. The cigarettes she smoked appeared to fulfil the role of a crutch, for a young woman about to fall.

'How did you come to know Mr Beaufort?' asked Nolan.

Laura flicked her eyes up to the young detective, slightly surprised by the certainty in his voice. It was if she were weighing up how much of the truth to tell.

'We met a few months ago,' she said, after a long pause and an even longer drag on her cigarette.

Nolan fixed his eyes on her but said nothing. Flynn noted this with approval. It was often the question that you didn't ask that revealed the most.

'Is this relevant? You don't seriously believe he was murdered?'

'We'll see, Miss Lyons. Would you kindly answer the question,' responded Flynn.

Laura sighed, smoked, sighed some more and then said, 'We met a while back, maybe four months ago. I was one of the very many, young women he dated. Of course, I thought I was the only one that he loved. We delude ourselves like that. Gentlemen, take note. Particularly with the worst kind of men. And Amory was certainly one of those, albeit a little better-dressed, well-spoken and with better table manners.'

Nolan coloured a little as he listened. He wanted to ask her why women went with men who were obviously no good. What were they looking for? What did they find? From what Nolan had observed, Amory, even in death, had clearly been good-looking, he was wealthy, gentlemanly, after a fashion and, all too obviously, bad. The combination of these character traits appeared to be irresistible to women. Even Flynn's daughter had fallen for this moonshine. He listened as Laura told him about first meeting Amory.

'He has a way about him. Had, I should say. He told me I wouldn't be interested in him. Of course, I became interested when I heard this. Then he said, something like, he supposed that I'd kissed a lot of boys. He didn't mind. He understood that boys would be after me all the time. Anyway, he told me my life story with men, and it rang true. Of course, he probably said the same to all the girls but, coming from him, it seemed real. And he had nice teeth to go with those eyes. Yes, those eyes. They were so sad. I fell for him like he intended. Then I read that nonsense story of his and realised that he used the same story, over and over again and we all fell for it.'

Laura looked at the two men and shook her head. She smiled ruefully, then said, 'I suppose I'm not giving a great impression of my sex, am I?'

Nolan felt like saying "nope" but held his counsel. Flynn made no comment but was quietly wondering what flannel Amory had come out with to make Bobbie agree to be his date on New Year's Eve. Was it just the fact that he had helped at the newspaper, or had she fallen for the same sob story?

Before they could ask any more questions, there was a knock at the door. Mulcahy rose and went to the door. It was Freddy.

'A Captain O'Riordan and two other gentlemen from the police department are downstairs looking for Inspector Flynn.'

'We'll be right down,' said Flynn. He turned to Nolan and Laura Lyons to add, 'We can finish this later.'

Laura left the room and walked down the stairs. She ignored Dick and went over to where Ethel, Chester and Alastair were sitting.

'What did they ask you?' said Ethel.

'They wanted to know about me and Amory. I guess it's no secret I knew him.'

'What did they want to know?' asked Chester, curious about the relationship.

Laura smiled bitterly and lit a cigarette.

'What do you think, Ches? We both know what he was like. I didn't say it in there because, well, what would it say about me? He was a predator with women.'

'If he's a predator,' asked Alastair, 'how would you describe Jack the Ripper?' He raised his eyebrows and calmly blue smoke into the air.

This irritated Laura. She snapped, 'Are you defending him?'

Alastair smiled sadly and spoke, as if reminiscing, 'No, my dear, I'm not. My brother had a way with women that I never had.' He paused, as if he'd just been struck in the gut. 'Yes, I know Amory's type, all right. I've never much cared for it. Would that more young women felt the same way.'

Laura would remember what Alastair had said later that night.

Kit, Mary and Bobbie were sitting by the window, watching the rain sheeting down onto the street far below. Mary took Bobbie's hand and asked, 'How are you feeling?'

Bobbie tried to smile but gave it up as a bad job.

'Honestly, I don't know. I liked Amory. Not that way, I might add. I could tell what he was like, and I wasn't going to be one of his conquests, but I did like him. I could see that he wasn't happy. That may have been part of his act of course, but I don't think so. I really do think he was unhappy, depressed even. If I were to guess why, it's to do with that young woman's death. Yes, I think this evening has convinced me of that.'

'Guilt?' asked Mary.

'Who knows?' said Bobbie. 'It might be. What do you think, Mary?'

Mary shrugged and said, 'I didn't know him well enough. I'm not sure the story he wrote tells me enough about him to draw many conclusions. If he and Archie are the same person, then it's clear that he was someone who found it easy to attract women. Laura, for instance. She's taken it rather hard.'

'Yes,' agreed Bobbie. 'I'm not sure she likes me. I wanted to tell her that there was nothing between Amory and me but, well, then it was too late and now it would seem ridiculous.'

Mary glanced sideways at Kit and said wryly, 'Come on Bloodhound. You're being awfully quiet. Have you solved this conundrum yet?'

Bobbie grinned at Mary as she said this. It was interesting for her to see two people around her age who seemed completely relaxed in one another's company, who could be playful towards one another while, at the same time, avoiding any disrespect. If she hadn't liked Mary so much, she would probably have been rather envious.

Mary appeared to have been involved in a number of adventures and she wanted to hear more of this. Perhaps she could write an article about the crime-solving British nobility. But then no one would believe it. They would seem like characters from a PG Wodehouse story.

Kit smiled back at the two young women looking up at him hopefully. He replied, 'There's no reason why either of you shouldn't get to the bottom of this, you know. You're both capable.'

'I haven't done anything like this before,' said Bobbie. 'You two have. Incidentally, I want to know more. Maybe, when this is all over with, you can give me the scoop on your intriguing past.'

'I think you'd enjoy it more if it was Mary telling you,' said Kit gallantly.

'I probably would,' retorted Bobbie before breaking out into a grin.

Mary nodded at this and then gently elbowed Kit in the ribs. 'Go on, you're not going to slither out of telling me what's on your mind, Christopher.'

'You're in trouble now,' pointed out Bobbie.

'Apparently,' agreed Kit. 'I think I want to read the story again. I suggest you do likewise. I think it's interesting that you said Amory was unhappy. I'm wondering if he was planning to finish off the job he intended from New Year 1917.'

Both Mary and Bobbie's eyes widened a little when Kit said this. Before either could ask Kit to say more, there was a loud knock at the door. Freddy sped over to open it. Three men entered.

The first man to enter was around the same age as Alastair and Flynn. He had a Trilby hat with white whiskers poking out from underneath. He was carrying a black Gladstone bag, and, under his black overcoat, he appeared to be dressed in a dinner suit. He certainly did not seem to be pleased to be where he was. The second man was, perhaps, in his early forties and wore a beige mackintosh, dripping with rainwater. The third man was bespectacled and looked more like a librarian than a detective. The man in the mackintosh introduced himself as Captain O'Riordan, from the Midtown precinct. He looked like the result of an affair between a yak and a bulldog. He was large, with a face squashed into a square head. A shock of red hair stood up on end, as if he had inadvertently stuck his finger in an electrical socket. In short, it was a face only a mother could love and O'Riordan's hadn't.

'Where's Inspector Flynn?' barked O'Riordan. He glared angrily at the dinner guests, before his mouth took up a shape that made Kit believe, for one second, he might spit tobacco onto the floor.

Nothing in the captain's voice suggested that Freddy should delay letting the other policemen know who had arrived, so he dashed off to the room where the interviews were taking place. Meanwhile, the new arrivals surveyed the apartment and the guests standing around the piano.

Addressing the group, the man they had heard introduce himself as O'Riordan asked, 'Any of you own this place?'

'I think you'll find him in his room. He's dead,' answered Dick rather drily.

27

The policemen gathered in Amory's room and watched as the be-whiskered man in the dinner suit examined the dead body. The light reflected off his bald head as he crouched over Amory.

'Well, he's certainly dead,' concluded Dr Amos Schwartz. He glanced up wryly at his old sparring partner, Flynn, and waited for the brickbats to fly.

'Thanks Doc,' growled Flynn. 'Anything you want to add to that, or you just going to keep us in suspense?'

Schwartz was caught between continuing the banter or showing due respect to the dead. He opted for the latter course.

'Until the autopsy, I can't be certain, but I think he's been poisoned,' he replied, rising to his feet.

Nolan pointed to the dead plants on top of the chest of drawers.

'Could the poison have been inhaled? We need to check, but it looks like these plants, which were sent to him this morning, might all have had their soil poisoned with something.'

Schwartz waved his hand dismissively before replying, 'No chance. Maybe that's what the killer wanted you to think.'

'Why do you say killer?' asked Flynn.

'Well, maybe he did it himself. You never know. But, I can tell you, for it to have acted so quickly, the only way he was poisoned was with something he ate or drank. You'd need a lot of a gaseous poison to kill a man in a room. Was the window open when the body was discovered?'

'Yes,' answered Nolan.

'Who discovered the body?' asked O'Riordan.

'I gather they busted the door down when he wouldn't answer,' said Flynn. 'I guess they all did.'

Flynn spent a few minutes updating O'Riordan about the unusual party that had been organised and the initial statements made by the guests. At the end of this, he officially put O'Riordan in charge of the investigation, ignoring the flash of anger that appeared in the eyes of Nolan. The young man would have to accept the chain of command. However, he fully intended keeping an eye on the captain and his handling of the case.

'Well let's speak to these good folk,' said O'Riordan when Flynn had finished.

'Before you do,' advised Flynn, 'you should read the short story that was meant to be the point of the evening. Nolan and I believe there is a link between what happened tonight and a suicide from four years ago. It might provide a motive if this is murder. And send Mulcahy to speak to the band. Two of them have a story to tell about this also.'

O'Riordan looked sceptical at this, but Flynn was too senior to argue with, so he nodded. Flynn led him and the other policemen out of the room, leaving Schwartz and Johnson from Forensics behind.

Downstairs, Agatha was pacing back and forth like a caged lioness. Kit and Mary watched her walking, with affectionate smiles stretched across their faces. Both understood how she was feeling, though. They desperately wanted to be involved yet they knew, for once, that this was as inadvisable as it was unlikely. They were potential suspects, although in Kit's view, he doubted if the police would seriously consider any of them to be so.

'Is something wrong, Aunt Agatha?' asked Mary after a minute of two of gazing at her.

Agatha shook her head in frustration. She replied, 'Old age. That's what's wrong.'

Mary turned to Kit, expecting him to make some clever rejoinder, but he was, once more, re-reading the short story. As there was nothing better to do, Mary and Bobbie sat either side of him and did the same. Somewhere behind them, they heard Dick ask Freddy to organise some coffees for the guests and the policemen.

Kit turned, momentarily, and looked at the young man. He seemed to be sobering up rather quickly or perhaps it was the prospect of being interviewed by the police. It would have occurred to him by now, as it had to Kit, that if a murder really had taken place, then Dick was probably going to be considered the leading suspect. Dick's eyes met Kit's. The American grinned and, as if reading Kit's mind he said, 'I best be ready, don't you think? I don't want them pinning this one on me.'

Chester chortled a little at this comment then stopped himself, as he realised it would seem out of place, given the gravity of what had happened. Unlike Dick, Chester seemed quite relaxed about the interview ahead. He sat with a consoling arm around Ethel who still seemed a little upset. He'd, long since, removed his tuxedo jacket, due to the heat of the apartment, which had reached almost tropical levels. Underneath his arms were tell-tale dark stains, but no one seemed immune from the heat.

Officer Mulcahy was with the band members now. Kit half-listened to what they were saying. The questions asked helped supplement the understanding of the evening's key moments and the times they took place. Nothing, in Mulcahy's manner, suggested that the band members were under any suspicion, despite the connection Tommy and Lanky had to the events of four years previously. Kit wondered if this would apply to Freddy also.

He returned his attention to the story. Like Agatha, he suspected they'd missed something obvious, at least it would appear so, when they realised what it was. Several minutes passed, as they read in silence. When they finished rereading the story as a group, Kit closed his eyes and tried to imagine the story once more but, this time, in combination with what he'd heard from Dick and Chester earlier, just before they had found the body of Amory. Just then, he remembered something that Amory had mentioned this morning. He turned to Bobbie.

'Bobbie, you said Amory had written articles for your newspaper. He mentioned one he'd written on the Ghost Dance. What else did he write about?'

Bobbie's eyes widened and she replied.

'Death.'

Kit rose to his feet and went over to the print by Remington. Underneath was a chest of drawers with the typewriter he'd noticed earlier. He opened some of the drawers and found what he was looking for. He held up a sheaf of newspaper cuttings'.

'I think we should read these too,' announced Kit.

The coffees arrived on the dumb waiter and Freddy brought them, first to the room with the detectives, and then to the party guests. Dick took his coffee and went over to the window, leaving Chester with Laura. It was obvious that he wanted to clear his head.

As they drank their coffees, Kit, Mary, Agatha and Bobbie read through Amory's articles, to see if they could provide any clue to what had happened. For Kit, the writing cemented a view that Amory's fascination with death went beyond intellectual curiosity.

'He seems to have taken a profound interest in how different Indian tribes view death,' said Kit. 'There are some common themes, apparently. They believe in an afterlife, rather as Christianity does. The manner of one's life, and death, seems important too.'

'Yes,' agreed Bobbie. 'I remember my editor was worried about some of these articles until Amory made just that point.

'He refers to the Mexican festival of *Dia de los Muertos,* in this article,' said Agatha. 'I can understand, at my age, having an interest in what happens next, but Amory strikes me as a little bit young for such musings.'

The police had now spent around fifteen minutes upstairs without calling anyone. Then, the door to the room opened and Nolan appeared. He motioned for Freddy to join them. The others watched him skip up the stairs.

Kit's mind was having trouble focusing on two things that were bothering him. He wished that he'd been able to spend longer in Amory's room. This would not be possible as the

Forensics man was busy with the doctor. They would remove the body soon and access would be completely barred.

'What's wrong, darling?' asked Mary looking at Kit with concern.

'I'd love to go up to Amory's room for a little longer. Something's bothering me.'

'I agree,' said Dick from beside the window. He put his coffee down and walked over to the group. 'What do you say we go up and take a look?'

Kit was not sure if he loved Americans, but he had a deep admiration for their spirit. Nothing was insurmountable for this extraordinary race of people. They refused to believe in the concept of impossibility. There was something to be said for such spirit.

'I'm game,' said Kit with a smile.

This was like a bugle call to Agatha. She said, 'I'll come too.' Then she noticed that Mary and Bobbie were also getting up from their seats. She shook her head slightly which was met with a frown from Mary and disappointment from Bobbie. 'Three of us is bad enough,' said Agatha. Then she added in a stage whisper, 'Leave the doctor to me. Just go with what I do.'

The three climbed the stairs while Mary and Bobbie looked on, intrigued by what they intended to do. Dick was somewhat curious himself, but was realising that neither the old woman, nor her nephew, were fools. Far from it in fact.

At the top of the stairs, Agatha said in a loud voice, 'Thank you for helping me. I must confess I do feel rather faint.'

Kit smiled as he realised what his aunt had planned. Dick nodded as he, too, understood what was about to happen. The door to Amory's room was half open so that the two men inside would hear everything. As they passed it, Agatha put her hand up to her head and announced, 'I think I'm going to faint.'

Kit helped her gently to the ground while Dick knocked on the door and said to the doctor, 'Doc, the old lady's fainted.'

Agatha glared up at Dick, for the reference to her age, which brought an unrepentant smile from the American. She resumed her collapsed pose intent on having a few sharp words with the young man later.

Schwartz was immediately out of the room followed by the Forensics man, Johnson. He saw Kit and Dick kneeling around Agatha.

'She just went,' said Dick. Then he looked up at Johnson, 'say, could you get us a glass of water.'

The Forensics man nodded and immediately descended the stairs while Schwartz knelt down to inspect her.

'Give me some room,' said Schwartz, impatiently. This released Kit and Dick to stand out of the way. Both men backed slowly into the room.

Once inside they looked down at the body which was now covered. Only his hand peeked out. It was still holding the revolver.

'Where is the other revolver?' asked Kit.

'That's what I've been wondering,' whispered Dick.

For the next half minute, they conducted a rapid search of the drawers and under the bed. It turned up nothing. Outside they could hear that Agatha had made an amazing recovery from her fainting fit. She was thanking the doctor and Johnson. While Dick's eyes were on Agatha briefly, Kit quickly lifted a shining object from the top of the drawers and put it in his pocket. Then he joined Dick in moving back to the entrance of the bedroom. Schwartz turned around; his brow furrowed.

'What were you two doing in there?'

'Just standing here Doc,' said Dick with an innocent grin.

'Well, get out of there. Here, help this lady up.'

'This old lady,' said Agatha, glancing sourly at Dick. The American did not seem in the least put out by the tone of her voice. In fact, Kit had the feeling that Dick was rather enjoying his aunt now.

They went through the motions of helping Agatha to her feet and then went down the stairs in silence. When they reached the bottom, they re-joined Mary and Bobbie.

'So, what did you find?' asked Agatha in a whisper.

'It's what we didn't find,' said Dick.

'No gun?' asked Agatha. Dick stopped for a moment and looked at her in admiration. He turned to Kit, who shrugged.

'It runs in the family,' said Kit by way of explanation.

'No gun,' confirmed Dick.

Agatha glanced at Kit with raised eyebrows. She said, 'Did you?'

'Yes,' replied Kit, which left Dick feeling frustrated at not knowing to what they were referring. Just as he was about to ask, Agatha spoke again.

'Do you realise what this means?' said Agatha.

'No,' interjected Alastair cheerfully before shrugging unconcernedly as his sister glared up at him. She answered her own question.

'Someone has the other gun and, one must suppose, the missing bullet, too,' said Agatha.

'Oh my,' said Bobbie as the implications became clear to her. 'You don't think...?'

Kit nodded to her and then said to the rest of the group, 'I think Amory intended that history repeat itself. This whole charade wasn't just a murder mystery. He's been playing with us all along. What was it he said at the beginning of the story? The quote from Shakespeare?'

'All the world's a stage, and all the men and women merely players; they have their exits and their entrances,' whispered Mary.

28

Freddy was feeling distinctly uncomfortable about the line of questioning being taken by Captain O'Riordan. The initial questions, around how he'd first met Amory, were innocuous enough. However, with each new question the tone grew more aggressive. Freddy sensed that O'Riordan was railroading him towards confessing that he had poisoned his master. And he knew something that the policemen did not know. Yet.

Just before Christmas, Amory had taken him aside and informed him that he had included him in his will. He did not specify the amount but, by the smile on Amory's face, Freddy guessed that it would be not inconsiderable. All of this had been said in front of Nat Thomas, Amory's lawyer. Once the police connected with Thomas, they would hear all about how Freddy could gain in the event of Amory's death.

As equations went, inheriting money from his dead master, plus colour, equalled motive in any policeman's book. Yes, Freddy was now feeling distinctly nervous and the men in front of him could see it on his face, they could hear it in his voice, they could probably smell it too, if you asked them.

Freddy took them through the events of the evening. The policemen were particularly interested in when he had served drinks to the guests. Had Amory taken anything from the others?

'No,' replied Freddy firmly. 'I gave him exactly what I gave the others.'

'Were you serving liquor?' asked O'Riordan.

Freddy looked wildly to Flynn and then back to O'Riordan.

Flynn took over at this point. It was only fair.

'Captain, liquor was served this evening in my presence,' admitted Flynn. 'I took some wine myself and it was rather good. A Merlot from Mr Beaufort's cellar, if I remember correctly. This was entirely above board as you know, Captain.' Flynn was not so sure it was but, if you say something confidently enough, it becomes the standard by which all truth is judged. Flynn fixed his eyes on Freddy. 'We'll need to test the bottles and glasses for poison.'

O'Riordan seemed distinctly unimpressed by Flynn's interruption. He had been making progress in scaring the wits out of someone he considered one of his main suspects. The idea that "the butler did it" may or may not be a staple of literature of deep artistic merit, but there was no reason that real life could not imitate art, in O'Riordan's view. With a sour glance towards Flynn, he began the interrogation once more.

'Did you make the dinner?' said O'Riordan, once more trying to put Freddy under pressure.

'No sir, it came from the restaurant. From the dumb waiter,' replied Freddy, trying to stay in control.

'Did you serve it?'

'Yes sir.'

'Did everyone have the same food?'

'Yes sir.'

'No one helped you serve it?'

'No sir.'

'Did you serve the drinks?'

'Yes sir,' replied Freddy.

'Did you see anyone else serve drinks?'

'No sir.'

'Did you poison Amory Beaufort?'

'No sir,' cried Freddy.

O'Riordan leaned forward and snarled, menacingly, 'We're going to dig out those glasses and bottles because, trust me, if there's poison in them, we'll find it and you'll have a lot of explaining to do.'

Now Freddy was close to panic. There was nothing in the eyes of the man in front of him that suggested anything other than a desire to pin the death of Amory on him. He needed a lawyer. How would he even find one never mind pay him?

Flynn could see fear in the eyes of the manservant. He did not automatically assume guilt, but there was something going on that the servant was not telling them. He was sure of this. O'Riordan was pushing him a little harder than he would have at this stage. When they should have been building up a picture of the events of the evening from the different perspectives of the witnesses, O'Riordan seemed already to be sprinting down the home straight and landing a confession.

'Do I need a lawyer, sir?' asked Freddy, as O'Riordan loomed over him ominously.

'Why would you need a lawyer? Got something to hide?' asked the Captain. In fact, Freddy knew he was hiding something that was material.

'Do you have a lawyer?' asked Flynn, suspecting that the answer was no. The look that Freddy gave him almost made him laugh out loud. That look said "are you kidding me?"

'No sir, I don't.'

'Then where, may I ask,' said O' Riordan, pretending to check his coat pockets, '...do you think I'm going to find one at this time of night?'

'Mr West is a lawyer,' pointed out Freddy.

Downstairs the group were absorbed in the articles written by Amory. Kit had to acknowledge that, as much as he had not fancied Amory the person, or the short story, the newspaper articles were uniformly excellent. They showed a side to the man that he had not seen in his short acquaintance in real life.

The articles were thoughtful and philosophical yet, also, at times, passionately eloquent on the wrongs done to the Native Americans by successive administrations. Kit recognised the anger he felt as he read them because he'd felt the same way about how his own country treated countries across the Empire. It was a mixed record, he conceded, and he accepted he was in no position to judge the Americans. What he'd read, painted a picture of someone who clearly had suicidal tendencies. Kit was fairly certain now of some things about the events of this evening and of what had happened at Princeton four years previously.

They did not see Nolan appear on the second-floor balcony. He stood there gazing down at the group poring over the short story, clearly in intense discussion about what it was saying. He was about to smile dismissively, when he thought about the acute observations from the Englishman and his aunt.

Perhaps he was being unfair.

It was interesting to see that Dick West had joined the group in discussing the case, while Chester Lydgate stayed with Ethel Barnes. Laura Lyons sat on the edge of the group but appeared to be taking no interest in the activity.

'Mr West,' said Nolan, 'may we have you for a few moments.'

Dick looked up and saw Nolan staring down at him.

'My turn for the third degree,' said Dick, half amused.

Nolan ignored the jibe. He said, 'Your services actually. You're a lawyer aren't you?'

'Yes,' replied Dick, a little surprised. 'I won't be representing myself.'

'Will you represent Mr Hughes? I think he feels he needs one.'

Nolan noted how all of the guests looked up sharply at this news. In particular, he saw a look on Kit Aston's face, that could only be described as horrified contempt. This reinforced the feeling that he'd had, listening to Captain O'Riordan trying to pin the death on Freddy that this was entirely the wrong direction.

'You seem surprised,' said Nolan, eyeing Kit.

Kit studied him for a moment. It was strange sensation having to look up at someone and communicate.

'I am. I think if this implies what I think it does, then we need to have a chat. You're missing something important.'

'Like?' asked Nolan. It sounded a little more sceptical than he'd intended. Old habits die hard, and he was an Englishman.

'Where is the second gun?' asked Kit. 'The one that might have the missing bullet?'

Nolan's eyes widened at hearing this. He nodded and turned towards the room where Schwartz and Johnson were finishing their work.

'Hey, Johnson. Any sign of another gun or a bullet in here? We didn't want to do a search until you'd been here.'

'No other gun and no sign of a bullet,' confirmed Johnson.

'Thanks,' replied Nolan ducking back out of the room. He took a step forward and looked over the railing back to the group. Dick West was already on his way up.

'Did they find anything?' asked Kit.

He wondered how they knew there was no other gun. Had they removed it? Unlikely, he thought. Perhaps they'd searched earlier. Either way, the fact remained, there was no second gun and there was a missing bullet. Nolan remembered how the story had talked about there being a pair of pistols.

'Did Mr Beaufort have two pistols?'

'Yes,' said Dick, arriving at the top of the stairs. 'He did and one is missing.'

'How did you know?' snapped Nolan. There was something about the lawyer he didn't like. They were of a similar age, a similar height. Both had been over to France. Yet, there was an air of privilege about him. Or perhaps it was arrogance. Or he was drunk.

'We searched the room and everywhere downstairs,' explained Dick, smiling like a recalcitrant child at an angry parent, uncowed by the prospect of chastisement. In the background they could hear shouting from the makeshift interview room. Nolan had no doubt who the owner of the raised voice was. He'd seen the captain many times in action and nuance was not one of the attributes that sprung to mind, when seeing him handle suspects.

Dick followed Nolan down the corridor and into the room. The sight that greeted them was shocking. O'Riordan was standing over Freddy. The manservant's head was in his hands, and he was sobbing. His body was shaking with the violence of his emotions. Flynn's face was set in stone. Dick met the eyes of the Inspector but could not read what was behind them.

'Looks like you're too late, pal,' announced O'Riordan with something close to a cackle. 'The houseboy has just confessed.'

The two men looked at Freddy who was rocking back and forth repeating over and over again, 'I killed him. I killed him.'

29 11:40pm

Dick West glared at the police captain. O'Riordan returned the compliment. He was in no mood to barter with a lawyer, after having his New Year's Eve interrupted. Dick turned to Flynn who he considered a much more sympathetic character. There was a strange look on the face of the inspector that West could not read.

'You can't be serious about this Flynn,' said Dick, ignoring O'Riordan. He pointed at the captain, 'I can well believe this idiot would believe anything, but not you.'

In fact, Flynn was perfectly certain that Freddy had no more killed Amory than he had, but he was keen to see how O'Riordan would handle the situation as it unravelled. And unravel it surely would.

Flynn said nothing, but Dick caught the half-smile. He set to work on Freddy. Kneeling down, he spoke into the ear of the sobbing manservant.

'Listen Freddy, answer me one question.' Dick saw O'Riordan rise, but he held his hand up and snarled at the captain, 'I'm his lawyer. Freddy, listen to me, did you knowingly add poison to anything that Amory ate or drank.'

'I gave it to him. I must have,' sobbed Freddy.

'I told you,' shouted O'Riordan, rising once more.

'Sit down,' ordered Flynn. He looked in no mood to be trifled with, so O'Riordan complied, reluctantly.

'Freddy, I'll ask you again. Did you know there was poison in what you gave Amory?'

Freddy looked up. His eyes were bloodshot and his face wet with the tears, of fear, anger, and frustration. He shook his head.

'How could I know? I didn't do it deliberately. You have to believe me, sir. He told me if he ever died that I would get some money, but I would never kill him, sir. I'd never do anything like that.'

A grin of triumph spread over O'Riordan's face. He said, 'You hear that. He knows he stands to inherit money. We have means, we have opportunity and I'm darned, lawyer-boy, if he didn't just provide the motive.' O'Riordan cackled at this. It wasn't a pleasant sound and Flynn recoiled from it physically.

'I'm taking him in sir,' said O'Riordan, with as much insolence as he could muster. 'In fact, sir, I'm taking you all in. We're gonna sort this out once and for all tonight.' He was going to say more, but there was a knocking on the door that interrupted his flow. 'Who is it?' he shouted angrily.

Outside the room, Nolan saw a group climbing the stairs to the landing. The young detective could see the urgency in Kit's eyes. Just behind Kit, Agatha, Bobbie and Mary had arrived on the landing.

'Freddy has confessed,' said Nolan, but there was doubt etched into every syllable. 'I imagine, West will rectify that. What's going on?'

'Detective,' said Kit. Something in his manner, in fact his whole demeanour, over the short period that Nolan had known him, gave the detective pause to wonder what was coming next. 'We think that we have all been part of a diabolical game tonight. We don't think that Amory's death was part of it, at least not in this way. It's my belief, that Amory intended to re-enact the events of four years ago.'

Nolan frowned at this. In a voice that could not hide his scepticism, he said, 'What do you mean?'

Kit took a deep breath and shut his eyes. He was trying to imagine the scene as it was playing in his head. Downstairs, Chester and the two ladies rose to their feet and stood underneath the landing to hear what Kit was about to say. Alastair, meanwhile, sat back in the armchair and contented himself with his cheroot and a glass of red.

'We'll never know for certain, but I believe that four years ago, Amory and Colette Andrews formed a suicide pact. I think they were both under the influence of drugs when they did so. Dick and Chester have alluded as much. I believe the plan was that they would do this at midnight on New Year's Eve 1917. Everything that Amory has written, points to this. I've looked at some of his other writing. He keeps it in the drawer downstairs. He has a fixation with death, with suicide, with the spirit world. Look at the painting on the wall. It is the Ghost Dance, practiced by the Sioux. It was meant to reunite the living with spirits of the dead. They didn't view death as the end, but merely the continuation of existence in another form. Amory intended to kill himself tonight, as he should have done in 1917.'

The expression on Nolan's face remained doubtful, but he was learning that the Englishman was no fool. What he said was fantastic, yet it felt plausible also.

'But Amory was murdered tonight surely? Or did he kill himself?'

'He was murdered,' asserted Kit. 'The manner of death does not match what happened four years ago and the ritual is just as important. I'm certain of it.'

'How does that change things here?' pointed out Nolan. 'Freddy has confessed, although he'll change his mind, I'm sure.'

'I'm not interested in Freddy,' said Kit, shaking his head. 'We have a problem. This whole evening was designed towards Amory fulfilling his destiny. He was going to kill himself, but I think in order to do so in the manner that he wanted, he needed someone else to help him. I think somewhere tonight, and I suspect it has to be in this building, someone is waiting to join Amory in a suicide pact.'

'That's ridiculous,' said Nolan. Yet a part of him knew otherwise. The intensity of the Englishman's eyes and the reaction of the others suggested that there was more to this. He glanced down and saw the members of the band staring up at him. He looked at Tommy.

'You said that you thought Colette Andrews was high that night,' said Nolan.

Tommy shrugged, 'I said she must have been to be wearing what she wasn't wearing if you take my meaning sir. I wasn't looking at her eyes. None of us were.'

'That's my point,' said Kit. 'Under the influence of drugs and, with someone like Amory, who knows what he could fill a young woman's head with. We need to find out if Amory had another apartment in the building. We don't have long. It's almost midnight. If there is someone else...'

'But if Amory's not there, maybe they won't do anything,' pointed out Nolan.

'We can't be certain,' answered Kit.

Nolan turned immediately and ran to the door where the interrogation of Freddy was taking place. He began to bang on the door.

O'Riordan ripped open the door to find Nolan standing there. He'd worked with the young detective for six months now and it was safe to say he didn't like him. He was pretty sure that the feeling was mutual. The opportunity had not yet presented itself where he could insert a spanner to halt the upward trajectory of Nolan, but when it did, he would be ready. For the moment he was content to bide his time and give him the most difficult cases. Unfortunately, Nolan's success rate was such with cases, that were recognised to be difficult, that it had the paradoxical effect of enhancing his reputation with senior officers.

'What do you want?' snarled O'Riordan.

'You should hear this,' said Nolan, indicating Kit standing behind him.

'Hear what? I don't care what some Limey says. This isn't some lousy dime novel. We're taking everyone down to the precinct.'

'Sir,' interrupted Nolan, who then made the mistake of glancing over at Flynn before retuning his attention to the captain.

'I'm in charge here son and I don't care what the Limey thinks. He is a witness and will be treated as such. He is not assisting us in this case. Out of my way, son.' O'Riordan turned to Mulcahy and said, 'Bring the houseboy.'

O'Riordan stomped out of the room and shouted down to Johnson, who was on the phone, 'Is the wagon here yet?'

'On its way, sir,' said Mulcahy covering the phone, but the ambulance is here. They're coming up now so we can take away the body.'

'Well tell them to send another wagon - we're taking everyone in,' shouted the captain. Then he turned to Kit, Mary, Bobbie and Agatha. 'All you need to go downstairs. We're going to have to take you in until we clear this mess up.'

Flynn followed O'Riordan out of the room. He was not pleased with how things were moving but, as a policeman, he could not disagree with the actions that the captain was taking. By taking everyone down to the precinct he was keeping his options open, on whether or not Freddy was the culprit. It suggested that he was more open-minded than he'd let on in the interrogation. In Flynn's view, this was a point in O'Riordan's favour.

'Do as he says,' said Flynn to Nolan, but indicated with his eyes that they should talk in the room when O'Riordan went downstairs. Freddy was led away by Mulcahy and O'Riordan followed. Flynn grabbed Nolan's arm and they went back inside the room. 'Quickly, what's this about.'

Kit followed them, uninvited, into the room, while the others followed the policemen down the stairs.

'Sir, listen to what he has to say,' said Nolan, indicating Kit.

Kit quickly summarised what he thought was happening elsewhere in the building. He finished by saying, 'We need either to get on the phone and find out if Amory has access to another apartment or if there is a key in his room. Either we speak to Freddy, or the reception or we search his room. There's no time, Inspector Flynn. If this is happening, then it will happen at midnight.'

Flynn nodded and recognised resolve in Kit's eyes. It was extraordinary and completely unbelievable, yet something about the Englishman was convincing. He nodded and said, 'Let me deal with O'Riordan. You two search Amory's room. Do it quickly.'

They left the room with Flynn heading in the direction of the stairs while Kit and Nolan ducked into Amory's room. The doctor and Johnson from Forensics had left now. They were alone. Kit indicated to Nolan with his eyes to take the drawers while he went directly to the wardrobe. He tore open the doors and began to search the pockets of the jackets hanging up. Nolan ransacked the drawers. After a minute or two they turned to one another.

Nothing.

Kit ducked down to the bedside cabinet. He opened the top drawer. Inside was a small wooden box. He took it out and opened it. Inside was a long copper Mortice key. He lifted it out and held it up.

'This looks like the key for the door of the apartments in this building.'

There was nothing to indicate if this was for Amory's apartment or for another in the building. Just then, they heard a commotion downstairs and Dr Schwartz directing people upstairs.

'They've come to take the body. Quick,' said Kit, but Nolan was already heading for the door.

They met the ambulance personnel on the landing carrying a stretcher. Kit glanced over the balcony down at Mary, Agatha and Bobbie who were standing with Dick West and Chester. Kit surreptitiously showed them the key they had found.

Two questions remained. Which apartment lock did the key fit? And how were they to find out? Kit looked up at the clock on the wall. It was now 11: 45pm.

They had fifteen minutes.

30 11:49pm

Amory's guests watched in solemn silence as his body was carried out by the ambulancemen. Kit resisted the urge to shout at them to get a move on. They were doing a difficult, thankless even, job on a night when they might otherwise have been with friends celebrating. Still, they moved with a ponderous dignity that had everyone on edge.

The time was now 11:49pm.

Eleven minutes.

Finally, the ambulance men were out the door, followed by O'Riordan, who felt the need to give instructions to them, despite the fact they had done this dozens of times. Schwartz followed them out, as did the Forensics man, Johnson. Freddy, too, was led out by the policemen, in handcuffs. He seemed like a broken man. He shuffled forward in a state of utter disbelief at how the night had unfolded for him. Flynn was now the only policeman in the apartment. They stood and watched the policemen exit followed by the click of the door of the apartment being locked.

Kit immediately went over to the phone and dialled a number.

'Hello,' he said. 'Is that reception? Good listen to me we urgently need to know if Amory Beaufort was renting another apartment or had an arrangement with another owner to have someone stay there. Thanks, I'll wait. I need to know now. Don't worry about the policemen. This is urgent.'

Kit gripped the phone tightly and stared back at the guests, who were all staring at him. Dick West put his hand into his breast pocket and extracted his hip flask. He took a swig and held it up for Kit in case he wanted a drink. Kit shook his head and returned his attention to the phone.

'Hello, yes, I'm still interested. I see. That's a shame,' Kit looked up at the others with a grim face and shook his head. Then another question occurred to him. 'Tell me, do you know of any residents who have not been in their apartment since before Christmas aside from Charles Dana Gibson and the Robsons? Yes, I'll wait.'

Kit felt like banging the wall in frustration. His eyes scanned the room, and then alighted on something. A voice came back on the line.

'Apartment 917. Thank you. Could you do me a favour and ring that apartment. Tell them to come up to apartment 1020. Tell them it's urgent, then can you call me back if you speak to anyone. Please can you do this immediately. It's very important. Thank you.'

Kit put the phone down.

The clock now read 11:51pm

Nine minutes.

The phone rang again a minute later. Kit nearly ripped the phone off its socket as he answered. His face was set to stone.

'No answer. Thank you. Look, is there any chance that you can go up to the apartment and open the door? This is an emergency. Well, may I ask why? I see, but this is a matter of life and death. Very well. Can you keep ringing? Thanks.' He put the phone back on its hook and looked to the others.

'Inspector Flynn,' he asked, 'can you check to see if this key works in the lock.'

Flynn caught the key that Kit threw over to him with a one-handed insouciance, that might have earned a compliment at any other time. He strode over to the door and put the key in the lock. He turned it.

The door opened.

Kit uttered an un-Kit-like oath that earned a silent look of reproach from Agatha.

'We have to go to reception,' said Agatha.

'If they're not going to let us out then perhaps we can use the dumb waiter,' said Mary. 'I've been looking at it for the last few minutes. I think I can just about fit into it. Bobbie, Ethel and Laura are too tall.' She relented from saying that Agatha was even smaller than her, but that made no allowance for the stoutness of age.

'Do you think it will support your weight,' agreed Kit. Then he looked at how slender his wife was before adding, 'Silly question. Ignore me.'

Mary sprinted over to the hatch, removed her shoes and, with the help of Dick West who removed one of the shelves, climbed in.

'Do you know how to work this contraption?' asked Kit. Dick nodded.

'Mary, this will take you to the kitchen on the second floor,' said Agatha. 'You'll need to get down to reception and take keys for apartment 11. It's on the first floor.'

'That's no good,' said Kit. 'The reception area will be full of policemen. Go to Ella-Mae. She can get the key. I'll tell the receptionist.'

Dick pressed the button and Mary slowly disappeared from view. Kit's heart was racing. Fear at the thought of what might be happening in 917 was mixed with anxiety for Mary in the tight space of the dumb waiter. Like most men, he hated not being in control of matters.

It was up to Mary and Ella-Mae now.

As the dumb waiter slowly made its way down the chute, Mary had plenty of time to wonder if she had made the right decision. The lift moved at a paralyzingly slow pace downwards. Mary was in a tight compartment which was in complete darkness. This was one of her worst nightmares. She felt the panic slowly rise within her.

How many floors did she have to travel? She shut her eyes and tried to ignore the feeling of discomfort. She was crouched over with her chin almost resting on her knees. Even when she reached her destination, she wondered if her legs would be so full of cramp that she may not be able to move.

After what seemed like an eternity, she heard the sound of loud voices. She was nearing the kitchen. Slowly light began to fill the compartment, until she arrived at the kitchen. The kitchenhands looked on in shock, and then in amusement, as the beautiful young woman emerged from the dumb waiter and smiled at them, as she rushed past through the double doors that led to the restaurant.

The noise that hit her when she burst through the doors was almost deafening. The restaurant was crowded and the aisles between the tables were like an obstacle course of men and women who, frustratingly, would not get out of the way.

Twice she had to push away the attentions of drunken men who spied her making her way between the tables. The cries of 'Happy New Year,' fell on deaf ears as Mary rushed past them.

It was 11:54pm now.

Six minutes to reach Ella-Mae. Five to get to reception and then back up to room 917.

Out into the corridor outside the restaurant, the elevator doors opened, and more party goers emerged. Mary rushed into the elevator and pushed the button for the eighth floor. The doors closed agonisingly slowly and then with a jerk the elevator set off.

At the eight floor, Mary rushed out and directly over to the apartment being used by Agatha and Alastair. She banged on the door. Ella-Mae opened almost instantly.

'Ella-Mae,' exclaimed Mary. 'Come with me.'

'What's wrong my dear,' cried Ella-Mae. Her eyes widened as she saw the alarmed look on Mary's face. Mary took Ella-Mae's hand, and they ran to the elevator. But it was gone. It had returned to the ground floor. No doubt there would be people climbing into it now and taking it to several floors. They hadn't time to wait.

'We'll have to take the stairs,' groaned Mary, cursing silently inside.

As they descended the stairs, Mary updated Ella-Mae all about the evening. Alastair's housekeeper stayed silent, to allow Mary to explain in her own way. On the fourth floor the elevator opened, and some people emerged. It was now empty. Mary sprinted towards it before the doors closed again and kept them open for Ella-Mae.

Moments later, they reached the ground floor. The lift doors opened to reveal a lobby full of policemen. She looked directly at Captain O'Riordan. Thankfully, his eyes were not focused on her. He was overseeing the arrival of the policemen, who would take the dinner party guests up to the precinct.

The two women darted out of the lift. Ella-Mae went straight to reception while Mary, head down, made for the stairs. She risked a peek around the corner at Ella-Mae and found herself looking up at Detective Nolan.

'How did you get out of the apartment?' he demanded. He seemed surprised more than angry.

'There's no time. We need the lift,' said Mary.

'Lift?' replied Nolan, utterly mystified.

Mary stared at him and then pointed to the elevator.

'Lift?' repeated Nolan, a little less mystified.

Ella-Mae appeared from nowhere, causing Nolan to jump out of his skin.

'She does that,' said Mary. 'We need the lift.'

Nolan was already moving guests away from the lift using his badge to indicate that it was for official business. The lift doors opened, and he motioned for the two ladies to get in. He joined them. As the doors of the elevator closed Mary caught the eyes of O'Riordan. Anger flared in his eyes. He pointed at the elevator and shouted, 'Stop them!'

The long hand on the clock on the wall at the far end of the lobby moved to 11:59pm.

Almost midnight.

31 11:57pm

'So what happens now?' demanded Chester, turning to Inspector Flynn. He adjusted one of his braces, which had Flynn fearing for a moment he would undress further. The sight of him in his sweat-stained shirt was quite enough for the time being.

The question from Chester was not an unreasonable one, given the circumstances. Flynn was caught in the middle of this situation. As much as he realised he disliked O'Riordan, his handling, so far, would not have differed markedly from his own. Aside from, rather hastily, assuming Freddy's guilt that is. However, there had been enough on the manservant to arrest him, even if Flynn's senses were telling him that he was the wrong man. Flynn knew that even his own intuition was not infallible. He had trained himself to be neutral in the face of everything except evidence.

Flynn held his hands up and proceeded to defend his captain, explaining, exactly, why they were being held and would all have to spend a few more hours explaining. in forensic detail, their memories of the evening, as well as more about themselves, their movements over the last few days, their relationship with Amory and a whole lot else besides. All of this would be checked, and counter checked. Anyone caught lying would be placing themselves in a difficult position.

Everyone's eyes turned to the clock. It was almost midnight, and they were wondering if Mary had reached Ella-Mae. If Ella-Mae had been able to get the keys or if she or Mary had been intercepted by the arriving policemen.

Flynn concluded by saying, 'Until then, we wait. Me included. In case you hadn't noticed, I am technically a suspect to. Is there any wine left?'

Alastair had taken charge of the bottle. He held it up to the light and replied, 'A couple of mouthfuls. Are you sure you can trust me?'

Flynn growled at him, 'No.' Then he took a glass off the table and held it out for Alastair to do the honours.

'It's rather hot in here now,' said Dick, taking off his jacket. 'Do you mind if I open the window?' He draped the jacket over the armchair he'd been sitting in on and off for much of the evening.

Kit was startled by the request. He had been staring at the Remington print, depicting the Ghost Dance, over the last minute or two. The painting depicted a line of Sioux with their back to the viewer in the background. In the foreground a man wrapped up in buckskin stood facing the viewer while a lone Sioux danced beside him. Two other figures were approaching. It was a fascinating piece by an artist Kit, who had an avid interest in the history of the old west, was familiar with and admired. Kit glanced towards Dick and said, 'No, please let me.'

As he was nearest the window, he walked over and opened it. To Flynn's surprise, he sat by the open window almost like he was standing guard. Flynn wondered why. He studied the tall Englishman with interest. He looked as if he had walked off the pages of a romantic novel, the sort Nancy used to read.

She claimed, with a smile in her voice, it was the only romance she had in life. Flynn felt a tightening in his chest as he recalled the laugh that would usually accompany such remarks. He would laugh louder than her. It was probably true. How he missed her.

Bobbie had, also, noticed how Kit had reacted to Dick's remark, about the window, with a certain alacrity. She, like her father, wondered why this was. Then it occurred to her why. If Amory had been murdered it meant either Freddy was the killer or, if not, one or the party was. And, unlike her father who resisted such temptations, Bobbie had already discounted the English guests. There was no obvious motive although she conceded everyone had the means and opportunity.

The band had hitherto not been included in her consideration. The fact that two of them had been at Princeton, on the night of Colette Andrews' death, did not alter that completely, but it was something that could not be disregarded entirely, either.

Someone in the room was a killer.

The band were now sitting among the guests. Kit took the opportunity to ask Tommy what he remembered about the New Year's Eve in Princeton.

'Well Lanky and I,' he said indicating rather unnecessarily, the big Double Bass player, 'were just talking about that. You don't forget a club like the Iroquois Club in a hurry. We'd never played anywhere like that before, even when we were playing for rich white boys.' Tommy stopped for a moment and then he grinned ruefully, 'Sorry.'

Everyone was smiling however, and, Tommy realised, no offence had been taken.

'I remember the incident as clear as day, but it happened really quickly. One minute we were playing and the next this beautiful girl wearing next to nothing comes in and, man, we all stopped playing, which I think made it even worse. There seemed to be one almighty argument over her and then she was taken out of the club, and we began playing again. Like I said, it all happened very quickly. Afterwards, the next day, we all heard what she'd done. Yes sir, it was a real shame you know. Such a beautiful girl.'

When Tommy had finished, Kit glanced towards the wall and at the clock. In fact, everyone was now staring at the clock, ticking towards midnight.

'I hope she makes it,' said Flynn.

'She will,' chorused Kit and Agatha together.

32 11:59

An apartment in New York: 31st December 1921

Finally.

The sound of laughter in the corridor and then the key turning in the lock. He was back. At long last. Where had he been? If liquor had a sound, then it was there in the cackling on the other side of the door. She stood up and faced the door, from the other end of the corridor. She folded her arms, in a manner that any man, with his senses still intact, would recognise.

It spelt danger.

However, the two men who spilled into the apartment were a couple of bottles past such sensibility. The first man looked up and said, 'Uh oh,' before bursting into a fit of giggles. The sight of the young woman, with fire burning in her eyes, was just too funny to go unremarked. 'You're in trouble Hal.'

The man named Hal took a few seconds to focus his eyes on the silhouetted figure at the end of the hall. Even in the dim light he could sense the fire burning within. Hal was completely confident in his own ability to cool the flames of anger and turn them, instead into the heat of celebration.

And Hal was in a mood to celebrate. Hell, he'd spent the last two hours celebrating with Ron. It was time to share his joy.

'Honey, I can see you're angry. Don't be. We made a killing tonight,' announced Hal.

The news, that Hal and Ron had made money, was greeted with a single raised eyebrow. Once again, a more sober man would have read this as a sign that, not only had the danger not passed, risk levels were actually rising.

Slowly, menacingly, she emphasised every syllable, asking, 'How did you do that, Hal?'

This was a reasonable question. He knew he was not out of the woods yet but, at least, she was open to talking. Perhaps an argument, over his rather submerged state, could be avoided and they could get down to the serious business of the evening. To ease her gently away from the icy path of righteous indignation towards the warmer climes of festivity and friendliness, Hal hit upon a moment of inspiration. A reporter friend of his had once said the secret to good writing was to show, not tell.

Hal decided to adopt this course. With a grin wider that Brooklyn Bridge and eyes that were still having trouble focusing, he took his hands out of his raincoat pockets, to reveal a bottle of gin, half drunk, and a wad of dollar bills.

'Whaddiya think of that honey?' asked Hal, in a voice overflowing with pride and optimism.

The young woman stared at the money and then fixed her eyes on the man she had thrown in with.

'How did you earn that Hal? That's more than you earn in a month.'

'Whassup Hal?' asked Ron, vaguely aware that the young woman seemed a little out of step with the mood of conviviality that he and his friend were exuding. He stepped forward a little menacingly towards the girl.

'Leave this to me,' slurred Hal. He turned to the young woman, 'Ron, my friend here, introduced me to a business proposition, my dear.'

Now that Ron was closer, the young woman noticed for the first time that he was dressed in a policeman's uniform. He was like no policeman she'd ever seen. To begin with, he was unshaven. On top of this, he was plainly drunk. There were stains on the uniform that didn't bear thinking about and his cadaverous appearance suggested his only connection with the law was when he was breaking it.

'Go on,' she said. Despite herself, despite the anger, she was curious.

Hal's eyes were beginning to focus a little better. For the first time, despite the lack of light in the apartment, he could see two things that alarmed him. Firstly, she was wearing an overcoat. In the hallway, a few feet from where he was standing, was her suitcase.

'Well, it's like this,' said Hal. 'Ron, my friend here, had this idea for making a little dough. Nothing violent or anything. Just making a little dough, from people who can well afford to spread a little good cheer on New Year's Eve.'

'What did you do?'

Hal explained their little scam, in between chuckles at the credulity of some people. Ron had stopped laughing though. It was plain to him that the story was not meeting a receptive audience. He didn't like this new woman of Hal's. He didn't like her one bit. Here they were, trying to make an honest buck, trying to get ahead on an awful night and this broad was proving a royal pain. He elbowed Hal in the ribs. His friend was startled by this.

'Hey Ron, what's that for?'

Ron nodded towards the young woman. His face curled up into a malevolent sneer.

'Seems this doll don't much like me, Hal. Seems she don't think much of what we've done.'

'Don't be silly, Ron, tell him honey,' said Hal.

The young woman's mood changed dramatically, and it was even further away from the forced friendliness of the man she'd thrown in with. Ron was right: she didn't like him. But she was afraid now. Hal was a friendly idiot. Good-looking, after a fashion, always friendly, optimistic. She'd liked his breezy manner and he'd always seemed flush with cash. Now she realised that there was a reason for this.

He was a crook.

His friends were crooks.

Worse, his friends were dangerous. Hal was not a man anyone would fear. He wanted to be loved, and people usually took to him. There was innocence about him that made him attractive. She had not seen this side of him before. Her chest tightened a little as she realised the two men were staring at her, waiting for a response. The anger had gone now, replaced by fear. She had to go.

Now.

A bell tolled somewhere. It was midnight.

33 Midnight

The sound of the chimes of midnight reverberated, like a child's cry in the night.

Kit's eyes, and all of the others, darted up towards the large clock on the wall. The two hands were now one. Both were pointing upwards. Towards Heaven, though Kit grimly. He realised he was holding his breath, before noting that he was not the only one. There wasn't a sound in the apartment. It was a vacuum while the world outside was spinning ever fast on an axis, to avoid falling over.

He scanned the eyes of Agatha, Alastair and then the Americans. They were all glued to the clock as the chimes rang out.

Two.

Three.

Four.

No one felt in the mood to wish the others Happy New Year, No one felt the need to link hands and sing *Auld Lang's Syne.* The silence in the apartment contrasted with the noise outside. Was it Kit's imagination that the sirens wailed louder. There were fireworks screaming in amusement at the helplessness of those inside. The air was full of electricity.

Somewhere, they could hear the people singing.

Should auld acquaintance be forgot,
And never brought to mind?
Should auld acquaintance be forgot,
And auld lang syne?

Should old acquaintance be forgot, thought Kit. Not Colette Andrews. She would always be remembered now. A beautiful young woman, fragile, innocent and sophisticated beyond her years. A life that had left her exposed and in thrall to malign influences, that sent her on the road to self-destruction. No one at this party would ever forget her.

The chimes continued.

Five.

Six.

'I'm leaving, Hal,' she said firmly. Her heart was racing and for reasons she could not explain, she was looking at Ron and not Hal. His eyes glinted with malice. She had to escape from *him*. The darkness of the apartment was like a physical presence. It was oppressive, a demon sucking life, love and hope out of every living thing. She had to escape.

Hal's eyes were full of pain and disbelief. He wanted to make it up to her. He knew that he'd overstepped the mark. She had to understand that. Anyway, all this was for her. She was smoking hot and dolls like this were high maintenance. This was his pitch, and it was falling short.

'No, honey, don't say that,' said Hal, trying, and failing, to sound jolly. Even to his own ears, he sounded a little frantic. 'Have a drink. Happy New Year, y'know. Let's celebrate.'

At hearing the desperation of his friend, Ron turned sharply to Hal. His face furious with disgust and contempt. No one should have to take this from a broad. No one that he would ever hang out with.

'What are you saying, Hal?' snapped Ron angrily. He glared at his friend. His lips had curled into the snarl of a wild animal.

She tore her eyes away from Ron and picked up her bag. His gaze had held her as if in a trance. Now was her moment. She had to escape the dark quicksand that was slowly pulling her under.

The chimes of The Holy Cross church rang through the noise of screaming fireworks, singing and shouting. She heard laughter somewhere and a child crying. She felt like crying too. What a fool she'd been.

Seven.

Eight.

She set her eyes on the door and marched towards it holding her breath. Her coat touched that of the fake policeman. Hal stared at her, but she would not return his gaze.

Nine.

The elevator doors opened. Mary, Nolan and Ella-Mae almost spilled out into the corridor. Mary looked up and down the corridor before spying the number she needed. She sprinted towards the door, arriving just ahead of Nolan. She shoved the key into the lock and twisted it to the right. As she did this, she heard the clock chime, but had long since lost track of the time. The sound chilled her as she realised it was midnight.

Heart thumping, she heard the lock click as the key turned. The door swung open into a short corridor that was in darkness. Mary sprinted forward followed by Ella-Mae before sliding to a halt as she reached the living area. The apartment's layout was just like the one they had left, but no lights were on. It was a large, high-ceilinged room with a second-floor interior balcony.

Mary's eyes took a split second to adjust to the darkness then she saw by the window a young woman, half in shadow. Dark streaks descended from her eyes but on her cheeks were white marks. She wore a headband. Attached to the back of it were some feathers. Then, Mary's eyes were drawn to the glinting object she held in her right hand. She was pointing a gun to her temple.

Mary and Nolan screamed in unison, 'No!'

But the young woman did not hear her, or did not want to. A clock in the apartment chimed.

The twelfth chime.

She pulled the trigger.

At one minute past twelve, Captain O'Riordan burst into Amory's apartment followed by half a dozen policemen.

'Where is she?' roared O'Riordan. His eyes found Flynn first and then fell upon Kit. 'Your wife. Where is she?'

'Doing your job, captain,' snapped Kit, angrily. He'd had more than enough of O'Riordan by now. The policeman's eyes flared in anger at Kit and, there and then, he made a promise to give the Englishman a hard time at the precinct, while he still had cause to list him as one of the suspects.

O'Riordan turned away from Kit, his eyes swinging around the apartment for some sign of Mary or his detective. Then he remembered that Flynn was nearby. He turned to the inspector, moderating his tone just a little.

'What's happening here? Did you know that dame had escaped?'

Flynn took a couple of steps towards O'Riordan. Despite being at least five inches shorter than the captain, he seemed at that moment to be towering over him. In a voice that was a menacing whisper, 'She went to investigate a possible suicide attempt. She did so with my permission. If you have a problem with this, then you know what you can do with it, Captain. And I can tell you, if these English people are right and something has happened downstairs, I will be kicking your rear end, from here to midtown, and then up and down Broadway. Do you understand?'

O'Riordan did understand. It occurred to him, at long last, that he had been pushing matters a little bit too far. Without a resolution to the case, and a fast resolution, he was staring into the eyes of someone who could make a lot of trouble for him.

'Where is Freddy?' snarled Flynn.

'In the wagon. There's a couple of them downstairs now,' replied the captain. His tone was noticeably less belligerent, but he was still not prepared to take any abuse from the English contingent. Just then he caught the eyes of Alistair, who was slumped across an armchair, calmly smoking a cheroot, with a smile on his face, like he was watching the Ziegfeld Follies perform. To add to O'Riordan's irritation, Alastair raised his glass which was clearly full of wine.

Agatha stepped forward. She ignored the sound of Alastair chuckling in anticipation. She said, 'Young man, we will be happy to accompany you to your police station, but you have been wilfully ignoring many things that we, and your commanding officer, have been saying to you. I suggest that you adopt a different tone and open your mind to the possibility that there is more going on here than you have, thus far, deemed it necessary to inquire about.'

'Like,' growled O'Riordan.

Agatha's eyes widened as she saw what was happening at the entrance to the apartment. Agatha's eyes flicked back to O'Riordan.

'Like that,' said Agatha, pointing behind the captain to the door.

34 12:05 am

Hotel des Artistes, New York: 1st January 1922

Everyone turned to the doorway. The uniformed policemen stood aside, to let the newcomers through. Mary and Ella-Mae flanked a young woman, who was wearing an overcoat draped over her shoulders. Her face still had the remains of white and black makeup, that looked as it had been scrubbed hastily from her cheeks. Behind them stood Nolan, holding a kitten.

'Maisie,' screamed Ethel. 'Maisie!'

She ran forward towards her sister whose eyes had barely moved, even when she'd heard her name called out. Ethel threw her arms around the young woman and began sobbing, 'What has he done to you?'

Kit sprang forward, also, and hugged Mary. There were, almost, tears in his eyes as he said, 'Well done, my love.' Bobbie Flynn went over to Mary and she, too, hugged her.

'You're a hero, Mary,' said Bobbie.

'Not just me, Ella-Mae, too,' said Mary, turning to Alastair's housekeeper. 'She's the one that reached her in time, before she tried the second shot.'

'What happened?' asked Kit, which neatly anticipated the question that O'Riordan had been trying to formulate, without filling it with profanity.

'Can someone tell me what the hell is going on here?' screamed O'Riordan, at last.

Nolan stepped forward, which was probably not a good idea, because the captain jabbed his breast with a finger, before saying, 'And you have a lot of explaining to do mister. Whose damn side are you on anyway.' O'Riordan's eyes flicked down to the cat and then back to his detective. 'And put that thing down.'

'Let me take it,' said Laura, coming over and picking the kitten out of Nolan's hands.

'What happened, son?' asked Flynn, stepping in between O'Riordan and Nolan.

Nolan indicated Mary with his eyes and said, 'I found Mrs Aston downstairs, with the other lady. The other lady took the key to the apartment from reception, and we took the elevator up to the ninth floor. When we reached the room, we found this young woman pointing this gun at her head.'

At this point Nolan took a revolver out of his pocket. It matched the gun that Amory had been clutching when they'd found his dead body.

'The gun was loaded with a bullet which, I am certain, came from the box we found in Mr Beaufort's room. We were too late to stop her firing, but the gun jammed. This lady, Ella-Mae, reached her before she could fire the second shot. I've never seen anyone move so fast.'

'You should see me whenever I catch sight of her,' interjected Alastair, earning a scowl from Agatha and Ella-Mae, but a grin from Kit and Mary.

Nolan continued, 'I checked the revolver. There's no firing pin. She couldn't have killed herself.'

'Who the hell is she?' demanded O'Riordan, who still had no earthly idea what had happened.

Flynn took over at this point, as the pieces of this particular jigsaw had now fallen into place, thanks to the English guests who he was now seeing in a wholly different light.

'This young woman is the sister of Ethel Barnes, the young lady you see over there. She was telling us earlier than her sister had walked out on her job and her house to be with a man. I think we can confidently say that the man she went to was Amory Beaufort who you've just taken away.'

'She looks like she's high on dope,' said O'Riordan.

'I expect she must have been to have attempted to kill herself,' agreed Flynn.

Dick West stepped forward and spoke up at this point.

'It's not dope, captain. It's something the Comanche used to take; a peyote and mescal cocktail. It has hallucinogenic properties. We knew Amory and Colette Andrews took this. Colette was probably on something similar when she died,' said Dick, beginning to choke with emotion, as he remembered the tragic events of four years previously.

'So? Why?' asked O'Riordan, still none the wiser as to what was happening.

Kit took over at this point.

'Amory Beaufort intended taking his own life tonight, at midnight. He had a fascination with death. If you read his articles for *The New York American,* that Miss Flynn writes for, you'll see this. He wanted to finish the job he'd started four years ago.'

Kit turned to Dick West and put a hand on his shoulder.

'I know you were in love with Colette and I'm sorry for what happened. Amory held a fascination for her, and he drove her to her death. Perhaps she was predisposed, I don't know. Whatever the truth, she and Amory had a suicide pact that night, four years ago. The plan was that they would each point a gun at one another's temple. and fire.'

Tears streamed down Dick's face as he turned to the gun that Nolan was hiding.

'There was no firing pin.'

'Correct,' Kit nodded. 'It was a murder-suicide pact that went disastrously wrong. The gun that Colette was holding jammed. Amory killed Colette, but he survived. I think he panicked at this point, realising what he'd done. The sound of the gun firing alerted Francis and soon he was banging on the door. Amory hid when Chester and Francis entered. As soon as they left to get help, he ran outside, onto the terrace and took the fire escape down to the ground floor. No one was around, because everyone had moved out to the corridor, to find out what had happened. Amory escaped around the side of the building and then entered, just in time to find Chester, who told him what he already knew: Colette was dead.'

'But why wait until now?' asked Bobbie, shaking her head. 'I didn't see any sign that Amory was depressed. He seemed his usual self, every time I saw him.'

Kit put his hands up and said, 'We will only know this if Amory has left a suicide note.'

'So if I understand you, we're looking for a suicide note, from a murder victim?' said Dick. There was a sardonic note to the comment. Clearly, there was precious little sympathy from this quarter.

'No,' replied Kit. 'We're looking for a murderer, also. And that person is among us now. I'm sorry, captain, but Freddy is not your man.'

O'Riordan stepped forward and glared up at Kit. 'He said sneeringly, 'OK bud, who should we be arresting, then? And what evidence do you have? That's something we find kinda useful over here.'

Kit smiled at this. He replied, 'We find it useful too, Captain O'Riordan. As it happens, I'm fairly sure that you have all the evidence you need, right here.'

Kit turned away from the policeman and strolled over to Ethel, who was sitting with her sister and helping her to the remains of some coffee. He sat down beside the two women and addressed Ethel.

'Ethel, did you know that Maisie was seeing Amory?'

Ethel paused for a few seconds before replying, 'I suppose I did now that I think of it. She never introduced us, but she described him, and it was Amory to a 'T', I guess. When I met him tonight, I wondered if it was him.'

Behind the main group, Laura sidled over to Alastair. She touched his arm which startled him slightly. He turned around to her and smiled that sad smile, when he saw the tears staining Laura's eyes.

'You were right Al,' said Laura. She shook her head and put her hand to her mouth to stop her teeth chattering. Alastair put his arm around her shoulders and led her over to a chair.

'Bitter experience,' he said, taking her hand. 'I suppose young women can be bedazzled by men like this. Perhaps flattered by their interest. They profess to love women. They don't, my dear. They love themselves and are utterly selfish.'

Laura nodded and managed to say, 'I was such a fool. I came here tonight to see him. Dick must hate me.'

Alastair glanced towards the group and saw Dick looking at them strangely. He probably did, thought Alastair.

'I'm sure he doesn't,' he said, hoping the lie would pass unnoticed.

'You're a good man Al,' said Laura. 'I wish I'd met someone like you.'

Alastair grinned at the compliment and knew she would have ignored him, just like so many other young women had, until he met Christina.

'Oh, I'd never have stood a chance with a beauty like you,' said Alastair, smiling.

Laura buried her head into Alastair's shoulder. Her mascara is going to ruin my jacket, he thought – Lord only knows what that Ella-Mae will think.

Silence fell over the main group, briefly. Everyone was still looking at Kit. He glanced towards the young woman sipping the coffee. She had a faraway look in her eyes, and she was rocking gently backwards and forwards. Kit glanced at the headband and the feathers at the back of her head which were at a strange angle. Then he stood up and walked back over to the other guests.

'Well?' demanded O'Riordan. 'Are we taking these people to midtown or what?' He was speaking to Flynn, but the police inspector's eyes were on Kit. Everyone's eyes were on Kit. Outside the room, they could hear the sound of singing and celebrations underway for the arrival of 1922.

Kit turned to Agatha, and asked, 'Did you?'

Agatha frowned for a moment before nodding. She said, 'Was I so obvious?'

Kit scanned the other party guests before grinning at his aunt, 'Apparently not.'

Everyone was mystified by the exchange that had just occurred. Just as O'Riordan was about to explode, Flynn held his hand up and said to the captain, 'Don't.' Then he turned to Kit, fixed a pair of sceptical eyes on him and added, 'Let's hear what he, or they, have to say.'

35

Kit paused for a minute and looked around the room. He was distracted by noise in the corridor as a few more policemen arrived at the front door of the apartment. Flynn turned to the policemen in the doorway and waved his hand at them to come in and be quiet. They filed inside in silence. Over by the piano, the band members stood up and trooped over to where the main group were standing on what, an hour or two earlier, had been a dance floor.

'All the world's a stage, and all the men and women merely players; they have their exits and their entrances; And one man in his time plays many parts,' began Kit addressing the group. 'That's how Amory's story began. I think, to answer your question, Bobbie and my own from earlier, perhaps this was his suicide note and confession. He waited, until now because it took him this long to pull together all of the people he needed to be part of the story. *His* story. I was struck right from the first moment I met Amory, that he was, perhaps, the most narcissistic man I had ever met, and I've known quite a few, believe me. Well, his world was a stage as far as I can see, and he was the lead actor, he was the director, the producer and the writer all rolled into one. We were his bit players, and we were his audience because people like Amory, needed both. That was his mistake when he and Colette agreed their death pact. It was too private. He needed a more public expression of his art, of his philosophy. He wouldn't make the same mistake twice. Except he didn't bargain for the one thing that narcissists can never consider. How other people think. One of the performers had their own script; their own idea of how this story should play out. And they acted on this. I think when it dawned on Amory what had happened, he made one last attempt at reclaiming his own story. He grabbed the one thing that would connect us all to the past and to what had occurred.'

'The gun,' said Dick West.

'The gun,' agreed Kit. 'I'll talk about the gun, in a minute or two, because it's more important than I first realised. But first, I want to talk about us, the guests. The players if you like. In situations like this, it's difficult to avoid putting yourself in Captain O'Riordan's shoes and wondering what he might be thinking. Dick and Chester perhaps have the most obvious motive.'

Kit saw Dick smile at this, but Chester seemed a little upset.

'I'm sorry Chester, but you have to admit,' pointed out Kit, 'he did steal Colette from you and Dick. That gives you some sort of motive.'

Then Kit turned to Laura, who was standing alongside Ethel and the young woman, who they knew to be Ethel's sister.

'And you'll have to forgive me, ladies, but each of you has a motive too, if you think about it.'

'Revenge, jealousy?' suggested Laura, getting into the spirit of the occasion.

'Very good,' smiled Kit. His eyes moved towards Ethel and her sister, but he said nothing. 'Freddy, we know, stands to inherit some money and he's already on his way to the precinct. Which leaves the boys in the band and the English contingent. Perhaps, I'm a little biased, but I can think of no earthly motive that we might have nor, I must say, the gentlemen from the band. So that leaves us with the people I have spoken about already. And make no mistake about it, notwithstanding Freddy's departure, the killer of Amory is among us.'

O'Riordan removed the cigarette from his mouth, with the intention of giving Kit his thoughts double-barrelled. Once more, Flynn put his hand on his arm. Kit saw the interaction and nodded to Flynn. Then, at this point he said, 'With due respect to the officers of the law with us today, I'm rather parched. Is there any wine left on the table?'

Agatha answered rather sourly, 'No, your uncle seems to have done a remarkable job clearing up the remains of what Mr Beaufort provided for us tonight. Without Freddy here, I have no earthly idea where we'll lay our hands on some wine, or anything else, for that matter.'

'Dick,' said Kit, looking at the lawyer. 'Did I see you with a hip flask earlier? One like Amory described in his short story.'

'I have one,' said Chester brightly. He was sitting by his jacket and fished it out of the breast pocket. He gave it a shake before adding, 'Still a bit in there if you like. It's a highball.'

'Just the ticket,' smiled Kit, before turning to Dick and asking. 'What do you have, by the way?'

'I had a highball also. It used to be our drink at Princeton,' replied Dick. He walked over to his jacket and took out the hip flask. It was identical to Chester's. He gave it a shake and said, 'Not much left in it.'

Flynn looked at the two hip flasks and a thought crossed his mind. He glanced towards O'Riordan who had a look on his face that suggested he wanted to shout now. One look from Flynn made him pause. Flynn was curious now; he wanted to see how this scene played out before his bellicose colleague messed up what the Englishman had in mind. He caught Nolan's eye also. The young man, at least, had the sense to stay quiet and wait to see what happened.

Agatha appeared with a small silver tray, containing three cocktail glasses and a cocktail shaker. She set it down on a table beside Kit. This brought a smile of appreciation from Kit. Mary frowned at Kit's aunt and wondered what was going on. Agatha and Kit sometimes had an understanding, that bordered on telepathic.

Kit took one of the hip flasks and emptied the contents into the cocktail shaker. He repeated the process with the other. Then he put the lid on the shaker and gave it a vigorous shake. The whole room watched in mute astonishment at what was happening.

Kit poured the contents from the shaker into the three cocktail glasses that Agatha had brought over. The clear liquid filled up each of the three glasses.

'I hate to drink alone,' said Kit looking up at everyone. All eyes were on him. Kit turned to Dick and Chester who were standing beside one another. 'Gentlemen, will you join me?'

Neither seemed particularly keen, but then Dick stepped forward saying, 'I'm sure you'll agree, I've probably had too much to drink tonight.'

'Is that a "no", then?' asked Kit. Dick shrugged and took the glass proffered by Kit. Chester was next. Kit fixed his eyes on him. 'Let's drink a toast to absent friends.'

‘If it’s all right with you, I’d rather not,’ said Chester coldly. ‘I think it’s clear that Amory has a lot to answer for. His behaviour has been beyond the pale.’

‘I agree,’ said Kit, still holding the glass out to Chester. ‘Perhaps you can suggest a toast then?’

‘I’d rather not,’ said Chester firmly. ‘I’m pretty submerged as it is.’

‘Go on Ches,’ said Dick, putting the glass to his lips. Chester’s eyes widened as he saw Dick do this. His eyes darted to Kit who moved forward slightly.

‘Really, Chester, I’d like you to drink this with us,’ said Kit before adding in an unusually strong tone, ‘I insist.’

‘No,’ said Chester. ‘I shan’t. You can’t make me.’

‘Why not?’ said Flynn, stepping forward towards Chester. ‘Take a sip. I want to see you drink this.’

‘No,’ said Chester, looking around him now and realising that all eyes were upon him. Perspiration was almost gushing down his face and the dampness under his armpits had spread to the back of his shirt. ‘No, I won’t. You can’t make me.’

‘What’s the problem with the drink, Mr Lydgate?’ asked Flynn. ‘Why won’t you drink?’

‘Nothing. There’s nothing wrong with the drink. I tell you I just don’t fancy it, that’s all.’

Ethel was now aware of the commotion, and she left her sister for a moment, to see what was going on. She saw that everyone was looking Chester.

‘What’s going on Ches?” she asked.

Kit answered on Chester’s behalf, ‘I felt like having a final drink for the evening, but Chester doesn’t want to join me or Dick.’

Ethel seemed confused. She glanced down at the tray with the hip flasks and then back at Chester. Moments later, she felt Kit put the glass in her hand.

'Perhaps you'll join us, Ethel?'

Without thinking Ethel put the glass to her lips. Chester screamed at her and leapt forward, swiping the glass from her hand. It shattered on the floor. Chester fell forward and landed on the floor also. He stared up wildly at the group.

Kit put the glass to his lips and drained the contents. Dick, seeing that Kit had drunk from the glass, did so too.

'You're mad,' whispered Chester. To be fair, most of the people looking on were in as much shock as he was. Mary gasped as she saw Kit drink from the glass.

Agatha stepped forward once more. She was holding up a third, identical hip flask. She gave it a little shake.

'I suspect there's not much in this one,' she said before adding archly to Chester, 'But I'm sure there's enough to prove there's poison inside, Mr Lydgate.'

36 12:30am

Chester was led away by two policemen, followed by Captain O'Riordan and Detective Nolan. Ethel was now being consoled, once, more by Bobbie and while Mary, accompanied by Ella-Mae, went over to her sister. Flynn and the others watched Chester being led out of the room, before turning to Kit and Agatha. He was still incredulous over what had just transpired.

'I've been a cop for nearly forty years, and I've never seen anything like what you two just pulled off. Any time you feel like joining the police department over here, just let me know. How on earth did you know?'

Agatha and Kit exchanged glances. Kit looked at his aunt and felt a wave of affection towards her fill him. All the way along the line she had been in step with him. She'd seen what he had seen, she had anticipated so much and needed only a look from her nephew to understand what had to be done. Kit took Flynn's arm, and led him away from the wider group, along with Agatha. Once they were a safe distance away, Kit began to speak.

'It was pretty obvious, once we knew poison was involved, that it would be either Dick or Chester. They had suffered most because of him, although I did wonder about Laura and if she had revenge in mind. But Amory himself was the first clue.'

'How?' asked Flynn, with no little exasperation in his voice.

Agatha answered for Kit, 'Well, the gun that Amory was hiding was pointed at a framed photograph on the bottom shelf of his bookcase. It showed the three of them, presumably when they were at Princeton. I think he was trying to tell us something, then.'

'About which one killed him?' asked Flynn, a little sceptically.

Kit answered this time. He said, 'It was impossible to say if it was Dick or Chester, just by the way he pointed, but I think he wanted to help narrow matters down a little. I think by drawing our attention to the pistol, he wanted to tell us that one was missing. Quite remarkable really.'

'He did all this while he was dying. Unbelievable I would say.'

'I've been in Amory's position myself, Inspector Flynn,' said Kit. 'A lot can go through your mind when you are dying.'

'Like getting help?' suggested Flynn, half smiling.

Kit grinned also.

'Yes, I wondered about that, but I think that Amory did not realise he was dying, initially. He felt unwell at first. He may have passed that off as too much to drink, or food poisoning. Then I think other things began to happen. Loss of control of muscles or pain. At some point he realised he'd been poisoned. This may surprise you, but I rather think he accepted what had happened. I think he viewed it as fair exchange. He'd already grabbed the gun to tell us about Ethel's sister. But then, perhaps at the last moment, he decided to try and tell us who might have done it.'

Flynn scratched his head. It was far-fetched and yet, on an evening when the impossible seemed to have occurred, a crime committed and cleared up, a young woman failing to commit suicide, the idea became more plausible the more he thought about it.

'And the switch you pulled off?' asked Flynn. 'How on earth...?' he began and then stopped himself.

'Mr West was drinking, periodically, from a hip flask,' said Agatha, 'which, if you remember, Mr Beaufort made specific reference to in the story. I noted that Mr Lydgate also had a hip flask but did not drink from it. And when we found Mr Beaufort dead, I saw the hip flask sitting on top of the bookcase.'

'I'm definitely losing it,' repeated Flynn, shaking his head once more. 'So you took the hip flask and switched it with Chester's? How did you do that without him noticing?'

'He took his coat off,' said Agatha. 'I switched it then. Christopher saw me doing that so we both knew what we wanted to do.'

'Don't forget,' added Kit, 'We'd seen Dick drinking from his hip flask, so we guessed that Chester had not tried to switch his with Dick's.'

'So when did Chester poison him?'

'Probably when we were dancing,' said Kit. 'He had plenty of opportunity to, for we were all on the floor, except Dick that is, and you had left. It was soon after the dancing had finished that we returned to our seats and Amory took the last fateful drink.'

'And his motive was revenge?'

'Yes, I think so. He loved Colette and she was stolen from him, first by Dick and then Amory. He blamed Amory for killing her, of course.'

'So why didn't he try to kill Dick?' asked Flynn, a frown creasing his forehead.

'I think he wanted to,' said Kit. 'Whenever Dick took off his jacket, I think Chester saw his chance and I believe he would have switched his hip flask for Dick's. That's why he left some poison in it. He knew that it would be found at some point and tested. Dick would be blamed for Amory's murder and would face the electric chair. That would have sealed his revenge and the fact that it was New Year's Eve would have put a seal on it for him.'

'Had we found the poison on him he'd have been a condemned man,' agreed Flynn. 'Utterly diabolical. I wouldn't have thought that of him, somehow.'

Kit nodded in agreement. He said, 'Nor I but, as he said himself, he faced everything that the Boche could throw at him and survived. He works on Wall Street. He may play the clown a bit, but I think he's someone you could easily underestimate. He's no fool, inspector.'

'Well, I should have realised that, after all this time, that anyone can be a murderer,' said Flynn, fixing his eyes on Agatha and then Kit. 'Let's go join the others. I suppose we can let everyone go now.'

Ten minutes later, another ambulance arrived to take away the sister of Ethel. Mary and Bobbie both hugged Ethel and wished her luck. Dick had departed earlier, with Laura, to go to the precinct, in the company of Inspector Flynn. Dick still had questions to answer, on the events of the evening, but he was also keen to secure the release of Freddy.

Soon the only people remaining were the English contingent, Bobbie Flynn and the band who were busy packing away their instruments.

'What are your plans now?' asked Bobbie to Mary.

'I'd like to see some of New York if I can. Kit and I are here for a month. I gather the owner of the apartment we are staying in wishes me to pose for him.'

'Who is that?'

Mary replied, 'Charles Dana Gibson?' She raised her voice, at the end, to ask if Bobbie was familiar with him.

'Oh my,' laughed Bobbie, 'You're going to be a Gibson girl.'

'So it seems,' smiled Mary.

'You'll be perfect,' said Bobbie, appraising her new friend.

'Are you going to write about this evening? It might be a chance to have a scoop.'

'Am I ever going to write about this?' said Bobbie excitedly.

Kit rose to his feet, as he saw the band trooping towards the door.

'Gentlemen, thank you for this evening. Can I ask if you have been paid or not?'

Fritz, their de facto manager, spoke up. 'Yes sir, Mr Beaufort was extremely generous.'

Kit went over to the German and held his hand out. Fritz looked at the hand and then he shook it warmly. Nothing was said, but in their eyes was the hope that, never again, would they be asked to do what they had done, only a few years previously.

'One more thing,' said Kit, reaching into his pocket. He took out his wallet and handed each of the band ten dollars. 'I can't say have a drink on me as that would be illegal, but you know what I mean.

The band accepted the money gratefully and then exited through the door. It was almost one o' clock in the morning as they reached the elevator. All of them were carrying bits of Arnie's drum kit, as well as their own instruments.

'That was some evening,' said Tommy, as they waited in the corridor.

'Man, I thought we'd never leave,' agreed Lanky.

'Nice guy,' said Lanky, holding the ten dollar note. This was met with nods from the others. The elevator arrived and soon they were heading to the ground floor. The doors opened and they spilled out into the lobby. It was quiet now. The police had gone and only the doorman remained. He nodded to the band as they walked out onto the street.

After the heat of the apartment, the night air stung their faces. The rain had stopped, thankfully, but the sidewalk was flooded. Streetlights glinted off the puddles.

'Man it was tropical out here,' said Lanky.

'Sure was,' agreed Arnie looking around him.

Just then a group of men approached them. Some were carrying cameras.

'Hey bud, is it true there was a murder in the building tonight?' asked one of the men.

The boys on the band looked at one another and smiled. Fritz put his hand up to his friends and said, 'Let me. You guys go home.'

'You sure?' said Tommy.

Fritz nodded and his three friends melted away from the group that was converging on Fritz. They heard him begin to talk about what they had seen. The German looked at the newsmen and smiled. While he felt sorry for the guy that had died, this was a big opportunity for them. Their names would be all over town in the morning. The phone would be ringing. Yes, it was sad for Mr Beaufort, but life goes on. He and his friends learned that the hard way, at Passchendaele, at Verdun and everywhere else they were sent. You had to look after yourself. Look after your own.

'Well gentlemen, what do you want to know? Damon, you go first.'

The remaining members of the band slipped away, unnoticed, until Tommy stopped. He turned around and looked at Fritz, surrounded by half a dozen newsman.

'I feel bad,' said Tommy. 'Maybe we should help him or something. Isn't that Damon, with Fritz?'

Lanky put a hand on his shoulder to stop him. They were on West 67th Street now.

'No man. You got something else you gotta do.'

Tommy frowned, and then he saw Lanky directing him with his eyes, towards something behind him.

Tommy turned around. Standing twenty yards away down the street was his wife and daughter.

'Dorothy,' he shouted. He ran towards her and stopped dead, just in front of her. There were tears in his eyes. He couldn't speak. He couldn't think of what to say. Dorothy was crying too.

'Pops, I'm sorry. I've been a fool. I don't know what I was thinking. Can you forgive...?' said Dorothy Jackson.

The rest of what she wanted to say, was buried in the bear hug from her father. There was nothing else for her to say and nothing else he needed to hear. She was with them again and that was all that mattered.

37 3:00am

Midtown Precinct, New York: New Year's Day 1922

Inspector Flynn marched down to the basement of the Midtown Precinct. He was tired, becoming increasingly grumpy, and beginning to regret having indulged himself, with having a few drinks with the English contingent. He'd enjoyed it at the time, but there is always a price to pay for indulgence. He was paying for it now, with his body screaming at him that it wanted to go to bed.

The clock on the corridor wall read a quarter after nine. Flynn glared at it and then Nolan, who he decided to blame personally for the inoperative clocks. Nolan was already fifteen hours into a shift, that should have ended three hours ago. He glanced up at the faulty clock and shrugged. Flynn was too tired to make any comment.

A uniformed officer opened the cell door that led to a bunch of cells in the basement of the building. The cells were full up from the detritus collected over the last few years. The men in the cells spied the arrival of the two policeman and began to cheer ironically. Flynn and Nolan received many new wishes and whole lot else besides. The cell they wanted was at the end of the corridor.

'Open this one,' ordered Flynn.

The clank of the keys echoed along the corridor causing another cheer from the man incarcerated. There were six men in the cell. All of them black. They were interested in the one wearing the white coat.

'Freddy,' called Nolan.

Freddy glanced up slowly. His face was cast in shadow, yet he still managed to seem pale. Flynn stepped inside the cell. A few of the men in the cell were about to rise, but Flynn motioned with his hands to stay seated.

'Up you get, son.'

'Why?' asked Freddy. There was no sense of insolence in the question, just resignation. Flynn wondered how to answer him.

'You're free to go, son. We know who killed Mr Beaufort,' replied Flynn. It seemed the only thing to say at that moment. Other questions circulated in his mind, though.

'Who?' asked Freddy. He put his hands on the concrete floor and slowly pushed himself up to a standing position.

'Chester Lydgate,' replied Flynn.

Freddy nodded, in manner that suggested he was not surprised, or perhaps, he had not fully registered what had happened. Flynn eyed him closely. It took a few moments before Freddy's eyes focused on the detective and then he met his gaze. The innate dignity and bearing of Freddy, slowly, began to reassert itself in his limbs and in his posture. Flynn seemed reassured that he'd understood.

'Thank you, sir, for letting me know,' said Freddy. The two detectives stood back to let him pass. Freddy straightened up to his full height and walked out of the cell with his shoulders back and his head held high.

Outside the cell, Freddy waited to be led upstairs and officially set free. As they walked along the corridor, a thought occurred to Flynn.

'Have you got a place to stay?'

The question seemed to confuse Freddy, for a moment, and then he realised what he was asking.

'Sorry, I've just realised that returning to the apartment is out of the question.'

'I'm afraid so, son. We'll send your clothes and belongings to a new address. Have you somewhere you can go?'

The answer was no but something inside of Freddy would not admit to this. He nodded and said, 'Thank you, sir. I'll let you know where to send my things.'

Back at Alastair and Agatha's apartment, Bobbie Flynn sat down at the table with Kit, Mary, Agatha and Alastair. She tried, and failed, to stifle a yawn, which promoted an amused look from Mary. Bobbie frowned an apology, which was met with a wave of dismissal from Mary.

The group had retired to Agatha and Alastair's apartment on the floor below. Ella-Mae brought over an open bottle of wine and set down some glasses.

Alastair poured the remains of the wine into the glasses and then set the bottle down and said,

'Well, I don't know about you, but I for one am looking forward to you three returning back to Europe, so that I can reclaim my easy life. How do you manage it?'

'It's hardly our fault,' pointed out Mary. 'I mean, trouble seems to follow us around.'

'You attract it young lady. You're as bad as these two,' said Alastair pointing to his sister and nephew. 'I thought you'd be a good influence and now look...'

There was a mock severity to his tone, that was fooling nobody. Including Bobbie Flynn, who put her hand to her mouth and giggled at this *cri de coeur*.

'And you're just as bad,' noted Alastair fixing his eyes on Bobbie. 'If I were you, I would stay away from this pair and my sister, stay away from crime reporting and find an interest in knitting patterns.'

'Amusing puppy stories,' suggested Kit, helpfully.

'Hat fashions,' added Mary, clapping her hands, as if she had just had a lightbulb moment.

Bobbie was now laughing openly at this.

'I shall bear this in mind,' said Bobbie but, she was, already, mentally writing her story. She turned to Mary and asked, 'May I interview you for the story I'm going to write.'

'You may,' grinned Mary. 'I might even see if I can persuade my dashing and rather smart husband to contribute to your piece. Perhaps we can have dinner tonight and you can finish it off then.'

'Would you mind?' exclaimed Bobbie.

'Of course not,' said Kit. 'Although I'm not sure your father will thank us for this.'

'Fathers are always right,' counselled Alastair. 'I can see you're going to be as much trouble as this lot.'

'I hope so,' said Bobbie and she clinked glasses with Kit, Mary and finally Agatha.

'I hope so, too,' said Agatha.

The End

Research Notes

This is a work of fiction. However, it references real-life individuals. Gore Vidal, in his introduction to Lincoln, writes that placing history in fiction or fiction in history has been unfashionable since Tolstoy and that the result can be accused of being neither. He defends the practice, pointing out that writers from Aeschylus to Shakespeare to Tolstoy have done so with, not inconsiderable, success and merit.

I have mentioned a number of key real-life individuals and events in this novel. My intention, in the following section, is to explain a little more about their connection to this period and this story.

Hotel des Artistes

Hotel des Artistes is a residential building located at 1 West 67th Street, near Central Park West, on the Upper West Side of Manhattan in New York City. It is a 17-story, 119-unit, Gothic-style building which opened in 1917. Many artists, writers and politicians have lived there, including early 20th century luminaries such as illustrator Charles Dana Gibson, Noel Coward, Harry Crosby and Isadora Duncan. It was home latterly to Gary Oldman, film director, Mike Nichols and the writer of Jaws, Peter Benchley.

Harry Crosby (1898 – 1929)

This book was inspired by the rather tragic story of one of the residents of the Hotel, the poet Harry Crosby. He was very much a product of the Jazz Age and could have stepped off the pages of an F. Scott Fitzgerald novel. Like many young American men of high social rank who were coined 'The Lost Generation', he went to Europe to fight in the War. After he returned, he drifted into a rather dissolute life and went to live in Paris becoming a poet. He included Ernest Hemingway among his friends. He and his wife had an open marriage, and his affairs were numerous. One of the young women with whom he was involved was called Josephine Noyes Rotch. The pair agreed a murder-suicide pact and on December 10th, 1929, their bodies were found, each holding a revolver with bullet holes in their temples.

Charles Dana Gibson (1867 – 1944)

Gibson was probably the most popular illustrator in America at the turn of the century. He was chiefly famous for creating an image of young, wealthy American women through his pen and ink illustrations, which featured in the top magazines, for many decades. The women depicted were known as the Gibson Girls. After the end of WWI his popularity faded as new illustrators came into vogue such JC Leyendecker, Norman Rockwell and Maxfield Parrish.

Frederic Remington (1861 - 1909)

Although he does not feature in the novel, a few words about Frederic Remington, one of my favourite artists. His fame at this time was based on his depiction of the 'Wild West' and Native Americans. Many of his painting contributed to the iconography of the Old West. The painting mentioned in the novel is Ghost Dance by the Ogallala Sioux at Pine Ridge. It depicts this extraordinary ritual. I cannot say if he witnessed it first hand, but I do know that he spent a lot of time, *in situ,* capturing ideas for his images that were later worked up in a studio.

Prohibition (1920 – 1933)

The basic facts of prohibition barely tell the extraordinary impact on American society. The 18th Amendment ended the production, sale, import and transportation of alcohol, nationwide. The law drove many Americans to hoard alcohol or become de facto criminals by consuming illicit booze created by criminal gangs and often sold through illegal bars called speakeasies.

The law ended with the ratification of the 21st Amendment, in 1933. This brought to a close one of the more extraordinary and, arguably, self-defeating initiatives in American history as it gave rise and strength to various criminal gangs, particularly the Italian American Mafia, led by men such as Al Capone.

The Ghost Dance (1889)

The Ghost Dance is first believed to have been practiced in 1889 by the Northern Paiutes living in Nevada. The dance was inspired by the visions of a Paiute named Wovoka, who was believed to be a healer. Wovoka also went under the name of Jack Wilson. The dance was held usually around an individual who leads the ceremony. Its popularity spread eastwards and was taken up by the Lakota (Sioux) tribe who also adopted it.

Tragically, it was the Ghost Dance that was being practiced during the appalling events at Wounded Knee, South Dakota in 1890 when US Calvary massacred more than 250 men, women and children of the Lakota with 51 wounded. Over 30 soldiers were killed in the episode.

Ziegfeld Follies (1907 – 1931)

The Ziegfeld Follies were a theatrical revue, a variety show, that ran for two decades and spawned several movies and theatrical revivals. The Follies were famous for the young women chorus line dancers who were known, imaginatively, as Ziegfeld Girls. The shows made stars of several entertainers, who went on to become household names including Bob Hope, W.C. Fields, Eddie Cantor, Louise (Lulu) Brooks and Fanny Brice, who is mentioned in the book and who Barbara Streisand played in the Oscar-winning *Funny Girl.*

Pat Garrett (1850 -1908)

How to describe Pat Garret, whose revolvers the character, Amory, in the novel professed to own? He was a legend of the Old West and, notoriously, claims to have killed William Bonney aka Billy the Kid. Garrett had a colourful life, to say the least. He was a buffalo hunter, a bounty hunter, a sheriff and was appointed by Theodore Roosevelt as a collector of customs in El Paso, before being fired by the President for incompetence and misleading his boss in the White House. His legend has only grown in the wake of his various 'appearances' on film and television portrayed by James Coburn, Patrick Wayne and Barry Sullivan, among others.

EXCEPRT FROM THE NEXT JACK MURRAY BOOK (to be published in 2024)

A LITTLE MISS TAKEN
Bobbie Flynn Mysteries Book One

Offices of the New York American, Park Street, New York: 2nd January 1922

New York, on New Year's Eve 1921, glittered like a diamond in a police searchlight the night Amory Beaufort was murdered.

Bobbie Flynn looked at her typewriter and smiled to herself. She liked the line she had just typed. She liked it a lot in fact. Then a cold feeling enveloped her. What would Thornton Kent think? All at once her confident ebbed away. Perhaps it was too dramatic. Hyperbole. He hated hyperbole. Except of course when it was Damon. Or Amory when he had been alive. Yes, when men like that handed in in their work it was as if Shakespeare himself had entered the offices of the *New York American* coining epigrams and sonnets to grateful sub-editors in need of intellectual stimulation.

The thought of her colleagues or, at least, former colleague, sent a surge of anger which throbbed from her temple and down through her arms to fingers that began to type rapidly on the keys. The words flew from the keys to the paper at a dizzying pace propelled by a rage that was only partially attributable to her auburn-red locks and Irish roots.

Twenty minutes later the report was finished, and she reviewed it grimly. In her estimation, and she was her own worst critic, the piece was well written, concise but provided sufficient human interest from someone who was an eyewitness to a murder and his capture.

Bobbie Flynn, only a couple of days earlier, had attended a party, a murder mystery party no less, where the host had become a victim. Thanks to the presence of her father, an inspector with the New York Police Department, and a few unusual English people who had a peculiar knack for detection, had ensured that the murderer was identified within hours of the murder taking place. Of course, such things are possible when English amateur detectives are involved as begs the question why they are not used more often in criminal investigations.

She read through the report twice. The first time was to see how it felt. To Bobbie, it felt just right. The second time was to check for grammar and punctuation lest some punctilious sub-editors reject a superb article on the basis of her heinous misuse of a comma, mid clause.

One of the more superior attributes possessed by women is that they are infinitely more collaborative by nature than chaps. Perhaps this is a misplaced lack of confidence in their own capability or a desire not to repeat the mistakes of their male colleagues who are singularly devoid of such humility when it comes to assessing their own competence.

Bobbie decided, rather as a good doctor might, to obtain a second opinion. She glanced into an office where her immediate boss, Buckner Fanley, sat scowling over a newspaper. A scowl was set permanently on the head of obituaries. This may have been ascribed to the serious nature of the columns that he oversaw him but to those who knew and, invariably, disliked him, this was, in fact, a permanent feature.

To describe him as 'head' was a vast overstatement of what was a small team. It comprised him and Bobbie. They detested one another and made no secret of this fact. Fanley saw Bobbie as a *parvenu* who only saw obituaries as a stepping stone to fashion, household tips or whatever it was interested the female of the species. Meanwhile, Bobbie had to endure the role of office dogsbody as Fanley allowed her to do the bulk of the research on recently deceased or prospective clients, or not, for entry to Paradise. The latter work was particularly morbid as the paper had to ensure its library of obits was up to date with latest news on the not-yet-deceased. Of course, Fanley was happy to put his name to Bobbie's work. All in all, their relationship simmered like boiling water on a stove.

Bobbie rose from her seat and ignored the sharp jerk of Fanley's head as he glanced up at his attractive young assistant walking past his office window. Bobbie gritted her teeth and headed for the open area where many of the reporters sat. She knew that every man Jack of theme would stop what they were doing and watch her pass along the rows of desks.

What was going on in their minds as they looked at her did not bear thinking about. Thankfully, everyone on the office knew that her father was a police inspector, a rather well-known one on fact. This acted as a form of protection against the unwanted attentions of prospective middle-aged lotharios who could probably still teach a young girl a thing or two given the chance, or so they claimed.

At the far end of the office was Thornton Kent's office. She could see the all-powerful editor pacing the room like a lion caged in a wardrobe. He didn't look happy but then again, he never did. Bobbie's eyes darted over to a table by the window that was set aside for the man that she had come to see.

Damon Runyon.

Runyon was the golden boy of the newspaper although at forty years of age he was no longer a child, he was certainly the shining jewel in the newspaper's firmament. His fame stretched beyond the sweaty confines of the newsroom, beyond even New York to the rest of the country thanks to his sports writing, in particular his writing about baseball and boxing.

Bobbie's eyes fell on the slender writer, crouched over his typewriter like an angry parent with a recalcitrant child. Ignoring the leering eyes of the other men in the room, Bobbie made straight for her friend and sometime drinking buddy. Her familiarity with the Broadway's speakeasies and criminal element almost matched that of Runyon. This was something that she tended to keep quiet from her policeman father who, not unreasonably would have taken a dim view both professionally and parentally of such associations.

Perhaps your chronicler is biased but men are genuinely amazing creatures. Whether it is due to the good Lord's sense of humour or a remarkable by-product of a few million years of evolution but the male genus of *homo sapiens* has an in-built alarm for whenever an attractive woman is in the vicinity. Although Bobbie was yet several tables away, and despite the fact that he was facing in another direction, Runyon glanced around and viewed the approaching young woman with undisguised pleasure.

He was a connoisseur of women, beautiful women preferably and funny women in particular. Bobbie Flynn qualified on all three counts in his book. This liking had never been sullied by any impropriety on Runyon's part beyond introducing her to some unusual Broadway characters and even more unusual cocktails.

'Red,' exclaimed Runyon, calling Bobbie by the name she was commonly known in the newsroom. 'What's cookin'?'

Bobbie waved a couple of typed sheets in his direction.

'Do you know that unpaid job you have as my proof reader?' she said with a grin.

Runyon scowled back at her without any malice, 'You use my good nature.'

'Would you prefer if it was your body?' said Bobbie, just loud enough to make several middle-aged reporters in the vicinity groan.

Runyon, picking up on the thread left dangling by Bobbie, countered, 'It's over kid. We had some laughs but move on.'

A few eyebrows in the room shot up at this. They knew of Runyon's penchant for younger women, but this would have been the ultimate scoop.

Moments later Runyon was on his feet cackling his smokers laugh. He hugged Bobbie and took the sheets of paper from her hand.

'Give me those, honey,' he said while sitting down to read. Bobbie perched on his desk and stared over him. Almost immediately he began to laugh. This is rarely a good sign and Runyon confirmed this a moment later.

'It's a good line but he'll never let it through,' said Runyon.

'Can't you say anything?'

'Why should I when I might steal it myself?'

'Beast,' laughed Bobbie.

'I'll see what I can do.'

Runyon read in semi-silence. There was the odd grumble along the way and his pen circled dangerously over the page like a bird of prey but did not swoop down to deliver its damning verdict. Finally, Runyon looked up. He smiled.

'It's good Red but Kent will throw a fit. You know he will,' observed Runyon.

'Will you take out a few things and...'

'...and you'll tell Kent that Damon had helped you. Nice idea. Might work. Once.'

Runyon brandished his pen, received a nod from Bobbie and then it descended like Madame La Guillotine to do its gruesome work. Bobbie watched the red flow and it felt as if she was being repeatedly stabbed. She steeled herself as she saw some of her best work butchered by her friend, but it was for a good cause.

A couple of minutes later she surveyed the carnage. Yet, when she read through the article, miraculously it was still coherent and, heartbreakingly, probably better for the surgery that had taken place. Whether the patient would make a full recovery remained to be seen. She glanced in the direction of Thornton Kent's office.

Butterflies battered the walls of her stomach as she prepared herself to march in and do battle for her story. Kent was aware that she was an eyewitness to a murder that had shocked the whole of the newsroom. Reluctantly, he had acceded to Bobbie's demand that she get to write the story. He had done so on the proviso that she make a decent stab at it. He'd laughed at his intentional pun.

Bobbie felt like running from the office, yet it was too late now. The whole of the newsroom was pretending not to be aware of the drama about to play out. The drama that might end in her walking out on her dream of being a crime reporter. These were the stakes and it felt as if everyone in the room knew this.

She was holding her breath as she hoped to catch the eye of the editor. At last, he looked up. Unerringly his eyes went straight to Bobbie. Or perhaps it was the shock of reddish-auburn hair that caught his attention.

With a single, graceful movement he waved at her to come in.

Bobbie sailed over towards the office stopping long enough to say, 'Hi Skinny', to a man that resembled a walrus complete with a handlebar moustache.

'Good luck Red,' said Runyon in a low voice and he meant it.

About the Author

Jack Murray was born in Northern Ireland but has spent over half his life living just outside London, except for some periods spent in Australia, Monte Carlo, and the US.

An artist, as well as a writer, Jack's work features in collections around the world and he has exhibited in Britain, Ireland, and Monte Carlo.

A spin off series from the Kit Aston novels was published in 2020 featuring Aunt Agatha as a young woman solving mysterious murders.

Another spin off series is features Inspector Jellicoe. It is set in the late 1950's/early 1960's.

Jack finished work on a World War II trilogy in 2022. The three books look at the war from both the British and the German side. They have been published through Lume Books and are available on Amazon.

If you enjoyed meeting the character Bobbie Flynn, then you may be interested to learn that a new spin off series featuring this character and her father will be out on 2024.

Printed in Great Britain
by Amazon